www.nobleromance.com
Love Bites
ISBN 978-1-60592-490-8
ALL RIGHTS RESERVED
Copyright 2010 Margie Church
Cover Art by Fiona Jayde

This book may not be reproduced or used in whole or in part by any existing means without written permission from the publisher. Contact Noble Romance Publishing, LLC at PO Box 467423, Atlanta, GA 31146.

This book is a work of fiction and any resemblance to persons, living or dead, or actual events is purely coincidental. The characters are products of the author's imagination and used fictitiously.

To Kate —
I hope you love my vamps. Thanks for coming!
Love, Margie

Love Bites

Margie Church

An accidental encounter turns into high stakes love when Jui Fabrice meets Wade Kairos in Germany. She has no idea he's a vampire and Wade has every intention of keeping his secret.

A vineyard cottage is the perfect place for Jui and Wade to make love until he discovers her unique link to his living years. He vows to stay away from her forever, but he can't let her go completely. Wade's repressed human feelings continue rising. He invades Jui's dreams and communicates telepathically with her at will. Evil jealousy consumes him when Jui becomes involved with Rob Hawthorne and she rebukes Wade for his controlling behaviors.

Then Wade's lifelong companion dies in a vamp war and his desolation is too much to handle alone. He turns to the only person who cares about him—Jui—and for one hot night, he becomes the man she's wanted all along.

The Ancient One, Ladislav Husek, learns of Wade's risky human behavior and gives Wade a taste of how viciously he'll die if he doesn't bury his tracks with Jui. Husek promises to turn Jui into his personal playmate and Wade has to choose. Can love prevail over evil in a relationship that never was supposed to happen?

Chapter One

Jui Fabrice rose early and left her hotel to take a cab into Old Town Heidelberg. She planned to lose herself, walking the cobblestone streets of Old Town, even if just for the day. Bright morning sunshine inspired her to stick her nose into most every shop on the Hauptstrasse along the Neckar River. The narrow street flowed to the Church of the Holy Ghost, and when the church's steeple bell sounded the hour, Jui smiled, happy to have plenty of Saturday ahead of her.

With a few purchases in hand, Jui chose one of the outdoor cafes for lunch. Tendrils of hair curled around her face and neck under the warm, late summer sun, making her wish she'd put her hair in a ponytail. A shaded table provided an escape from the heat. She chose a seat with her back to the wall so she could enjoy the colorful scenery. The hem of her skirt ruffled in the breeze, giving life to the bold, puce-colored orchids woven into the white fabric. Jui fluttered her wide-necked, emerald-green, peasant blouse to cool off a bit and then rested her chin on her hands, waiting for a waiter to show up.

A few tables away, a handsome man sitting with two beautiful women caught her attention. His companions flirted blatantly, rubbing their generous curves against him and nibbling his neck like pastry. The olive-skinned, tawny-haired man took it all in like Lord and Master.

Jui gazed over the top of her sunglasses at their naughty escapades. *Get a room, will you?*

A waitress brought Jui the lunch menu and a glass of water and then left. While she skimmed her choices, the low sounds of the stranger's voice kept distracting her and Jui couldn't help spying on the trio from behind her bound menu and dark glasses. When one of the vixens kissed the stranger, Jui's breath caught in her throat and she felt a warm pulse between her thighs.

The handsome stranger returned the kiss with similar

boldness, cupping the woman's head in his large hand. Their jaws flexed while they kissed, hinting at the passion behind it.

Another shot of desire raced through Jui's body. She couldn't drag her eyes away from the alluring scene.

The man ran his long fingers down the woman's slender arm and didn't even try hiding the intimate contact he made with her breast at the end of his journey.

Jui's words stuttered in her brain. *Holy shit.* His other companion leaned against his shoulder, with her luscious lips pursed in a pout. Jui wondered where the woman's hands were.

The waitress interrupted her lustful thoughts with a request to take her order.

Embarrassing heat filled Jui's face when she realized she hadn't even read the menu.

Glancing over her shoulder toward the trio, the waitress said in perfect English, "He's a dangerous one. Stay away from him."

For a second, Jui considered lying, but the man had already garnered her interest. "Who is he?"

"His name is Wade Kairos. He's a wealthy playboy — as you can see."

Jui heard a tenor of disapproval in the waitress's voice. "Does he live in Heidelberg?" As soon as the words left her lips, Jui wondered why she even cared.

"I have no idea. I see him occasionally during the summer, but I'm sure he spends the winters someplace much warmer." She jerked her head toward the threesome. "It's suiting."

"What is?"

"His name. Wade means 'traveler', Kairos is Greek for 'opportune moment' and he takes advantage of every opportunity." The waitress gave Jui a meaningful glare.

"Well, they ought to get a room."

The waitress chuckled. "He always brings playmates. You should come back in the evening...."

Jui changed the subject by placing her lunch order and then settled against her chair, determined not to play Peeping Tom any longer. The heat of someone's glare unnerved her, however, and she soon caved into the curiosity. Even at a distance, Jui could see the flecks of yellow and green in Wade's eyes. His gaze riveted hers, as if compelling her to stare at him, whether she wanted to or not. She bit her lower lip while gawking at his chiseled features. A shiver soft as a caress ran through her body, making Jui realize how attracted she was to him. She dragged her gaze away, only to hear his deep, baritone laugh. *Is he laughing at me?* She bought herself a spine and met his bold gaze again.

A seductive smile curled his lips to show even, white teeth. The handsome stranger named Wade Kairos tipped his head toward her. His full lips parted just a hint farther as he smiled.

A rush of emotions, cloaked in confusion, raced through her. *Is he flirting with me?*

Wade nodded again.

Jui dropped her gaze, flustered at the uncanny coincidence that he'd seemed to answer her question. His laughter floated above the other café patrons' voices, landed on her ears, and whispered into her soul. Suddenly, she felt warmer and connected somehow to the handsome stranger with the mysterious eyes and compelling smile. *Holy crap, the romantic lore of the city and the castle are getting to me.* She removed her dark glasses and studied the illustrious Mr. Kairos, who seemed to enjoy her attention as though he was sitting next to her. *Did he just say, join me?* Her brows furrowed. *How could I have the hots for a man I haven't even met?* She looked away, stabbing into her lunch.

While she ate, his voice and the soft laughter of his companions wafted to Jui's ears. Her German wasn't great and she only caught bits and pieces of their conversation. She wished she could move away but decided she wouldn't let him get the best of her. Digging into her schnitzel with renewed zest, she ignored the sound of metal chairs scraping on the patio stones.

"I'm Wade Kairos."

He chuckled when Jui almost dropped her fork. *Damn it, what an arrogant bastard!*

Wade extended his hand in greeting; a large silver ring with an onyx face graced his index finger.

Jui took her time wiping her mouth with a white linen napkin. "Are you always so forward?" *My god he's tall, and those shoulders....*

He answered in English with a soft German accent. "Only with beautiful women."

Jui shook his hand. The electricity flowing between them startled her. "Jui Fabrice," she said in an all-business tone.

"Such an unusual name for an American," Wade said without letting her hand go. "Jui—that's Sanskrit for 'flower', is it not?"

Jui wasn't fazed by his seductive pronunciation of her name–*Zjoo-ee*. "If you already knew, why ask?"

"American women are so bold. I find them enticing." He gave her another one of his captivating smiles.

"I'm not on the menu," Jui said in a crisp tone and slid her hand from his.

"I would never be so gauche. A gentleman waits for the offer." The statement hung in the air between them, laden with innuendo. "Are you here on holiday?"

"I don't think my plans are any of your business, Mr. Kairos." Jui ogled his female guests. "And anyway, from the looks of things, you're spoken for."

"Touché. How rude of me to ask you for dinner when—when I am otherwise detained."

His voice teased her ears like black velvet. The rich tones tangled around her body in a silken sheath, almost making her sigh with the way his voice naturally relaxed her. "Your reputation precedes you, Mr.—"

"Please call me Wade."

"—Kairos. And I haven't got time for a fling."

Wade chuckled while his female companions seemed oblivious to his flirting. "A fling? My dear, a night in your arms could never be described as a mere fling." He spoke in German to the two women clinging to him. "Would you please excuse us for a moment?"

"I understood that," Jui said in perfect German.

A humorous glint filled Wade's hazel eyes. "*Sprecht Du Deutsch?*"

"Enough," Jui said in German and then switched to English,

"but I prefer my native tongue when I need to be clear."

"I'd love to introduce your tongue—to mine."

Jui reached underneath her chair for her oversized, hot pink purse and fished out her wallet. "I'm certain your companions can help you out in the tongue department. I noticed they aren't bashful or inexperienced," she said, while taking out enough euros for the check and a tip.

"I've offended you." Wade picked up Jui's hand and pressed his cool lips against her skin. "Forgive me," he said gazing into her eyes. "Please let me make it up to you. Have dinner with me tonight."

Jui pulled her hand away. She rubbed the spot where he'd kissed her, trying to erase the sensations from her skin. "I have other plans. If you'll excuse me, Mr. Kairos."

"Wade."

When she stood, Jui realized the man was over six feet tall. She held her breath as he reached for her sunglasses and handed them to her.

"Green eyes. Sleek, long, black hair like a panther in the night. Beautiful Jui, the green-eyed flower."

With a shaking hand, Jui pushed the sunglasses back on her nose. "Excuse me—Wade."

He lifted a tendril of her long hair to his nose and inhaled. "Don't make me wait." He let the curl drop back onto her shoulder. "I'll call you." With a girl on each arm, Wade ushered them back onto the Hauptstrasse.

A half-smile curved Jui's lips. *You don't even know I'm staying at the Heidelberg Crowne Plaza. Even if you are just about the hunkiest man I've seen in a long time, you're still a cocky know-it-all.* She shrugged off the heady encounter. *Wade Kairos is one for the books.*

Chapter Two

The sandstone and rust-colored Heidelberg Castle sprawled above Old Town like a winged creature, holding in all its secrets and legends from the past. After a fire nearly destroyed the romantic home, previous castle owners had rebuilt and added new wings over the years. Jui stared at the footprint embedded in the pavement in front of her. She read in a castle brochure that a lover jumped from the window above her to escape a jealous husband. He landed so hard his footprint forever marked his passage. Jui dubbed the imprint a cheap tourist trick, began the long walk down the stairs to Old Town, and caught a cab back to the Crowne Plaza.

The message light blinked on her hotel room telephone. *I hope the message is in English.* A day of broken German conversations had taxed her brain. Jui skipped the messages, opting to leave a scarf over the annoying light, and laid down for a nap.

In her dreams, Jui watched herself dance at a ball, wearing an elegant, aqua-colored gown. The setting amused her since she had never worn a gown, not even to her high school prom. Her dance partner—a man with long, caramel-colored hair—seemed so comfortable having her in his arms as he whisked Jui around the dance floor. With a chiseled jaw and the most dramatic hazel eyes she'd ever seen, he damn near swept her off her feet. When his gaze met hers and he spoke without moving his lips, she became confused.

Come to me, Jui. We'll share an experience you'll never forget.

Her brain absorbed the invitation, but she didn't respond. She continued to dance like a mannequin with the man wearing long black tails. Her non-response seemed to perplex her dance partner. Again, he bid her to come to him.

Jui awoke, laughing at the ridiculousness of the dream, and reminded herself to call her sister, Sylvie. *Vie could use a good laugh.* She glanced at the clock and figured out the time difference. *It's the middle of the night at home.* Still giggling about the strange dream, Jui went into the shower to get ready for the evening.

*****

With sandals clattering on the butter-colored marble tiles, Jui hurried through the lobby to meet her coworkers for the evening.

"'Bout time, Jui," Rob said to her as she arrived. "Another minute and we'd have left you here."

She gave the group an apologetic smile and said, "I'm so sorry. I took a nap and overslept."

The group of six moved out of the hotel lobby to the waiting cabs.

"Where are we off to?" Jui said.

Stephanie answered with clear excitement in her voice. "The burning of the castle."

"The what?" Jui asked.

Rob provided a more succinct explanation. "Today is the first Saturday of the month. They light the castle with Roman candles and then shoot off fireworks. The event is supposed to be spectacular."

Stephanie said the desk clerk suggested watching from a boat on the Neckar River and partying the evening away.

"Sounds fun," Jui said, ducking into a cab and sliding in next to Rob.

Their thighs pressed together during the cab ride as the trio squeezed into the back seat. Rob slung his arm behind her, perhaps to give Jui a little extra space, but she doubted his intentions were honorable. During the past year, Rob Hawthorne had asked out Jui repeatedly and each time, she'd declined, saying she didn't think romantic relationships between coworkers was a good idea. The taxi's movement caused her body to shift into his even more. Soon Jui felt his thumb stroking her bare shoulder. She reached up and scratched her arm.

"Oh, sorry," he said when she caught him in the act. His brilliant, boyish smile made his blue eyes shimmer. He laughed easily and often, and right now, he seemed to be doing his level best to charm Jui.

Jui jostled against his muscular body during the ride down cobblestone streets. She liked his spicy cologne and soon recalled the enticing scene from the café earlier that day. Strong visions of handsome Wade locking lips and grinding against his voluptuous playmate made her temperature rise. *Maybe I've put off Rob Hawthorne long enough.*

The group left the cab near the docks where large party boats, decorated with lights and banners, awaited this evening's revelers. Jui and her friends managed to get on one vessel together and accepted noisemakers to rattle during the fireworks.

Music from the various boats combined in the nighttime air to create a cornucopia of sounds. Jui stood next to Rob, watching the fireworks explode into myriads of color. She joined the hooting and hollering during the thunderous explosions and toasted the spectacular effects with large glasses of German Bier. She laughed at Rob's crazy antics and comments, in part, because the man had a great sense of humor, but mostly because the beer made her tipsy.

After tossing back the last of her beer, Jui said, "I have to get something to eat."

Rob craned his neck, moving closer to her. "What? I didn't hear you."

She shouted over the band and the crowd. "I'm hungry."

Rob shook his head, indicating he still didn't understand what she said, so Jui pulled his head toward her lips. "I said I'm hungry."

In the flickering firelight, she noticed the intensity of Rob's eyes moments before he planted a lingering, gentle kiss. When he pulled away, the next round of fireworks illuminated his face, displaying his broad smile.

"You look pretty pleased with yourself."

He flagged down a waitress passing around large, soft pretzels and offered one to Jui with another easy grin. "I've waited a really long time to kiss you."

The band struck up a popular German polka and everyone locked arms and swayed left and right to the music. Each time Jui's breast pressed against Rob's upper arm a zing of pleasure spiraled through her.

When the song ended, Rob turned her in his arms and kissed her boldly. The strength of his body and the obviousness of his desire were impossible to ignore.

Cupping her chin, he spoke in a low, husky voice. "Spend the night with me."

Thunderous explosions and nearly seamless flashes of light signaled the grand finale. Bold intent shined in his eyes and Jui kissed him again, silently acquiescing. Afterward, she leaned her back to Rob's chest, with his arm wrapped across her shoulders. The gentle rocking of the boat provided just enough movement to caress his cock with her buttocks. Her desire rose with each of his soft moans.

Rob nibbled her neck, just below her ear. "When are we getting off this damn boat?"

Jui smiled and stiffened in his arms, hoping to add a little more heat to Rob's fire.

He whispered into her ear. "Wait 'til I get you back to the hotel. I'll make you pay for teasing me half the night."

"Tease, did you say?" She gave him a wicked smile and broke from his embrace. The night air cooled her skin, sending shivers up and down her body. "You must be mistaken." She glanced down at the noticeable bulge in his jeans and then licked her lips. "I didn't do that."

* * * * *

Once they got off the boat, Rob and Jui made their excuses to the rest of their group. Jui giggled after they parted from their co-workers. "Do you think they know?"

Rob feigned ignorance. "Know what?"

"You know...."

Rob stopped in the middle of the sidewalk and drew Jui back into his arms. "That I'm going to make you come so hard your toes curl?" He kissed her again. "Do you know how long I've wanted to make love to you?"

She smiled, hearing about his hot plans for her. "I hope

we won't have to wait long for a cab."

They walked arm in arm along the crowded, narrow street. One voice in particular sounded so familiar, she glanced over her shoulder to put a face with it. Her eyes widened when she realized Wade and his small entourage of lovelies followed twenty feet behind her and Rob. Wade passed under a street lamp, tossing Jui a knowing smile and a nod of acknowledgement.

Wade's wicked smile made her shiver and suddenly, the waitress's words of warning came back to her. "*You ought to come here after dark...he's dangerous.*"

Soft laughter cut through the silence. She glanced backward once again. His eyes gleamed as he drew nearer.

"Hey, watch out!" Rob said as Jui stepped off the curb without looking. "You're going to get run over."

Now Wade stood only a few feet away and Jui was torn between watching the seductive character behind her and acknowledging the man she'd promised the night.

Wade gave Jui another silky smile, before pulling one of his dates into a searing French kiss.

Jui gasped at the sexy performance and her body throbbed with jealous arousal.

"Anxious?" Imitating the scene behind them, Rob drew Jui into a kiss. She didn't even close her eyes as her lips and tongue mechanically twisted with Rob's. Instead, from the corner of her eye, she watched Wade and his kissing companion. Likewise, Wade never took his gaze off her while he tended to the buxom woman in his arms. She swore she heard him laughing even though his lips were otherwise occupied.

When Rob finally took her hand and led her into a waiting taxi, Jui noticed Wade's watchful gaze followed her.

* * * * *

During the cab ride to their hotel, Jui stroked Rob's rock hard cock through his jeans. Goose bumps raced over her body when she noticed the cab driver using his review mirror to watch them make out. Their wanton behavior in front of the cabbie turned Jui on more than she expected.

Rob slid down in his seat, tugging at the tight fabric confining his stiff shaft. "Can't he drive faster?"

Jui kissed and nibbled Rob's neck, enjoying the sensation of his evening beard on her lips. She ran her tongue along the coarse whiskers on his jaw while eying the rear view mirror. Her gaze locked with the driver's and the corners of her mouth curled up in a provocative smirk.

With a wink to the driver, Jui curled her leg over Rob's lap, letting her skirt slide up her bare thigh. Rob caressed her ass while she dry fucked his thigh. He groaned under her assault and she responded by stroking his cock with the heel of her hand.

The driver cleared his throat. "We've arrived."

The sound of his voice turned down the heat, but didn't put out Jui's fire. Rob wiggled his hand in his snug, front pocket to retrieve a fold of euros and thanked the driver.

"It was my pleasure," the driver said.

They walked through the lobby holding hands and Rob flicked his middle finger against Jui's palm, signaling his intent. Jui was hornier than hell and satisfying her ache was the only thing she cared about at that moment.

"Your room or mine?" Rob asked between kisses in the empty elevator.

"Yours." Jui liked the idea of being able to leave when she wanted, not the other way around.

With his room door closed behind them, Rob asked, "Would you like a drink?"

"A drink of this." Lust had drenched her body twenty minutes ago, and Jui wasted no time reaching for Rob's jeans and unzipping them. His eyes smoldered as she shoved his shorts to the floor and took the head of his cock in her mouth.

"Oh fuck yeah, Jui. Suck me hard. Like that," he said as his shaft slid into her open throat until his balls rested against her chin. A minute later, he pulled her off him. "You're going to make me come. Stand up."

Undressed to her bra and panties, Jui waited for Rob to make the next move. The way his eyes swept over every inch of her sent a hot puddle of moisture to her throbbing pussy.

"Are you going to window-shop or buy?"

His eyes smoldered with desire. Rob carried Jui to bed, raking off her navy blue underwear as he laid her down. He mounted her in a single motion.

"Ahh," Jui moaned, feeling some relief from the sexual itch she needed Rob to scratch. She wrapped her legs around his narrow hips. "Fuck me like in your wet dreams."

Rob pumped his cock in Jui's pussy with a smacking force. He leaned above her with eyes closed, biceps and shoulders bulging, and drove into her.

"Did you fuck me this way in your dreams? Does my pussy feel better than your hand?"

"You're so hot. Better than I imagined, a million times better."

Jui raised her hips, feeling her orgasm building as he strummed against her G-spot. All her muscles tightened, slowing his ability to thrust at will. He howled monosyllables as he reached his own release. Realizing she'd be left in the cold if she didn't take matters into her own hands, Jui reached down and rubbed her clit until her pussy pulsed around his softening cock. Rob barely seemed to notice.

A moment later, he rolled off her. He threw an arm over his sweaty forehead and chuckled.

"What?" she asked, running her fingers through the tight blond curls on his chest.

"Sex with you was way better than I'd fantasized." He pulled her closer and kissed her, stroking her tongue with his. "Much better." He climbed out of bed. "I'll be right back."

Jui watched Rob walk into the bathroom. His muscular flanks and back told her he spent a lot of time at the gym.

He came back with a warm cloth and towel. "You okay?" he asked while wiping his cum from her skin.

"That was good."

When he finished, Rob took her in his arms and soon fell asleep.

His gentle breaths tickled Jui's ear while she laid there, wide awake. She retrieved her mental scorecard. This was a naughty practice Jui and her girlfriends started after her friend, Sheila, complained about the crappy night in the sack

13

she'd had with her newly ditched man. Jui scored the columns in her mind. *Kissing-eight. Hand action-six. Cock length-six. Thickness-five. My satisfaction-four. He forgot cunnilingus.* Jui stifled a giggle. She loved the word. She exaggerated the word's pronunciation in her mind and put accents on different syllables. *"Oral sex" just doesn't sound as good as cun-nil-ing-us.* A little giggle escaped her lips and Rob stirred.

Overall, she gave him about a six. She gazed at her sleeping bed partner and wondered if she should wake him and offer a chance to improve his score. *The number would have been higher if his cock was just a little longer and a little thicker, too. One of these days, I'd like to be with a man who's really hung.* The giggle track replayed in her head. Jui rolled out of bed. She glanced back to see if Rob noticed her absence, but he hadn't moved a muscle. She got dressed and let herself out.

* * * * *

Back in her room, Jui decided to play it cool with Rob. *Fun guy but not too great in bed.* She stripped down and rinsed in the shower. Her muscles were tender in all the right places. *Maybe he has potential. We'll see how things go when we get back to the States. Lord knows getting involved in an office romance with Isaac turned out to be a total disaster. I definitely don't want to go through an ugly breakup with a colleague again.* Jui toweled off and then soothed her skin with moisturizer. *But Rob really seems to be into me. Maybe I can teach him a thing or two about how to please a woman.* She drifted off to sleep with a smile on her face.

* * * * *

Wade entered her dreams and smiled, tuning into the sexy subject in her mind. *So your romp with the blond American wasn't as satisfying as you'd like?* The king-sized bed shifted as his weight joined hers. He studied her face, so peaceful in repose, and whispered into her mind, "*Come to me, Jui, I'll show you what it feels like to be with a man who can satisfy you in ways you can only imagine.*"

The way Jui frowned told Wade she understood him. He used mental telepathy to speak to her again. "*Don't fight me, Jui. Let me in.*"

Jui moaned and shifted her weight. For an instant, she stiffened when she made contact with his chest.

Wade monitored her thoughts, which were jumbled in the airy space between wakefulness and sleep. "*You're not dreaming, Jui. I'm here. Come to me.*" He gazed at her luscious naked body, half exposed to his view. His mouth watered and his teeth ached in anticipation of joining with her.

She turned over, presenting her back, rejecting him.

With a feral growl of frustration, Wade fell into the shadow cast by the moon and disappeared.

Chapter Three

In a rush of wind, Wade Kairos returned to Christophe's chateau situated in the Bavarian Alps, 200 kilometers south of Heidelberg. His mid-thigh-length black coat rustled when his molecules reorganized into his image. Wade stood in his bedroom, still furious over Jui's rebuke. He roared his displeasure with the next breath he took, loud and angry, until his whole body shook from the force of his vocal explosion. A swift swipe of his hand across the oak bureau sent everything flying and he shoved the heavy piece of furniture on its side. The cuckoo clock slid down the wall, crashed as it hit the floor, and made crazy, ceaseless annunciations. The mere sound further enraged Wade. He picked up the hapless clock and flung it with all his strength out the open balcony doors. The cuckoo noises diminished to silence.

Wade whirled around to choose another target.

His friend and mentor, Christophe, surveyed the damage with an arched eyebrow. "Trouble in paradise?"

Wade returned the elder vampire's cold glare and commanded in an inhuman voice, deep and breathy, "Get out. I don't need your lectures." Anger still ruled him as he jerked out of his coat and then wrenched the bureau out of the plaster wall, exposing a gaping hole. Seeing the destruction, another threatening roar erupted from Wade's throat.

Christophe used telepathy to demand Wade regain self-control before he frightened away tonight's willing guests.

The pitch of Christophe's thoughts ached in Wade's seething brain, getting his attention. Wade snarled. "How many?"

"Six are still available. Have you fed tonight?"

"Some."

"Join me. The sun will be up in a few hours."

Wade followed Christophe to the living room. A freestanding bronze fireplace in the center warmed the room with flickering orange and blue flames. Contemporary leather furniture designed to complement the natural curves

17

of the body provided visual rhythm. Rust and dark green-striped pillows magnified the cream and cocoa accent pillows scattered around the room.

Christophe handled the introductions. "Ladies, I'd like you to meet Wade Kairos. I'm certain he'll enjoy your company as much as I."

Wade gazed at the women, none of whom looked older than twenty. Each wore provocative lingerie, which also didn't surprise him. Women flocked to Christophe for romance and exotic pleasures, but Wade knew their addictive desires stemmed from what he jokingly called Christophe's "love bites." Their human partners described the sensation like a branding iron pulsing through their bodies with the most powerful sexual tension they'd ever experienced. The true cause of their lusty experience, a vampire bite, brought eager women to Christophe's homes all over the world, and Wade had sampled many.

Wade sat on large, comfortable floor cushions among the enthusiastic hotties. Jui's rejection still pissed him off, and despite needing to feed, seducing four women didn't appeal to him tonight. Resigned, he leaned backward between the legs of an eager blonde and rested his head against her generous breasts.

The young blonde massaged Wade's shoulder muscles. "You're very tense. Can we help you relax?"

Her breath smelled sweet and Wade's hypersensitive hearing tuned into the rhythm of her heart.

"Yes, how can we relieve your stress?" another asked while unbuttoning Wade's black silk shirt. She spread the soft fabric and pressed her lips to his chest, licking and kissing his cool skin.

Wade moved the woman's long, straight, black hair away from her face so he could watch her ruby lips go to work. Another pair of nimble hands moved up his thigh to his cock. By the time her skilled fingers reached their target, an impressive looking bulge formed in his tight black jeans.

He closed his eyes, wanting to give whatever the women wanted from him, taking what he needed. He flicked his tongue along the firm, satiny flesh on the blonde's slender arm. The young woman smelled like oxygen, fresh and alive. Her pulse increased as he wrapped his lips around her slender wrist.

"Yes please, Wade, I've been waiting all evening," she said in a whisper.

His razor-sharp teeth pierced the layers of her skin and the delicious radial artery below. Her blood tasted like warm port wine. Wade was just getting into his living meal when a pair of eager lips wrapped around the head of his cock and a firm tongue stroked his balls. He flexed his knees, distracted by the talented women pleasuring him.

The blonde's heart rate slowed and her breaths grew shallow against Wade's chest. Wade and Christophe enforced a firm rule about turning humans. They didn't. He released her wrist, licking away the droplets of dark red blood appearing from the small punctures. He'd almost taken her too far. She moaned and leaned back against the pillows.

Wade forgot about his blonde snack when another woman climbed aboard his rigid member. Her beautiful, midnight black skin contrasted with the lips of her glistening, bright pink vagina. Inch-by inch, his cock penetrated her. A wide grin spread across Wade's lips. He enjoyed women with full hips and eager attitudes. Wade got into the seduction game.

The woman leaned forward and bit his shoulder. "Fuck me," she said, while meeting his gaze. "You know you want to."

Wade stifled a smile. His interest lay in a long sip of the woman's blood. Letting her think a good fuck was foremost in his mind always worked to a vampire's advantage. He held her hips and pumped into her wet pussy.

The dark-skinned woman's eyes rolled in her head but she begged him not to stop. Her long fingernails raked his chest. A mere mortal would have dripped blood afterward. She didn't seem to notice that didn't happen; Wade didn't care. The woman was wet and willing so Wade didn't mind using her to wipe the bitchy American out of his mind. He flipped her onto her stomach and took her from behind. Gazing across the room, he saw Christophe enjoying his own delights. He sent Christophe a message. *You still fuck pretty well for an old man.*

Christophe's silent laughter filled Wade's brain.

Wade lay across the beautiful woman's back, inhaling the scent of her sweat. The strenuous activity opened her veins, making her blood flow quicker through her body. Her heartbeat echoed from her chest into Wade's ear. He reached around to massage her swollen clit. "Come hard, let me feel you pulse around my cock, the same way your heart pulses in my ear."

The black woman groaned louder when Wade intensified his strokes.

He growled into her ear, growing impatient. "That's it. Feel me in you, branding you, owning you. Come." As her orgasm began, Wade sunk his teeth into her carotid. He caressed her breasts, two generous handfuls, keeping her still until he finished feeding. He moaned in appreciation for her delicious gift and let her think he'd achieved orgasm. She didn't need to know vampires can't orgasm. Wade listened to her heartbeat slow to its normal rate and then dropped a little lower. He laved her neck with his tongue, licking every droplet from the little punctures wounds. They healed in seconds, eliminating uncomfortable questions with even more uncomfortable answers later.

The beautiful woman collapsed on her side, appearing exhausted. Her eyes were glassy slits and a satisfied smile curled her full lips. "Kairos, you can fuck me any time."

* * * * *

The sun snuck above the horizon by the time Christophe ushered their female guests out the door. He stretched languidly and told Wade, "Time for bed."

Shaking his thumb toward the departing women, Wade said, "They sure put a better spin on my night."

"I wonder if any of them ever wonders about us — what we are." Christophe leaned against the front door and chuckled. "Sometimes I wonder what I'd do if one of them showed up in a bad mood carrying garlic and holy water."

The old vampire folklore made Wade laugh, too. "Show

them the kitchen?"

Christophe shook his head, still laughing. "Shall we climb into our coffins?"

When they reached Wade's bedroom, Christophe said, "I think your next degree ought to be in remodeling or construction. If you're not going to outgrow your immaturities, at least you could learn to repair them."

Wade smirked at his companion's acerbic remark. "But you always enjoy the men who come to do the repairs. They give you an opportunity to explore your wilder side," he said, taking a jab at Christophe's sexual appetite for men as well as women.

"I think I can manage to secure companions without bringing them here under the guise of home repairs. At the very least I think you should take an anger management class."

Wade couldn't help laughing over the absurd remark. "Or perhaps I should take up jogging to relieve my stress? Asshole."

"So what filed your fangs tonight? Or shall I ask, who?" Christophe threw Wade a pointed glare.

"These little mind games are so tedious. In a few hundred years, you and I won't even speak to each other. Maybe I should learn some of that cloaking bullshit to keep you out of my head."

Christophe laughed. "So what are you planning to do about the elusive Jui?"

Wade let out a deep breath and ran his hand through his hair, pulling out the braided tie. He examined the soft leather between his fingers. "I don't know."

"Why didn't you just take her and move on?"

He paused a minute and then met Christophe's stern gaze. "I don't think I've ever been rejected before. The woman was impervious to all the bait I laid. When we met this afternoon, I know she was turned on enough to leave with me, but I wasn't alone. Tonight she was intrigued and aroused...."

"But?"

"But nothing. She acted like *she* had cloaking abilities."

"Does she? Is she truly human?"

Wade nodded. "She is."

21

"Why bother? I don't like that look in your eyes, Wade. Getting emotionally involved with a human is dangerous and risky for you and for all of us."

"I don't need your fucking lectures."

Christophe glared at the younger vampire. "It's not a lecture. It's the truth and I'm not the only one who won't tolerate your bullshit. I can only protect you so much from the others. We'll talk about Jui later. Goodnight."

* * * * *

Wade stripped off his clothes and then pulled back the bedding. He moved on the soft fabric beneath him like a cat stretching in the sun, flexing his feet, and twisting his torso to work out the kinks in his back. While waiting for sleep to claim him, he tried not to hold a grudge against Christophe for his protective behavior. He was, after all, responsible for turning Wade.

Wade recalled the excitement of sitting in Christophe Strasse's physics class more than seventy years ago. The illustrious Strasse taught at the University of Heidelberg and he and Wade hit it off the moment they met. Wade enjoyed their vigorous discussions about physics more than anything.

Emptiness always filled his soul when he remembered the fateful day that changed him forever. Wade never saw the car that sideswiped his on the Autobahn near Munich. He regained consciousness cradled in Christophe's arms.

"*I couldn't let it happen,*" Christophe had said. Then seemingly, without effort, he lifted Wade and carried him away from the crash scene before they were discovered.

Cloaked by the forest, Christophe had tried to explain Wade's new consciousness. "*Surviving the crash wasn't humanly possible. You have a brilliant scientific mind and the world will benefit from everything you can teach us. You'll have a place in history – with me.*"

Wade had struggled to understand. His voice sounded like a croak. "*Am I dead or alive?*"

"*Neither.*" Wade never forgot the pain in Christophe's

eyes as he'd confessed what he'd done. *"I'm not what you think I am. I mean, I'm a teacher, that's true, but I'm not...not human."*

"You're not making any sense."

Christophe had stuttered through his explanation. *"I'm a vampire and now...so are you. I couldn't let you die. I wanted you to live with me and teach with me...so I turned you into...what I am."*

For weeks, Wade had trouble absorbing the enormity of what Christophe had done to him. He'd taken solace in the fact Christophe hadn't abandoned him in his new existence. In fact, Christophe had done everything possible to make Wade's transition into vampirism as easy as possible and to help him cope with new identities and living arrangements as the years passed.

* * * * *

Jui's wakeup call came much too early. She thanked the hotel operator and fumbled with the receiver until the handset rested back on the cradle. Stuffing a pillow over her head, she turned over with a groan, wanting to go back to sleep. But slumber evaded her.

Jui thought about getting dressed and checking on Rob. *Too eager.* She had a nagging feeling that something happened last night when she got back to her room. She wracked her brain but remembered only hazel eyes. *Man, I gotta get back to the States for a little more variety in eye color.* She rolled out of bed chuckling.

Jui loved sexy underwear, and today she chose a cerulean lace panty to wear under her tight, faded jeans. The panty resembled more of a suggestion than a real garment. She skipped her bra and pulled on a form-fitting, white t-shirt that showed off her breasts. After tying her hair at her neck with a tie-dyed sash, she grabbed her black leather jacket. A village to the north was holding a wine festival and Jui thought spending her Sunday at the vineyard might be relaxing and interesting.

She took the train to Weinheim, then rented a bicycle and followed the crowd to the vineyards. At the first one, she

bought a tasting glass emblazoned with the vineyard name. She sampled one wine after the other until the alcohol and the afternoon sun made her lightheaded. Jui chuckled about her carelessness and stopped for lunch in one of the large storage barns converted into a quaint café. While she ate a rich slice of Black Forest tort, she decided which wines she liked best. Afterward, she walked back out to the fields to place her order.
"Just in time," the clerk told her as she wrote up the sale.
"Excuse me?"
The clerk pointed to the threatening sky. "The afternoon rain."
Jui glanced at the dark clouds moving in. "Every day?"
"Almost, this time of year. The showers won't last long, but find a place to hide or you'll be soaked."
"May I wait here?"
Pointing, the woman said, "Run to that little cottage."
No sooner did the words leave the woman's lips than the first drops fell. The cloudburst gained momentum, peppering Jui as she ran to the cottage. She lifted her arms to shield her head from the sudden downpour, but her efforts were of little avail. She twisted the doorknob and pushed on the door. *Locked.* A skeleton key rested in the lock and she cursed a hundred times before she wiggled the stubborn key the right way. She hustled over the threshold and pushed the door shut behind her. Jui shrugged out of her damp leather jacket and looked down at her soaked clothing. The front of her shirt clung to her skin and Jui giggled, imagining she won the vineyard's wet tee shirt contest.
The sound of someone clearing his throat startled her. Turning, she narrowed her eyes and frowned, trying to remember the man's name.
"Wade, Wade Kairos. We met yesterday." He got out of the rocking chair and said, "I've forgotten my manners. Please let me help you." He extended his hand and took Jui's wet leather jacket from her.
"Are you following me?"
"If I was following you, how could I possibly arrive before you? Did you plan to seek shelter from the afternoon rains in

24

this guest cottage?"

Jui studied Wade, uncertain whether to believe him.

"I assure you, our meeting is mere coincidence. You can see I'm half-soaked, too." Wade flicked the collar of his button-down shirt. The forest green fabric with gold flecks accentuated his olive-toned skin. "And my hair," he said, leaning toward Jui, "see, it's damp, just like yours."

Jui already noticed the way his hair coiled loosely in the humidity and admired the golden tones woven in the caramel color.

"You're staring, my dear."

"I'm sorry," she stammered. Jui closed her eyes and tried to shake the feeling Wade was in her head somehow. "It seems so odd to keep running into you—I mean, of all places to...."

"Share a rainstorm?" Wade stood inches away from Jui. His sensitive hearing picked up her increased heart rate. Goose bumps rose on her arms and her beautiful nipples ripened before his eyes. His musky scent and the sensual pheromones released by his body were stroking her olfactory lobe as surely as his tongue soon would. Wade's mouth watered. He couldn't wait to join with her.

Jui rubbed her arms as though chilled and glanced around the small cottage. "Excuse me a moment. I'll be right back."

Her shapely hips swayed as she left the small room. He invaded her thoughts and learned she was confused about the powerful attraction she felt for him. A smile curled his lips and remained when she immerged from the bathroom toweling her hair.

"May I?" he asked.

Unmistakable indecision filled Jui's eyes. She glanced upward where the rain pummeled the red tiled roof.

"The rain shower won't stop for awhile. You might as well make yourself comfortable." He reached for the towel and the plush fabric slid from her hand into his.

"Sit, please," he said, indicating a padded stool near the window. Lace curtains hung on the windows even in this simple gardener's cottage.

Jui perched on the stool while Wade stroked her thick, dark hair with the white cotton towel.

"You have beautiful hair," he said. "It's so luxurious. I wish my hair was more so."

Jui stood while reaching for his damp locks.

His gaze held hers as she made contact. His entire body stilled. He studied her, trying to penetrate her thoughts and gage her reaction to touching him. Her unique response frustrated him again. *Any other woman would have fallen into my arms already, offering herself like pâté on a delicate cracker.*

"Your hair is so soft. It feels like mink."

Wade wanted to be sure he understood the translation. "The small animal from which they make fur coats?"

"Yes," Jui said, still stroking his hair as though it was the finest silk. "Mink is the most wonderful feeling against your bare skin."

As he dropped the towel, Wade's hand brushed across her puckered nipple. He imagined the sensitive peak got even firmer after the intimate, albeit innocent, contact. Frustration rose when he couldn't access her mind. His determination to make this defiant creature come to him grew.

Jui ran a well-manicured fingernail along his jaw line. The scruffy whiskers there made the gentlest crackling sound against her nails. When she reached the cleft of his chin, she drew his lips to hers and dared to sap the strength from his body with a bold kiss that communicated the depth of her passion.

She curled her leg around his calf, keeping him close after they kissed. "Does your chest feel like mink, Wade Kairos? Is your treasure trail soft on a woman's lips?"

He grasped her smaller hand in his and brought it to his chest, sliding their enjoined hands under his shirt. "I believe my body could pleasure you in many ways." Wade maintained a calm exterior, but when he attempted to penetrate Jui's mind, the steel door he slammed against unnerved him. He had no sense of what Jui thought or was feeling. He hadn't felt so inept in over seventy years. *Since I was human.*

Wade's nostrils flared as he inhaled her sexual pheromones and the richness of her blood. After unbuttoning his black and gray-striped shirt, Wade pulled the garment from his black jeans. Jui never glanced up at him during the process and he wished he knew why. He spread the fabric.

A soft moan escaped her lips when her fingers curled in the soft hairs beneath her fingertips.

Wade's mouth watered; his bloodlust grew. He drew his open palms downward and then moved them in a circular motion around the fullness of her breasts.

Jui raised her eyes to his. The dark green orbs smoldered with desire.

He sensed no fear. He raised her tight t-shirt over her breasts. "Come closer, my little minx. See if the softness you desire is truly felt." He cradled her against his chest, while pressing kisses along her shoulder, up to the delicious pulsing spot below her left ear. Wade flew solo, unaided by telepathy. He focused on what flowed through her veins, listening to Jui's respiration and heart rates. *They're steady. She's not very aroused.* Wade mentally commanded his cock to harden. He drew Jui closer to him, letting her feel the growing length of his cock. He rubbed it against her thigh with a gentle rhythm, dry fucking her until he heard her body respond. Then he bit down, relishing the sweet, first taste of her blood, warm and life sustaining.

Fire zipped through Jui's body, erotic and wild. She reached into his waistband, sliding her fingers through his soft treasure trail until she encountered his cock. Even semi-flaccid, it felt long and thick against her palm. Jui'd never experienced one so large. She looked forward to Wade Kairos' results on her sex scorecard. She unzipped his jeans, eager to take him fully in hand, and discovered her fingers couldn't encircle him. She whimpered with anticipation as wet heat soaked her pussy. Anxious to see all of Wade, Jui stepped away.

His lips left her neck with a light popping sound. He bowed his head while Jui slid his jeans down his muscular thighs, stooping until his cock danced in front of her lips. She cupped his heavy, smooth balls and ran her tongue up his length. Her body quaked with excitement. She wondered if she could accommodate his size and could hardly wait to find out. The veins along his tumescent length pulsed against her tongue. His rod filled her mouth and stretched her throat.

"*Holy shit,*" her brain screamed, "*this guy is huge.*" His size made sucking cock even more exciting. While her lips and tongue worked on Wade, the rest of her body, specifically her soaking wet pussy, looked forward to feeling him inside her.

Wade stroked her hair while she sucked him. "Does sucking my dick turn you on, Jui? Are you wondering how it'll feel to have me buried inside you?" he asked in a tone meant for seduction. He lifted her shirt higher on her slender back, letting his fingers trace the outlines of her shoulder blades as they moved with each back and forth glide of her head. The edge of a birthmark came into view and Wade slid her shirt to the side to see the unique mole. The light brown mark resembled a small figure eight. The mark looked familiar but there had been so many women in his life over the past seventy years. Many he'd only been with once; some he enjoyed a season before he and Christophe moved on.

Jui stood in front of him with a wet, seductive smile on her face.

"The rain stopped and someone is coming."

"I don't hear anyone," she whispered and then nibbled on his lower lip.

Wade pulled her t-shirt down. "Cover yourself."

She frowned. "What's the rush? Nobody's coming."

"Someone is and I don't want whoever it is to think badly of you. A man is simply a rogue." No sooner did Wade have his jeans back on his hips, than the doorknob rattled.

Jui was still tucking her shirt in her jeans when the door swung open.

"I'm sorry, I didn't...," the man stuttered in German.

Wade replied in the man's native tongue. "There's no problem. We took shelter from the rain." He tuned into her angry thoughts about the man's ill-timed interruption. "We were getting ready to leave, weren't we?"

"Yes, thank you for the use of the cottage," she said in halting German.

They left the small cottage and Jui took his hand, forcing him to slow his pace. "Wade, can we go somewhere—together?" she asked, biting her lip until a droplet of blood appeared on the delicate tissue.

Wade wiped the dark red fluid with his thumb, licked it, and then smiled at her. "Another time, perhaps. I think the moment has passed."

Jui raised her eyebrows, surprised and embarrassed at the remark. "I'm sorry. I thought—we had something going—wow, I'm glad...."

"Glad what, Jui? Glad you didn't give into temptation with a dark stranger?"

A string of curse words ran through her brain but Jui leveled her gaze at Wade. Regaining her composure, she said, "You'll never know what you missed. See you 'round, Mr. Kairos." Jui turned on her heel and walked away without giving him a chance to respond.

She hopped on her bike and pedaled toward the village to catch the train to Heidelberg. "Arrogant bastard," she muttered and then groaned in frustration. Glancing at her watch, she thought she might be able to catch Rob after dinner. She phoned him.

"Where are you?" he asked.

"Riding my bike back to this little village. I went to a vineyard today."

"I wondered where you went. I left you a few messages."

"I'll be back in an hour. Maybe we can pick up where we left off...." She hoped the suggestion tickled Rob's libido.

"Sounds good. When I woke up and you were gone and I couldn't reach you all day I thought I'd done something wrong."

Jui felt a little slimy knowing she was going to use Rob to get her rocks off, thanks to the arrogant man she'd just left behind. "Not at all. Be waiting, I'll come right to your room."

"I'll order some dinner and drinks."

Jui bumped along on the cobblestone street and her voice started to shake with the vibrations. "I can't wait. See you in a little bit." She shut her phone and slid it into her back pocket.

"Your loss, Wade, you conceited jerk."

Chapter Four

Wade arrived in his chateau bedroom moments after Jui disappeared from his sight. The wall plaster still looked wet after repairs and a new oak bureau stood ready for service. He sat in an overstuffed, leather chair and put his feet up on the ottoman. His shoes slid off and landed on the floor with a couple of soft *thunks*.

He needed to feed but his brain was paralyzed. He'd seen a similar birthmark once before. Remembering felt like a million years ago—and yet, only a breath ago.

Claire.... He was thirty years old at the time, and studying for a master's in mathematics at the University of Chicago. At any time of the day or night, Wade could be found reading in the library or in the laboratory, working with his colleagues.

Classical music was his only vice, and he'd never missed a university chamber orchestra concert. A beautiful cellist captured his attention the very first time he saw her. Her body swayed to the music she played. Discrete inquiries produced her name: Claire Seaforth.

Wade waited for Claire a few times after concerts to compliment her performance, but she'd met his kind words with cool disdain. Miss Seaforth paid little attention to anything or anyone unrelated to her goal of becoming a concert cellist. Nevertheless, he had continued to attend her performances and after tenacious inquiries, learned where she rehearsed.

After months of gentle cajoling, Claire agreed to have coffee with Wade. Their relationship was public and proper. He escorted her on his arm and after several months of the ritual, he chastely kissed her on the cheek. Deep in his heart, Wade knew Claire was the woman of his dreams.

When Claire had invited him to a private performance of her quartet at her uncle's home, Wade hadn't hesitated to accept. He was eager to spend every minute he could with her and thought the invitation was an important step toward cementing their relationship.

She'd met him at the door on the appointed day, wearing a loose-fitting gown resembling more of what Wade imagined she slept in than performed in. A fire glowed in the brick fireplace in the large living room and no one else seemed to be around.

Puzzled, he'd asked if he'd come on the wrong day. She'd answered with a smile and a gentle tug of his hand to draw him inside.

She'd seduced him in front of the fireplace and spent the entire afternoon and evening in his arms making love.

She was the most exciting woman he'd ever met—an amazing mixture of primness and seductress. No one would ever have guessed Claire Seaforth wasn't the schoolmarm she appeared to be. The slender, green-eyed nymph with the figure-eight birthmark on her left shoulder was a passionate woman, eager to give as much as she received. Wade couldn't have envisioned a more satisfying lover. When she'd accepted his marriage proposal a few weeks later, he couldn't believe his ears.

Despite their pending marriage, Wade had wanted to go to Europe to study under Strasse for a year. Claire had understood. She planned to audition with the French Philharmonic and they decided to meet for romantic trysts all over Europe. Their goodbyes were sorrowful but neither thought that fateful day in September, 1940, would be the last time the lovers would see each other.

He'd raged over being turned a vampire but realized death was also a "life sentence." His life with Claire was over no matter what. He'd hovered as a shadow to witness her unfathomable grief at his memorial service, where a body was unavailable to bury. As the coffin containing a few of his personal effects lowered into the ground, Claire became inconsolable.

Misery overwhelmed him now, as if the event happened only yesterday and he asked himself the same questions he'd asked himself thousands of times since his burial. *What could I do? Present myself to her as a vampire and ask her to spend eternity with me like this?*

He paced his chambers. The gnawing urge to feed grew with each footstep. Wade tuned into the household noise and picked up the sounds of Christophe and a male he assumed was the latest repairman. With a snort, Wade fell into the shadows to prowl the streets for his dinner.

* * * * *

In his library later that evening, Christophe read at his computer. He appreciated modern technology and its connectivity to brilliant minds around the world, but he also loved the scent of leather-bound books and they lined the shelves on his walls. Sensing Wade's arrival, he glanced up. "You've been gone a long time."

"I came back earlier, but you were otherwise engaged," Wade said, giving Christophe a smirk.

Christophe snorted. "A-positive, not my favorite."

"I think the guy I just dined on drank his dinner."

A frown knitted Christophe's eyebrows. "What made you so desperate you took the first come, first served route? You know better." The scowl on Wade's face cued Christophe into a deeper thought level. "Why are you torturing yourself over Claire? I thought you put her out of your mind when she died forty years ago." He studied the tall man standing in the shadows and understood Wade's grief for his past life. The anger Christophe carried about being turned never dissipated either. He'd never met a vamp who loved eternal life and the endless loneliness that filled their existence. Unchecked, the longing meant nothing but trouble for every vampire.

"It's Jui," Wade said. "She has the same birthmark on her shoulder Claire did."

Christophe didn't hide his frustration over the tiresome subject. "Sheer coincidence."

Wade snarled with a fierceness that would have sent a human scurrying for cover, but Christophe was used to his outbursts.

"Don't you think I've said the same thing to myself a hundred times already?"

"What does this woman mean to you? She's a meal, a roll in the sack," Christophe shot back, his frustration growing.

"She should be those things but she's not." Wade rested his hands on his hips and paced in and out of the library lamp's shadows. "She rejects me, brushes me off with a flick of her wrist, and gets on with her life. And I can only read her thoughts accurately when bullshit is running through her brain, like which shoes she's going to wear or what time her next meeting is. Being blocked from her mind drives me crazy."

"What is the point of all this aggravation? Feed on her, fuck her if you want, and move on."

"I came close," Wade admitted. "Actually, I did taste her and I intended to do more — she did do more — and then I saw the birthmark."

He spoke in no uncertain terms. "You're talking dangerous nonsense and if Ladislav Husek or one of the Prophets gets wind of your indecisive little games you'll be exterminated. Death by Husek's hand won't be pretty." Christophe transported himself across the room. Looming in front of Wade, he said, "Park your human heart someplace in a lab beaker and act like a vamp for a change. Are you going to let her see the darkness in you — the yellow eyes, the bloody fangs — and tell her you love her or want her to love you? What can you offer her?" Exasperated, Christophe turned away and spoke over his shoulder. "The truth will destroy you. We've been down this path before and I won't rescue you from yourself again. You go rogue one more time and I'll kill you myself."

Yellow flames flickered in Wade's eyes. "You wouldn't kill me."

Christophe didn't skip a beat. "I can and I will. When Claire died, I understood how hard putting those human emotions to rest was, but I won't let you go through emotional suicide again. You left a body trail wherever you went and jeopardized the safety of vamps because of your reckless behavior. I won't pick up one more morning newspaper and read about a 'mysterious illness' plaguing the residents of some nearby city. You'll incite panic and humans will kill untold numbers of innocents before they ever figure out what we are and where to find us."

* * * * *

Jui hurried back to the hotel. Her stomach growled and she hoped Rob made good on his promise to order room service. The train ride home cooled some of her passion, but she still got angry thinking about the time she wasted pleasuring Wade. *I should have taken what I wanted as soon as I discovered that awesome cock.* She groaned every time she pictured his thickness, his length. "So close," she said under her breath. "He could have scored my first eleven."

When the elevator stopped on her floor at the hotel, she went to change clothes. Even though she planned to have sex with Rob, there was something un-cool about leaving on her wet panties. Wade made them wet, not Rob. The lacy fabric floated out of her hand and into her hotel laundry bag. She stood there a minute, wearing only her t-shirt, and cursed the ill-timed arrival of the vineyard worker. After putting on a black thong, Jui brushed her hair and realized she left her favorite hair tie at the little cottage. "Ah shit, isn't anything going to go right today?"

* * * * *

Rob, wearing only a faded pair of jeans, answered Jui's knock.

His half-dressed appearance and boyish smile put the zing back in Jui's libido. *Dinner can wait — first things first.* Jui gave him a needy kiss to wipe the fiasco with Wade out of her mind. Moments later, she used her thumbs to slide Rob's jeans off his hips.

* * * * *

"Are you hungry? I can order dinner." Rob said after they made love. He kissed her collarbone and flicked his tongue on her earlobe. "Or perhaps you'd like a little more of this," he said before kissing her again.

Jui giggled in his embrace. "I think I should go back to my room. It's getting late and we have a full day ahead of us tomorrow. In case you forgot, the investor's meeting for Heart Strings Cove starts at nine."

Rob ran his hand down the curve of her waist to her hips. "Stay, spend the night," he whispered, holding her close.

She stopped him just before he distracted her with more of his seductive intentions. She smiled and kissed his forestalled hand. "As much as I'd like to...." She rolled out from under him and sat on the edge of the bed. "I really should get some sleep so I'm fresh for tomorrow's meeting." Jui gave Rob an accusing smile and said, "Somebody kept me up late last night."

Rob smirked. "I don't know what you're talking about." He grabbed Jui by the waist and rolled her back onto the bed with him. After a few languid kisses he said, "I can't convince you, can I?"

"Not tonight." She gazed at his chest, hating to say what was on her mind. "And Rob, can we keep this between us? You know the office grapevine—just until we decide."

"Decide what?"

"I guess whether this thing between us is just a fling or something else. I don't want to rush us because of office gossip."

"That's putting your feelings out there," he said, rolling away from her.

"I didn't mean it the way it sounded. You remember Isaac, don't you?"

"The old creative director?"

"Yes. He and I dated for a while. It got pretty serious for me. I thought I was in love with him. I thought he was 'the one'." Jui blushed over admitting her relationship blunder. "When I found out he was using me just to get on my father's good side, things got really ugly between us and that's the reason he left Saint Claire. I'm just wary, okay?"

"I get it. We'll play all cool and professional in the office."

She grasped his hand and squeezed a little. "Thanks."

Rob lay in bed with his arms folded behind his head, watching her dress.

When she finished, Jui came back and kneeled on the bed. "I'll see you in the morning," she said and then gave him a quick kiss.

"Sure, goodnight."

* * * * *

When she returned to her room, Jui showered. The sound of the water splashing on the tiled floor reminded her of the rainfall this afternoon—and Wade. She dried her hair and recalled Wade's long fingers wrapped on the towel as he'd dried her hair. Rolling her eyes, Jui dismissed the romantic fantasies as a waste of time and energy. She climbed into bed and quickly drifted asleep.

Wade pulled her into his arms and pressed her naked back against his naked body.

Jui moaned in her sleep. *Mink, he feels like mink.* She moved against him, letting her body create a gentle friction against his. *Wade.*

He spoke directly into her mind. *Let me hold you while you sleep, minx.* His arms encircled her, keeping her near. His breath fell against her neck.

She moaned in annoyance, unable to twist around to face him. *You shouldn't have left me this afternoon. I wanted you so much. Make love to me.*

Shh, lay still. Let me hold you, shh.

She twisted free of his tight embrace, triumphant and expecting to show Wade Kairos it wasn't worth the effort to deter Jui Fabrice from a mission. She blinked awake and found her bed empty. She touched the indentation on the pillow next to her, slid her leg to where he had laid. The sheets were cold. Confusion filled her.

"He was here," she said, stroking the indented pillow. "I'm certain." Jui laid back down. "I couldn't have dreamed his presence with so much detail." Baffled, she hugged the pillow he'd used and stared at the ceiling. *I know I felt his body next to mine. I know it.*

Wade hovered in a shadow state on the balcony. If he'd

stayed any longer, he would have tasted her again and made love to her. He read her thoughts — she wanted him and felt disappointed his presence seemed only a dream. *Should I appear to her?* He left in a rush of the wind. *She can't handle the truth.*

Chapter Five

Jui got up extra early on Monday morning to prepare for her nine thirty investor's meeting. Her father was counting on his team of executives to advance his corporate vision. She didn't plan to let him down.

After applying a dusky red lipstick, she pursed her lips. With a glimmer of a smile, Jui announced to her reflection in the mirror, "Time to make some music." She picked up her leather briefcase and walked out, closing the door behind her.

In the hotel's conference room, Jui found her spot at the head table and unpacked her briefcase. She felt an intense gaze, absorbing every detail about her, and glanced up. A frown furrowed her brow. *What in the hell is Wade doing here?*

He stood in the back of the room in the company of four men and acknowledged Jui with a slight nod.

Her stomach quivered a little at seeing him again. *Maybe he's more than an elusive stranger destined to live forever in my fantasies.* A small smile flitted on her lips. *Oh yes, Wade sure conjures up delicious fantasies.* Noticing Wade returned to his conversation, Jui glanced around the room and spotted Rob Hawthorne.

"Good morning, everyone," she said, joining Rob's group. Careful to keep her body language and expressions professional, she asked, "Are you ready to begin, Rob?"

Glancing at his Rolex, Rob said, "Yes, we should get started."

Throughout the two-hour-long presentation about a new outdoor amphitheatre called Heart Strings Cove, Wade's eyes stayed on her but he seemed a million miles away. She couldn't figure out why he was even in the room. At the conclusion of her marketing presentation, Jui asked if there were any questions.

Wade raised his hand. "May I ask how the company name was chosen? The company is not a religious organization, is it?"

A wistful smile graced Jui's lips while she explained. "No, we are not a religious organization. My father named the company in honor of his mother, Claire. She was a gifted concert cellist with the French Philharmonic, and his father, Claude, was the conductor at the time my grandmother performed with the orchestra. Originally the company was named Claire Symphonic Construction. My father changed the name to Saint Claire Symphonic after my grandmother died."

Jui glanced around the room, looking for more hands, but not before she noticed the tension in Wade's face. "Are there any other questions?" Seeing no other raised hands, she said, "Okay, I hope to see you tonight at our dinner party — seven o'clock. Thank you for coming this morning and we're excited about working with all of you on Heart Strings Cove."

Jui mingled with the investors afterwards. "I'm looking forward to meeting your wife," she said to one investor who seemed too interested in her personal life.

"I'm not married, Miss Fabrice," the man said. An unspoken suggestion glimmered in his blue eyes. "I'm still looking for the right woman."

"I hope you find her." Jui turned to Rob. "I have some work to do and a few calls to return. If you'll excuse me, I'll be heading back to my room."

"I'll phone you to discuss tonight's details."

Wade approached Jui from behind and grasped her elbow. "May I have a word before you leave?"

Jui's temperature rose and she hoped she wasn't blushing like a schoolgirl. Just his casual touch sent her pulse racing. "Certainly. Please excuse me," she said to Rob and the rest of his group.

Wade led her to the terrace. The breeze caught her perfume and he savored the scent. His mouth watered with the desire to taste her. He tamped down his dark desires, determined to keep his promise not to feed on her or make love to her. Once he discovered her unique connection to his living years with Claire, Jui was off limits to his teeth and his bed.

"Mr. Kairos?"

His nostrils flared at the coldness of her tone. "I think we're a little past that formality, don't you?" He searched her mind and heard her laughing at him.

"Maybe. I'm surprised to see you here."

"But not displeased. Did you think I'd disappeared from your life?"

"Frankly, yes, but I think it's weird we keep running into each other."

Pleasurable memories of her life-sustaining blood flowing down his throat flickered in Wade's mind. "Literally and figuratively, I might add. The field worker's timing couldn't have been worse."

"This is what you wanted to discuss? Missed opportunities?" She turned to leave and Wade stopped her. Jui glanced down at their enjoined hands; she raised her eyes to his.

"You're angry with me," he said in a soft voice. "I share your frustration."

"Don't flatter yourself. I'm an adventurous American in a romantic and foreign land. You're a handsome stranger who keeps popping up. I'll get over you."

Anger rumbled in his throat and he swallowed the emotion. "And if *I* don't get over *you?*"

"Please. We hardly know each other—first and last names, more or less. I'll be going home in a few days and our little sexual fantasy will be over. Don't lose any sleep over me."

Wade crooked his eyebrow. "Because that other man, the sales director, Robert Hawthorne, shares your bed?"

Jui swung her hand and he grasped the feminine weapon before she could slap him. He pressed her fingers against his lips and left behind the barest suggestion of his tongue.

Jui glanced toward the terrace door. "My relationship with Mr. Hawthorne is none of your damn business, now or ever. You're an investor on this project—"

"No, I'm an engineering consultant. I'm quite well-known for my mathematical prowess."

Jui jerked her hand free. "Mathematical prowess, my ass. I'm beginning to think the vineyard worker's arrival was providence. Keep your distance."

"Until this evening," he said to her retreating form.

* * * * *

At three o'clock, Jui walked to her appointment in the hotel salon. She gave herself a pep talk all the way there. The full bikini wax made her want to gnaw off her knuckles and she wondered how she'd ever survive a French or Brazilian wax even if a hot-looking guy did the work. Afterward, she closed her eyes and relaxed while the therapist massaged soothing moisturizers into her legs, but tensed like a spring when the therapist got a little too close. *The agony we go through to look good.* But by the time her hair and nails were done, Jui floated in a state of relaxed bliss.

"Too bad I'll be spending the evening with a bunch of contractors and investors instead of dancing," she grumbled while walking through the lobby toward the Palatina Room.

The wine-red carpet with matching, upholstered chairs gave a regal touch to the dining room. Floor-length, gold draperies patterned in green, royal blue, and almond were tied back to reveal the street level scene. White linen tablecloths and china edged in gold awaited Saint Claire's forty guests.

Jui saw Stephanie overseeing the last details with the hotel catering manager. "Everything coming together all right?" she asked, joining them.

"Seems so. I'm sure there'll be a disaster or two but nothing lurking so far," Stefanie said. She gave Jui the once over. "Looks like you got the royal spa treatment. Must be nice."

Jui smiled back at her coworker. "You have time to get dolled up. It's only five."

"A whole hour. Geez, what will I do with myself?"

"The life of a public relations manager is full of pain — and so is a bikini wax."

They giggled over the truth of the remark.

"Maybe overseeing seating arrangements is more fun after all," Stephanie said through her snickers. "Rob will probably like your little surprise a lot."

"Not funny. I have no idea what's happening — or not, between he and I." Jui gave her a serious look and said, "I'm not looking to get tangled up with anyone."

"Famous last words, boss. Do you want to give me a code phrase to rescue you if Rob gets possessive?"

Jui rolled her eyes. "I knew I should have been more discrete. That damn Wade."

Stephanie's ears pricked up over the mention of a new name. "Wade? Is this a Wade I know?"

"Forget it. I shouldn't have said anything. Just please, keep my 'purported relationship with Rob' quiet. At least until there is one to gossip about."

"I'm just teasing you. Of course I'll keep my mouth shut... but about this Wade...."

"I'm going to spill something disgusting on you tonight if you don't knock off the teasing."

Stephanie giggled at Jui's discomfort. "Sure thing. I'll shut up right after...well, I'll think about keeping my trap shut."

Jui looked around the room. The hotel staff was putting fresh yellow and white rosebuds on every table. "The room looks nice. I'm sure we'll have a great time—afterwards!"

The two broke into girlish laughter again and then Jui told Stephanie, "You'd better hurry if you hope to look better than something the cat dragged in."

* * * * *

Jui's black satin, v-neck cocktail dress accentuated her curves. A silver ring cinched light gathers of fabric just off her hip and the skirt floated a few inches above her knee. The sleeveless dress slung low in the back, giving prime time to her toned back and shoulders. A teardrop diamond necklace hung from a delicate silver chain around her neck and a silver comb kept layers of sexy ringlets out of her face. She put on a pair of silver, strappy heels and then viewed the results in a full-length mirror.

"What a shame to waste this great dress on a bunch of old guys. Well at least Rob is around," she said with a more enthusiastic smile.

Jui entered the Palatina Room with confidence and grace. She moved through the crowd, greeting her guests, and eventually ended up next to Rob.

"Good evening, Rob, gentlemen," she said, acknowledging those in his group. "Have you found your seats for dinner? I think we're about ready to begin."

Rob placed his hand on the small of her back and escorted Jui to her table. "If we didn't have this business dinner, you'd be out of that dress and on your back," he said for her ears alone. "I hope this evening won't drag. I have other plans."

Jui gave him an innocent look. "Turning in early?"

"Something like that." He held her chair for her and waited for her to sit down. "Enjoy your dinner," Rob said to Jui's table guests and then joined his own guests.

* * * * *

Jui shoved the traditional German food around her plate with her heavy silver fork. Course after course went back to the kitchen almost untouched until one of the waiters asked if she would like something else.

"I apologize," she said to the concerned waiter. "I'm just not a big fan of German food. I'm sure everything is well-prepared—everyone seems to be enjoying their meal."

"You must be very hungry. How about a traditional salad?"

"I didn't mean to cause a fuss," she said to her table guests after the waiter left. "Herr Wergen, you were telling us about the promotions planned for Heart Strings. Please continue."

Wergen dove into a detailed explanation. "We want Heart Strings Cove to be a wonderful place to experience all kinds of music. I'm certain the children's concertinos will be very popular for families. We are looking into some beat box artists to attract the university students and teenagers during the summer. Oktoberfest can be celebrated there and even holiday events, until the weather turns too cold." Herr Wergen was breathless with enthusiasm by the time he finished. "I've barely touched the surface of all the wonderful plans we have for Heart Strings Cove!"

"Saint Claire Symphonic will do everything possible to

ensure your sound quality is stunning. We've worked on some of the best music studios and performing halls in the world. We know what makes a performance hall remarkable. Yours will be no exception, I assure you," Jui said.

*****

Wade stood in front of the large corporate logo displayed in the Palatina Room. An outline image of the company's namesake elicited many difficult emotions for him. Echoes of Claire playing the beautiful instrument swept through his memories. How enraptured she was when she played, and the way she looked after she finished—sated. His soul ached with sadness over their lost years together and Wade wondered for the millionth time if he made the wrong choice by letting Claire think he was dead. *It's been too late for a long time.* She'd been dead to him for seventy years and gone from the Earth for forty. He glanced toward Jui, who appeared to be enjoying her dining companions, and proceeded to the balcony.

A few minutes later, Jui excused herself from her table and made her way to the restroom. She stared at her reflection in the ladies' room mirror. Wade's somber demeanor in front of the company logo had bothered her. *Why should I give a rat's ass about what Wade does or doesn't do?* She nibbled the inside corner of her lip while drying her hands on the soft towel the attendant gave her. *From the moment I put a face to his voice, I felt connected to him somehow.* Her heart raced every time she imagined Wade holding her in bed last night. A big part of her wished the dream had been real. His touch was magnetic. "Hot" barely described the sensation when he kissed her neck. *"Volcanic" is more like it.* A frown tugged at her lips while she contemplated reality. *In a couple of days you'll be going home and you'll never see him again. You're only asking for trouble by dwelling on these crazy fantasies.* Jui applied a spritz of perfume and fresh lipstick. *What about Rob?* Jui shut her lipstick and pitched the tube into her silver evening bag. *We aren't even a couple.*

Saint Clair Symphonic's guests were eating dessert and enjoying after dinner drinks by the time Jui returned. She played the cordial hostess as she moved among the tables, making pleasant chitchat. Near the balcony door, Jui glanced behind her to see if Rob was paying attention to her. He wasn't. She snuck onto the balcony.

"What do you want?" Wade said without turning.

She shut the balcony door behind her and leaned against the frame. "How did you know it was me?"

"Your perfume. No one smells like Jui Fabrice."

"Anyone can buy this--"

"I didn't just recognize your perfume—your scent is uniquely yours. I can smell your body and all its secrets."

A shiver ran through Jui. "Why were you staring at the logo for so long? You looked sad."

Wade faced her. Deep shadows masked his face. "She was your grandmother."

"Yes, what about her?"

"You bear a resemblance to her."

"That makes you sad? You're a strange man."

"I thought you would be honored. She was a beautiful woman and I'm sure she was proud of you."

His seductive charisma drew her in. "I never met Grandma Claire and I don't look much like her, except for my hair and the figure-eight mole on my shoulder. I can't even whistle. I thank my mother for my talents. She's a businesswoman, too." *Why am I telling him this?*

Wade extended his hand to her. "Come here."

Her heels clicked as she crossed the wooden balcony. She put her hand in his. *Not a working man.* Her pulse gained speed as she gazed into his beautiful, hazel eyes. "What?" she said in a low voice.

"I won't hurt you."

A gentle sigh left her lips when Wade drew her against him.

"I'm here because you wanted me to be. You're in my blood, in ways you cannot fathom. When you go home to America, I won't forget you."

"Why do you care, Wade?" she said, resting her cheek against his shoulder. "Do you only want a night of unforgettable sex?"

His gentle laughter rumbled in his chest. "My body gives me away. I would make love to you like no man ever has. I can promise you our intimate moments would be much more than just satisfying our baser pleasures." He lifted her chin with the knuckle of his right index finger. The silver ring he wore glimmered.

"What is the matter now?" she said, searching his eyes. "You look so sad again."

"We'll be oceans apart. You're wise to try to find happiness with Mr. Hawthorne."

Jui's voice reflected her anger. "Don't tell me where to find happiness. I don't like being ordered around, personally or professionally." Jui knew she ought to dismiss the dictatorial man like crumbs on her suit, yet she remained in his arms, imprinting his body with hers.

Dipping his lips toward hers he said, "We shouldn't be together."

"Why?"

Before Wade could take the kiss she so desperately wanted him to steal, the balcony door opened.

"Jui, what's going on?" Rob asked.

Wade stiffened and swore under his breath.

Jui wiped away imaginary tears with the back of her hands.

"Jui, are you okay?" Rob asked.

She gave Wade a meaningful glance and then sniffled. "I am," she said, facing Rob. "We were talking about my grandmother and how she inspired my father and I guess—I guess I got a little emotional." Jui painted a gentle smile on her face and stepped out of Wade's embrace. "Thank you for understanding, Mr. Kairos; I apologize for my silly tears." She walked over to Rob. "We should rejoin the party."

"Sure," Rob said, opening the door wide.

"Are you coming, Mr. Kairos?" she asked over her shoulder.

"Right behind you."

Jui launched into a nasty, silent rant about Rob's poor timing.

"Another time, Jui," Wade added, as if he'd read her thoughts.

The hint of his promise to remember her sent lust-inspired shivers to Jui's core, yet his uncanny ability to supply answers to unasked questions unnerved her. *How the hell does he do that?*

Once they rejoined the party, Rob said, "Are you sure you're okay?"

Jui dismissed his worries. "Yeah, fine. I was just being silly."

"I've never thought of you as a 'silly' woman."

"Goes to show what you know." Jui left Rob standing there to ponder her snarky remark. *He's a nice guy; don't treat him like an idiot, Jui. Besides, Dad likes him. Wade Kairos is somebody you need to forget about. Tomorrow evening you're going home anyway.*

* * * * *

Their last guest bid his goodnight and Jui and Stephanie plunked into chairs.

Stephanie groaned, taking off her high-heeled shoes. "My feet."

Jui chimed in, equally pained. "I hear ya, and I could use a massage or a long soak in the tub."

"The night was a success, don't you think?" Stephanie said. "I didn't hear any complaints, and people stayed 'til the very end."

Rob nodded. "Seems so, and we got some new project leads in Germany."

"Cool," Jui said. "Let me know when you want to discuss them."

"If you're not too tired, we could have a drink before we call it a night."

Jui recognized her opportunity to patch things up between them. She gave her watch a perfunctory glance and said, "I think I can manage a drink."

Stephanie picked up her patent leather shoes and yawned.

"Looks like the hotel staff have everything here pretty much under control. I'm headed for bed. I'll catch up with you two tomorrow. We leave at five, right?"

Jui slipped her shoes back on and walked out with her assistant. "Ah huh, you have a whole day of R and R. Maybe you should check out the spa," she said with a wink.

Rob glanced between the two women, uncertainty filling his blue eyes. "Do I want to know?"

A mischievous smile curled Stephanie's lips. "No. Well, yes."

"Never mind," Jui said in a warning voice. "Let's get out of here."

Stephanie left Rob and Jui on the third floor. When the elevator door closed behind her, Rob asked, "Were you serious about having a drink?"

"Sure, I could use one. My throat is raw from talking all night and I think my brain is totally scrambled from talking in German so much, too."

The elevator door opened on the fourth floor. As Jui and Rob walked down the hall, she heard soft female laughter mingled with a low male voice. Turning the corner toward Rob's room, they encountered a young woman in Wade's arms. The couple leaned against the door making out. The shock of seeing him with the young trollop stung like a wicked slap across her face. *You bastard. You almost made a fool of me twice. I won't let it happen again. Mark my words.*

Jui and Rob walked past the amorous couple without a word, but Jui glanced back when they reached another corner. Wade was kissing the woman's slender neck but met Jui's gaze for an instant. His eyes smoldered between animal passion and regret and then he returned his attention to his date.

"Wasn't that Kairos?" Rob asked once they were around the corner and out of earshot.

"Yeah."

Rob reached into his pocket and retrieved his room key. "The guy sure gets around."

"Who gives a shit? We need him for engineering. Who he spends time with is his own business." She grasped Rob's lapel. "I have better things in mind than worrying about what

49

that man whore is up to." His lips were warm and inviting as the kissed. "Don't you?" she asked afterward.

Perhaps her response was a bit strong but she didn't want Rob to ruin the mood with any more talk of Wade Kairos.

"Kairos who?" Rob asked, apparently taking her hint.

Once the door shut, Rob slid the chain lock into place. "What would you like to drink?"

"Cognac, if there is any. Daddy's buying." She sat on the bed, kicking off her shoes. "That's the last time I want to put those on tonight." She wiggled her toes and flexed her ankles. "What I wouldn't give for a massage therapist right now."

Rob handed Jui a Hennessey cognac in a small snifter. "I'm sure I can help." He knelt in front of her and began massaging her feet and calves. "Feel good?"

Jui closed her eyes. "Mmm."

"I couldn't wait to get you back here tonight." He slid his hand up her thigh. "Every time I looked at you I got a hard on. I wanted to sneak up here before dessert. I would have made you soaking wet but not let you come. The idea of you so hot and anxious for me to make love to you...." Rob groaned while leaving a wet trail with his tongue from her knee to mid-thigh.

Jui finished her cognac in one gulp. "Higher. See what's under—or not under—my panties."

Rob took her hand and helped her stand. He reached under her dress and caressed her ass. Then he slid down her black lace panties and buried his face in the fabric of her skirt, nuzzling her mons.

"Aren't you curious?" Jui asked.

"Aren't you impatient?"

Jui ran her fingers through Rob's thick, blond curls and pressed his face harder against the apex of her thighs.

Little by little, he raised the hem of her dress, kissing his way up. He sucked in his breath when he discovered her very trimmed pussy.

"What are you waiting for?" she asked.

Rob helped Jui out of her dress and then laid her on the king-sized bed. Crawling between her knees, he asked, "Where was I?" He made glancing strokes across her swollen clit with his tongue. "Right about here." He fastened his lips onto her waiting heat.

Later, as he mounted her from behind, Jui said, "Like that, Rob, yeah, right—right—" Her breath left her body in short pants as her hips smacked against his, taking everything he could give.

He gripped her shoulders, forcing her to slow down and let him manage the pace. "I want to come with you, Jui," he said, each word punctuated by the sound of his hips slapping against hers. "Right now." Rob cranked up the pace and pulled out at the last moment, ejaculating onto her ass. He stroked his cock, milking every drop. "Fuck yeah." Afterward, he rubbed his essence into her skin and then French kissed her cum-drenched tush.

"Lower," she said.

He rimmed her with his tongue. "Like this?"

"Absolutely."

"If I'd known you liked anal sex, tonight would have had a different ending." Rob lubricated his middle finger in Jui's pussy and then pressed it against her asshole.

"Two of them," she said. Jui rocked against his fingers while massaging her clitoris. "Feels good, don't stop."

With his free hand, Rob caressed Jui's breast. "Come on baby, I know you're loving it."

"I'm almost there. Finger me harder."

Rob increased the tempo of his thrusts into her ass and tweaked her nipple between his fingers.

Jui groaned as pleasure reverberated through her body. She clenched her teeth, feeling all her energy focus on her aching pussy and ass. Rubbing her wet clit faster, she said, "Harder. I'm right there." A squeal of pleasure ripped from her lips as her pussy pulsed under her fingertips. "Don't stop yet; finger fuck me through it. That's it."

* * * * *

Later, Jui rested her cheek on the soft mat of curls covering Rob's chest while he stroked her arm and shoulder.

"You're so adventurous in bed. Very, very sexy," he said, pressing a kiss to her head.

Jui couldn't suppress a sly smile. *You have no idea what you missed, Kairos.* "I hoped you'd think so. You're pleased?"

"Why wouldn't I be? Hot, naughty women are the stuff wet dreams are made of—at least mine are."

"I guess working in a man's company, in a male-dominated industry, taught me not be too shy about my goals and ambitions. My father won't promote me just because I'm his daughter and if I sit in the background like a shrinking violet, I'll be left there. I've worked really hard to prove I deserve to be the company's vice president of marketing and I love the challenges. But there's not much room for silly female emotion and behavior if I want to succeed."

"I'd never use 'shy' or 'silly' to describe you. I'm still surprised I found you crying on Kairos' shoulder—of all people."

"Do we have to talk about him?"

"I didn't think we were talking about him. I thought we were talking about you."

Jui's tone turned cool. "So I shed a few tears. I'm allowed to, every once in awhile."

"The scene looked like more than a few tears—was there more to what I saw?"

"No and there never will be. I guess our paths could cross again during the Heart Strings Cove project but what you saw was a moment of weakness." She leaned on her elbow and said, "Now can we drop the subject and get some rest?"

Rob kissed her. "Sure, it's forgotten."

Jui turned on her side and scooted against Rob, spoon-style. She let out a loud, contented sigh.

"You okay?"

Jui couldn't help laughing. "Yeah, I was just thinking about my sister."

"That makes you giggle?"

"When my sister, Sylvie, and I shared the same bedroom as kids, we used to have a contest every night to come up with the most creative-sounding sigh. It became a ritual for me even after we had separate rooms. Sorry"

"Maybe you *are* silly every now and then."

Jui giggled. "Don't let my secret out."

"My lips are sealed. Get some rest."

She squeezed her eyes shut and got out her mental scorecard to rate Rob's performance tonight. *Definitely higher marks. With a little more practice, he might score a nine. You're kinda strange, you know that, don't you, Jui?* Another giggle escaped her lips.

"Are you going to sleep or not?" Rob asked, sounding groggy and a little annoyed.

"Sorry, I guess I'm used to sleeping alone."

Jui laid there wide awake until she heard Rob's deep, even breathing. The image of Wade in the hallway with another woman popped into her mind and chipped at her wall of cool reserve. *If Rob hadn't opened the terrace door, what might have happened?* Hot tears scalded the edges of her eyelids and she squeezed them shut tighter, determined not to let the hurt feelings overpower her. She remembered how exotic his voice sounded, how much she wanted him to touch her everywhere. Pent-up emotions had her throat in a vice grip. *Why do I even care?* She asked herself that question a thousand times before she dozed off.

"*Jui, we can't be together.*"

Hearing Wade's voice in her dream confused her. "*Where are you? Why?*"

"*It's complicated but you know I want you. You make me weak with desire.*"

"*Then why? Tell me. Is it because I'm leaving?*"

His voice sounded regretful. "*No, it's because of who I am.*"

"*Who are you? You pop in and out of my life like the wind.*"

"*If I tell you, you'll fear me, hate me.*"

"*You're not making sense. And if we can't or shouldn't be together...are you married?*" Even in her dream, Jui wondered why that question hadn't occurred to her sooner. His soft laughter filled her mind.

"*Not the way you think.*"

"*The way I think? Could you be less cryptic for once?*"

His voice caressed her spirit. "*You're in my soul and that's why I'm with you. Make a life with Rob if that'll make you happy.*"

I can't give you the things you need."

She couldn't keep the hurt out of her voice. *"You haven't tried. Do you always give up so fast?"*

"I can't give you what you want out of life."

Jui's tears welled up again. *"How do you even know what my needs are?"*

"I once wanted the same things, planned for the same things."

"You're not making any sense. You're talking like something is wrong with you. Are you saying you can't have children or you're sick?"

"It's bigger than that. Let me go. When you beckon me this way...I'm always going to know if you need me but we have to stay apart."

Containing her anger and disappointment made Jui's chest ache. *"You're a liar and a coward. I wish you'd walked away after we met in the café and left me alone, instead of making me think there's something between us."*

His anguished face appeared in her dream. *"I should have. I knew better but you're different. I couldn't."*

"Hold me," she whispered through her tears. *"Hold me and say goodbye."*

Wade joined her in bed. *"Come here minx,"* he said, gathering her close.

Jui's heart twisted like a wrung sponge. Her silent tears soaked his chest.

"Shh, you'll wake Rob, just lay in my arms."

She molded herself against his lean body and rested her thigh intimately over his. *"Don't say goodbye. I don't want to leave things this way. I feel like there's something special between us and I'd really like to find out if that's true."*

With a soft growl, Wade kissed her. He bruised her lips with his, twisting them over hers, drinking her sweetness. He wound his fingers through her long hair, pulling her head back and then he opened his jaw wide. He coaxed her tongue into his mouth, stroking it, teasing it. The heady experience took him down the short, slick path to joining with her. His body simmered in bloodlust. Vampire desire flickered behind his closed eyelids and the volcanic passion she felt the first time he tasted her was a bite away. *I could turn her. She would*

be mine forever. The thought horrified Wade and he broke from the molten kiss and embrace.
We can't, Jui, we can't.
"Jui, wake up, you're having a bad dream, wake up, honey."
Her eyes flew open, but the instant she saw Rob's face, they slammed shut again. Throwing her forearm over her eyes, Jui burst into tears.
Rob drew her quaking body into his arms. "Hey now, you look like you saw a ghost. You had a bad dream," he whispered. "I'm here. I'm right here."

* * * * *

Wade materialized deep in the Bavarian forest, silent now except for occasional calls and rustling from nocturnal birds and creatures. The moment his body stabilized, the scent of musty death filled his nostrils. Rage and disgust took turns shaking his tall frame. His roar, as vicious as a pack of lions, filled the moonless night air. Wade took out his fury on the forest using inhuman strength. Trees fell in his path and boulders turned to dust when he slammed into them. He uttered no words in this grief-stricken state. Instead, he expressed himself in terrifying, uncontrolled devastation.

A distinct scent caught Wade's attention. He turned his head toward the pungent aroma and lifted his chin as he sniffed. *Mold. Lots of it.* Grunts and crunching sounds grew louder in the dark forest. His chest heaved from exertion but Wade wasn't in any mood to settle down and disappear yet. A murderous smile curled his lips and he stood still, waiting for the animal to appear. Out of sight, the beast huffed and snorted to warn off whoever—or whatever—had dared invade its territory.

Wade immitated the sounds of another dominant male boar, coaxing his adversary from behind the massive pine tree.

The wary hog appeared.

Wade tore off his dinner jacket, already ripped to shreds from his lumberjack escapades. He taunted the large animal with a series of aggressive snorts.

Mud and debris matted the dark gray, one hundred fifty-pound animal. Coarse bristles stood up on its spine and the challenger grunted at Wade, seeming to invite conflict. It was too early for mating season but never too early for a dominant male boar to claim its territory. The wild hog pressed his snout to the ground like a bull preparing to charge.

Cloaked in boar language and behaviors, Wade attacked in the inky darkness. He grabbed the pig's upright ears and rolled with it. Searing pain engulfed Wade's leg as the hog's sharp tusk laid open his left thigh.

Before Wade could get on his feet, the animal huffed several times and then charged like the battle victor. The aggressive hog slammed into Wade, shoving him backward to the ground. Wade squealed and snorted even louder as a sharp tusk pierced his chest this time. He relished the pain and abuse his powerful adversary inflicted and thirsted for more.

The relentless boar chomped down on Wade's injured thigh, and Wade rolled away in pain, limping, and oozing fluids. The wild pig charged without warning. Wade stunned the beast with a powerful punch to the forehead, subduing the animal. The dazed creature lay on its side, grunting with short breaths.

Dragging his left leg and holding his ripped torso, Wade circled the downed pig. He screamed human words for the first time. "Get up!"

The sound of his voice seemed to revive the boar. The hog scrambled to its feet and then ran at Wade. The boar nailed him in the legs and knocked him flat on the ground. Fireworks went off in Wade's right eye when the pig's hoof shattered his cheekbone. Before the beast passed by, he grabbed a hind leg and dragged the snorting challenger backward.

The captured animal flailed, using its powerful legs and sharp hooves to inflict as much damage as possible on Wade's vulnerable head and shoulders.

Impervious to the abuse, Wade twisted the animal onto its side. With a triumphant roar, he sank his razor-sharp teeth through bristled hair, thick hide, and into the boar's jugular. The matted mud, stench of swamp water, and decayed matter clinging to the struggling hog didn't bother Wade at all. Their heated battle made blood surge through the pig's body and gush from the large, open vein beneath Wade's hungry mouth. The earthy-tasting nourishment ran down the his chin, soaked the shreds of his shirt, and mingled with the bloodlike fluids seeping from his own wounds. Wade gorged on the defeated animal in joyful self-loathing until sated.

Meanwhile, wolves skulked outside the circle of conflict, seemingly anxious for their nocturnal brother to finish his meal and leave them theirs. Wade flung the nearly dead boar toward the wolf pack. Their ravenous snarls of thanks rose in the forest as they finished the job Wade started.

Wade sat on the damp forest floor. His tattered shirt hung from his maimed body—his skin smeared with blood, dirt, and debris. Indescribable pain engulfed him. He spat into his hand and then rubbed the saliva on his gaping thigh wound to begin the healing process. Then he stretched out on the ground and tried to catch his breath. Blistering pain in his ribs and chest indicated the boar had tried its best to kill him. He wished the wolves could finish him off, too, but no matter how hard the pack would try, Wade would still be an undead.

He swore, realizing his right shoulder was dislocated. *Christophe is going to have to help with this one.* Wade rolled his eyes, not looking forward to another famous Christophe lecture about his volcanic temper. He applied more saliva to his torso until the pain subsided and his breathing became easier. Wade was back on the road of eternal life.

The idea of living alone forever hit him again like a punch to the gut, delivering more pain than all his other injuries combined. He hadn't felt this wretched since Claire died forty years ago. *I can't force Jui into this kind of existence. I won't.* With the high-pitched screech of an eagle, Wade headed home.

* * * * *

Christophe materialized in Wade's bedroom. He stood in front of his haggard companion. Sizing up the half-destroyed man, Christophe asked, "What in hell's name happened to you?"

"Fix my shoulder, will you? It's dislocated."

Christophe didn't waste any time. Whatever Wade did to get himself in this predicament, Christophe figured the man deserved.

Wade's bruised and dirty face crunched into a threatening snarl as the joint popped back into place. Afterward, Wade ran his hand through his matted, long hair and pulled out a handful of forest debris.

"You did the right thing," Christophe said after listening to the ticker tape of anguish running in Wade's mind. "You can't turn her. She won't bring Claire back."

"This isn't about Claire! She's dead and I know Jui can't bring her back."

"Then why can't you leave her alone? You're playing a dangerous game that will end in tragedy. Either you'll get careless and turn her and then she'll hate you forever, or you'll endanger other vamps with your reckless behavior. Could you really exist with her hating you for all eternity? Vamps are known to be quite vicious in their thirst for revenge."

Purple and red bruising on Wade's swollen, filthy face made him appear ferocious but his words sounded hollow. "I know. That's why I left her."

"Then why are you still consumed by the human?" Christophe shot back.

"She wants me. I read her thoughts when she slept."

Christophe was incredulous. "Dreams? You're reading her dreams. What's next, fucking tea leaves?" he said, laughing at the foolishness of his companion.

"It's not about sex. She doesn't let me invade her mind and we had an immediate connection."

"The only connection you should have with a human is with her neck or some other ready vein. Stop acting like a besotted fool." Christophe shook his head. "I'm so glad this doesn't happen to you more than every half-century. If you were turned as a teenager, I'd have killed you already. This lovesick behavior makes my stomach turn." Changing the subject, Christophe said, "I have business to tend to in Memphis, of all places. Come with me. Get her out of your system."

"What's in America?" he asked, still picking twigs and

leaves from his tangled locks.

"Gerhardt Meuhler."

"You're never going to let him go, are you?"

Christophe's temper flared. "Tell me you enjoyed knowing Claire lived her life with somebody else while you were still in love with her. Tell me you don't regret a moment of your dead years. Muehler has roamed this Earth at will for more than three hundred years. I hate him for turning me and I'll never quit hunting him until he dies by my hand or I have proof someone else killed him!"

"When are you going? I need a few days rest—after this," Wade said, indicating his bloodied visage.

Christophe heard Wade's question but was distracted by memories of Meuhler flickering in his mind like a scratchy-sounding, black-and-white film.

He saw himself teaching mathematics at the University of Heidelberg, in the late 1700s. Only the most serious students had been allowed in his classroom. Christophe was forty-seven years old—ancient back then, but compared to his true age now, he was a young pup.

The university had retained its close ties with theologians, dating back as far as the Holy Roman Empire. Christophe enjoyed many animated, intellectual conversations with one theologian in particular—Gerhardt Meuhler. The men became close friends, exchanging ideas about the merits of science and God and the role the Church should play in a man's life. These were wicked exchanges in the theologian's opinion and almost always ended with Gerhardt telling Christophe he was damned to hell. Christophe always laughed him off, thinking Gerhardt was the one with all the absurd ideas, but promised to go to Saturday confession to assuage him.

One evening, after a very heated argument about creationism, Gerhardt...changed. Before Christophe's eyes, Gerhardt transformed into a yellow-eyed, fanged creature with arms of steel. Christophe became powerless in Gerhardt's clutches. In shock and sorrow, Christophe felt the life draining from his body.

When his new consciousness appeared, he heard Gerhardt whisper, *"I told you you'd be damned for all eternity."* Gerhardt had turned him into a creature of the night, inhuman and immortal. For more than two hundred years, Christophe never relented in his hunt for revenge on Gerhardt.

The disgusting stench Wade brought with him snapped Christophe back to the present. "Boar? You tangled with a wild boar."

Wade unbuckled what was left of his pants. "And a few other things. What do you care? At least I didn't come back and demolish your house."

"I'll give you a free pass to the blood bank to show my undying gratitude."

"You didn't answer my question. When are you leaving? I can't go anywhere in this condition."

Christophe looked with disgust at the gaping wounds in Wade's thigh and torso. "Come when you're able. I'm leaving in a few hours."

Christophe disappeared and Wade slid out of his briefs, shoving them in a pile with his foot on his way to the shower. Ice-cold water drizzled over his battered body while he lathered his dirty skin, avoiding the angry red flesh tears as much as possible. Afterward, Wade spit on his hand several times and applied the healing saliva to his stomach and thigh, which still oozed the vampire equivalent of blood. With painstaking effort, he got all the debris out of his long hair and vowed never to wrestle with a boar again.

Wade stared at his disfigured reflection in the mirror and pressed his cheekbone gingerly. He yowled from the pain shooting into his swollen eye socket. Wade applied more spit on the split skin and decided to leave his busted face alone for now. *Vampire physiology sure comes in handy at times like this. I'll feel better after a few hours rest.* Stretching his sore, battered body in bed, Wade closed his eyes. Seconds later, he heard Jui weeping and then her lies to Rob.

* * * * *

"I had this terrible dream about my sister, Sylvie," Jui said between loud sniffles. "I don't know what happened, but it feels like she died."

"It was a dream," Rob said, passing Jui a few tissues to dry her tears. "Do you want to call her? Maybe you'll feel better if you do."

Jui dismissed the considerate suggestion. "I'm sure she's fine. It was just a dream, and we're going home tomorrow. I'll see her then." She gazed into Rob's blue eyes, which were so full of compassion, and hated the way dishonesty made her feel.

"What?"

"You're a really great guy. I don't know why I didn't realize it before." She put her arms around his neck and hugged him. "Thanks for tonight."

"Tonight is just the beginning."

Chapter Six

Wade slept for the next twenty-four hours, letting his abused body regenerate damaged cells and repair broken bones. He awoke ravenous and tended to that need before any other. He materialized in the shadows of the Cocoon Club in east Frankfurt. Renowned for its music, beautiful women, and privacy, the club would provide Wade with the nourishing blood for which he thirsted. Bodies twisted in the psychedelic lighting and couples enjoyed conversation or something a little more intimate in one of the cocoons for which the club was named.

Techno music pounded in his ears while he worked through the crowd. Dressed in a black silk shirt and slacks, Wade walked onto the dance floor. He used his classic good looks and vampire pheromones and went to work on two women gyrating to the music.

A curvy blonde and a tall, slender brunette with deep blue streaks dyed in her short, spiky hair made a Wade sandwich out of him. The blonde pressed against his back and he didn't object to her playful nibbles on his neck or her suggestive comments in his ear.

The brunette, who'd introduced herself as Lana, acted more aggressive. Her hands rubbed down Wade's chest, to his thighs, and clung to his hips while she joined her lips with his. Her pierced tongue tickled his and hinted at an evening filled with naughty pleasure.

"Are you interested?" the blonde named Mikla whispered. Wade rested his head against her shoulder to give her access to his lips. She wound his leather-bound ponytail around her fist and kissed him.

"We'd make a fabulous trio," Lana suggested in his ear.

Wade led the women off the dance floor. His dead heart pumped with excitement, not because he was about to get laid, but because dinner was about to be served. "Where shall we go?"

63

"Go?" Lana said with a suggestive look in her eye. "I thought we'd stay here."

Mikla led them down the dimly-lit hallway to an adjoining restaurant. Just before the restaurant entrance, she stopped before another door. She retrieved a set of keys from her gigantic silver purse and after looking up and down the hallway, turned the key in the lock. A smirk curled her lips and she beckoned Lana and Wade to follow her inside.

Emergency lighting illuminated the ten by twenty-foot storage room. Hedonistic Lana wasted no time on pleasantries. She kissed Wade, stroking the underside of his tongue with hers, and nipped at his lips while she unbuttoned his shirt. Wade got in the game and mentally commanded his cock to awaken since Mikla was already unzipping his pants. By the time his slacks were off, Wade was hard and ready.

While Mikla sucked Wade's cock, he latched on to Lana's neck. Her knees buckled when his surgically sharp teeth penetrated her soft skin. To distract Lana even more, he wiggled his fingers under her short skirt and into her wet pussy.

Mikla released Wade's cock and turned, bending over and presenting Wade with her ass. Wade braced his hips against the wall and fucked Mikla from behind until he finished drinking Lana's musky-tasting blood. He released Lana and she sank to her knees at his feet. Wade leaned forward to take a satisfying turn on Mikla's neck. She came instantly but Wade continued to drive his cock into her hot pussy until he'd gotten his fill of her salty blood, too. When he was through, Wade said goodnight, leaving both women panting and dazed.

He returned to Christophe's chalet. Sated and exhausted, Wade climbed back into bed. Tomorrow he expected to be in fighting shape to help Christophe chase down Gerhardt Meuhler. With a drawn-out exhale, Wade rolled over, hoping this time they'd find the primeval bastard and kill him once and for all. *Christophe isn't the only one tired of scouring the Earth for the cagey vamp.*

* * * * *

Exhaustion permeated every fiber of Jui's body. She twisted the key and then shoved her heavy, oak front door wide open. In the foyer, she paused to disarm the security system. After two trips from the garage, all her luggage lay in a heap in the living room.

Panoramic living room windows displayed a spectacular sunset over shimmering Lake Washington and the Cascade Mountains. Deep-hued reds and blues progressed to jet-black in the evening sky. Jui crossed her arms while staring over the water and wondered if some of her encounters with Wade were figments of her imagination. *Certainly he was real at the dinner party and in the vineyard, but what about the dreams? They were so detailed, so authentic.* Overwhelming sadness filled her whenever she thought of never seeing Wade again. *Why do I feel so connected to a man I barely know?* Her ringing phone interrupted the soul-searching thoughts.

"Hello?"

"Hey Jui, it's Dad."

"Hi, I just got home. How are you?"

"I'm fine. I already heard from Rob, so great job on the Heart Strings meetings. Sounds like it'll progress nicely."

Jui leaned against her granite kitchen counter and watched the sun fade while she listened to her father.

"The new business opportunities he told me about are very exciting," Terry Fabrice continued. "Rob is a real asset."

Jui heard the implication in his voice. "Yes, Dad, I know he's a really talented sales director and wonderful to work with."

"It sounded like the two of you had a nice time together."

Jui's temper rose and her tone reflected her anger. "Really."

"Don't work yourself into a knot. He just said you had some good conversations and fun on the boat cruise."

"Well, that's true," she said, "I guess Isaac burned me pretty badly. I'm sorry for jumping to the wrong conclusion. I just got home, so if it's all the same, I'll check in tomorrow. I'm beat."

"Actually, we have a problem I need you to take care of," he said, sounding all business.

"Can't it wait?"

"There's still a problem with the new production studio

in Memphis. Can you call Blake first thing and see what the hell is going on?"

Jui groaned. Between jet lag and the time zone difference, sleep would be a precious commodity tonight. She listened to her father describe the situation and agreed to place the call bright and early. By the time she hung up the phone, her cell phone was blinking with a message. She retrieved it.

"Hey Jui, it's Rob. Just checking to make sure you got home okay. I had a great time with you and I can't wait to see you again. Give me a call."

Jui deleted the voice message and shut off her phone.

* * * * *

Dressed in a comfy sleep shirt a little while later, Jui turned out the lamp. Night ensconced Seattle and the stars played in the clear, early autumn sky. Large, oval-topped windows gave her a wonderful opportunity to admire the nighttime gems while lying in bed. She wondered if Wade saw the stars tonight, too, and thought of her. *Why are you still wasting energy on him?* Jui turned over and slept.

* * * * *

The alarm blared at five in the morning. After a loud, tired-sounding groan, Jui slapped the snooze button and fell back asleep. Another alarm on top of her bureau went off a minute later. She hated setting two alarms but knew if she didn't, she'd miss the production studio's site supervisor.

After quieting the buzzing annoyance, Jui trudged back to bed. Sitting cross-legged, she rubbed her eyes with her fists, trying to rejuvenate some life in her bone-weary body. She swayed and plopped backwards against down-filled pillows.

"I'm too tired," she whined to her pitch-dark bedroom. "Why can't somebody else deal with Memphis for a change?" Her eyes stuck shut and bleary sleep invaded her brain.

"Gotta get up," she said, shaking off slumber's grip.

Jui combed her hair and washed her face with cool water. After dressing in a buttoned-down, gray blouse, she padded over to her laptop on the other side of her bedroom. She logged on and then contacted her Memphis superintendent, Blake, using Skype. To him, Jui appeared to be working at her desk. Little did he know, her bed occupied the other side of the room and she wasn't even wearing pants.

"Morning, Jui," Blake said. "How was Germany?"

"Good, thanks, but I hear you guys are still in the muck down there. What's shakin'?"

The superintendent explained the problematic dead spots in one of the sound studios. "No amount of re-engineering, materials changes or head scratching seems to work," Blake said.

Jui blew out her cheeks, tired and frustrated over this continuing problem. An idea popped into her mind. "I met a man in Heidelberg—Wade Kairos. Do you know him?"

"No, should I?"

"Apparently he's an engineering genius. Maybe I can track down Mr. Kairos and ask if he can consult."

"We're losing ground fast. If you think he can help, by all means...."

"I'll do what I can and get back to you."

"The sooner the better," Blake said.

Jui logged off and was glad she got up so early. Checking her watch, she calculated the time difference between Seattle and Germany. *It's mid-afternoon in Heidelberg.* She searched her contact list for Heart Strings Cove and found Martin Wergen. After a brief conversation, Martin provided Wade's cell phone number.

Jui stared at the digits she'd written while her heart thumped with anticipation. Even after rehearsing a couple of sentences, making sure she sounded composed and professional, butterflies played tag in her stomach. She hung up after one ring. Jui cleared her throat and took a deep breath. "Stop acting like an idiot. This is business." She pressed redial.

"Wade Kairos."

The sound of his deep, mellow voice made Jui's breath

catch in her throat. She was transformed instantly back into a high school girl with a terrible crush. "Wade, it's Jui," she said in a cool tone.

After a pregnant pause, he said, "What can I do for you this morning?"

Her mind spun with all kinds of clever answers but she discarded them all. "I have an engineering problem at one of our new sound stages in Memphis, Tennessee. I wondered if you could give our superintendent a call and consult on the problem."

"How was your trip home?"

"I'm tired. I didn't get enough sleep and it's super early here." Jui shook her head, wondering why she fell for the bait. "Can you call my guy in Memphis? This project is riddled with challenging problems and this one won't go away."

"Are you coming to Memphis, too?"

"This isn't my area of expertise. I don't show up unless Blake or the client makes a request. Wait a minute. I didn't ask you to go to Memphis. I asked you to call."

Wade's soft laughter fondled her ear and stroked her soul. "I'm on my way to America. My partner, Christophe, asked me to join him on business there."

Jui's heart almost stopped. The prospect of seeing Wade thrilled her but...."I thought you said we need to stay away from each other."

His voice remained low and seductive. "I need to stay out of your bed. I didn't say we shouldn't work together."

A hummingbird sigh could have knocked Jui over. Temptation rose and with it, desire.

"Jui?"

"I'm here. I'm—I'm...."

"I embarrassed you, I'm sorry. I shouldn't have mentioned our intimate relationship."

"I don't know if I can just work with you. I'm the one who wanted more of a relationship than a roll in the sack. You're the one who keeps running, so I think it's best if we don't see each other. If I need to come to Memphis, I'll show up when you aren't there."

"I love to hear you say, 'come'."

"Please give Blake a call and send me your invoice." Jui rattled off the appropriate phone numbers, including her cell phone. "But only call me if it's business." She admonished him. "Goodbye, Wade. Take good care."

Although Jui ended the call on a confident, professional note, disappointment pervaded her spirit. It would be so easy to catch a plane under the guise of keeping the client happy and "accidentally on purpose" run into Wade. *Child's play, actually.* Jui unbuttoned her blouse, hung it on the back of her desk chair, and went back to bed. She flopped onto the mattress, pulled the soft blankets around her shoulders, and decided to make plans with Rob today.

* * * * *

Jui's phone rang in the middle of the afternoon.

"You sound as groggy as I feel," he said in response to Jui's sleepy greeting. "Are you up or just using the phone?"

"I'm lying in bed. Kinda lonely, if I do say so myself."

"I know how to remedy the situation," he said.

"Maybe we can discuss your solution over dinner."

"We could talk about it." Rob rolled onto his side and propped himself on an elbow. "I bet with the right choice of words, dinner would barely last through appetizers."

Jui giggled. "Do you like sushi?"

"Sure."

"How about dinner at BlueC?"

"Six-ish?"

"Yeah, I'll meet you there. I live pretty close. We can come here after—"

"Appetizers?" Rob laughed. He groaned while stretching his body. "Maybe you should come over here and let me make love to you the rest of the afternoon. We can work up one hell of an appetite, go to dinner, and do it again at your place afterward."

"You have everything all figured out, don't you?"

"I think you're smiling big time. I hear it in your voice. What are you wearing?"

"Right now?"
"Yeah."
"Never mind. Nothing sexy, if that's what you mean," Jui said.
"Well, wear something hot tonight. I love taking sexy lingerie off a woman. I'm particularly looking forward to stripping the lace off you with my teeth."
"I'll think about it."
"Wow, what a way to ruin a good hard on."
"I'm just teasing. I'll find something suitable, just in case."
"Plan on it, Jui, I am."

* * * * *

Later that day, Terry Fabrice called his daughter at home to find out where things stood with the Memphis studio. Jui explained she'd referred Wade Kairos to Blake.
After a long pause, he asked, "Did you say, Kairos?"
"Yeah. Do you know him?"
"How old is he?"
"I don't know—thirty, maybe? Why?"
"I haven't heard that name in a million years. Do you know if he's Wade Kairos, junior or the first?"
"I have no idea. Why are you asking? Do you know his family?"
Terry snorted in disbelief. "Your grandmother, Claire, was engaged to a man named Wade Kairos. He died in a traffic accident in Germany and she married my father a few years later."
"Must be some other relative, a namesake."
"I found a picture of him after your grandma died. Tall, broad shoulders, brown hair—wore it in a ponytail—must have been a rebel even seventy years ago."
Jui's heart flip-flopped. "Lean, rectangular face. Expressive, hazel eyes. Straight eyebrows. Large hands. Long fingers."
"I didn't look *that* closely. It was a picture, after all," he said with a laugh.
Jui's face flamed as she realized she'd drifted into a

70

"Wade fantasy." She tried covering her blunder. "He came to the dinner party and we got to talking. He mentioned Grandma Claire, but he didn't mention any significant knowledge of her."

"That's odd because the Wade Kairos your grandmother was going to marry was a gifted mathematician, too."

"Yeah, that is strange. Anyway, Blake seemed pretty confident Wade knew how to handle the problem."

"Wade, is it?" her father asked with a suspicious, teasing sound in his voice.

Jui moaned like a teenage girl whose father figured out the name of her newest crush. "Shut up, Dad. The studio problem is finally getting fixed. I gotta go. I have dinner plans tonight."

"Sure. Tell Rob I said hello."

"You can be so exasperating sometimes, you know?"

"Yeah, like I care," Terry said with a smile in his voice. "Have a nice evening with Rob."

Jui hung up the phone, embarrassed about her Wade comments and her father's dead-on assessment of her relationship with Rob. She didn't like her father knowing about her romantic involvements, especially because she worked for him. *Is it the speculation about a real relationship with Rob that bothers me or maybe I don't want Wade to think I'm unavailable.* Jui clucked her tongue against the roof of her mouth while pondering the questions.

"Holy shit, Jui, are ya nuts?" she exclaimed. "The guy is usually half way across the world, and right now he's on the other side of the U.S. Get a frigging grip. He doesn't want you!" The truth stung, making Jui emotional. She began a pep talk. "But Rob does. He's smart, sexy, and fun."

She ran upstairs and dug through her closet, looking for the right outfit for her date. *Something to keep Rob's attention on me, and my mind on him.*

* * * * *

Jui got out of the cab in front of the crowded BlueC restaurant. Appreciation showed in Rob's eyes when he spotted Jui walking toward him. She wore a mid-thigh, tartan plaid skirt and a dark green sweater with a very deep v-neckline. Her black lace bra peeked out in all the right places. Black lace also trimmed the hem of her hip-hugging skirt, and chunky, silver buckles glimmered on her black leather boots. Glossy ringlets surrounded her face and shoulders. Her makeup was soft, except for plum-colored lipstick that accentuated her lips.

Jui sat next to Rob and after the hostess left, he said, "I think we should get dinner to go."

A satisfied smile filled Jui's face. She leaned over and gave him a light kiss. "Hi, sorry to make you wait."

"Believe me, it was worth it just to watch you walk in and have every guy in the place know you're with me."

"Glad to boost your ego," she replied, still smiling. "Let's eat; I'm starved."

Dinner arrived and Jui giggled when another bit of sushi rice escaped her lips.

Rob took his time plucking a kernel of rice from the deep valley between her breasts. "You missed one."

Their eyes locked as she slowly extended her tongue, beckoning him to give her the errant grain.

"I think it's time we got out of here," he said in a deep, husky voice.

"We haven't had dessert yet."

Rob put his hand on her bare thigh and positioned himself so he could caress her undetected. "Are you sure you want that kind of dessert?"

"I like ice cream."

Rob moved his hand higher. He wiggled his fingers, silently asking Jui to spread her thighs. Another inch or two and he'd be able to slide into her panties.

Jui relaxed in her chair to comply.

Rob discovered the fragile panty lace and swallowed hard. He whispered into her ear while probing her wet folds, "You feel like melted ice cream."

A blush rose on Jui's cheeks as he slid his long, middle

finger into her. He kissed the slender column of her throat while her pulse raced under his lips. "Let's go home. It's time to get you out of these wet panties."

* * * * *

Rob's cobalt-blue Lexus sports car hugged the rolling streets of Seattle, barely making a hum when it idled at the lights. Jui's capricious behavior in the restaurant fueled Rob's ardor, and he leaned over to kiss and fondle her during every red light. Knowing passersby witnessed their audacious behavior excited him even more.

Jui shoved her townhouse door closed with her heel and drew Rob into a hungry, wet kiss.

He rubbed up her thighs, lifting her skirt and then hooked his thumbs in the waistband of her flimsy panties and tugged upward until he knew they cut into her tender pussy lips. Rob hurriedly pulled off Jui's sweater. His lips left wet trails on her luscious breasts, which spilled over the tops of her bra.

Jui unzipped his pants and pulled out his cock. "Fuck me, I want you right now," she said through gritted teeth.

Rob unhooked her black lace bra and tossed it aside. He latched on to her nipple, suckling hard, and nibbling the pebbled flesh with his teeth. Her wanton behavior unleashed his reckless side. He moved the wet fabric between her thighs out of the way and lifted her onto his hips. Leaning against the kitchen wall, he impaled her on his hard cock, making her cry out.

Jui threw her head back and rocked on Rob's hips, urging him on. "Fuck me hard. I need you."

Rob bounced her against his hips until a sheen of sweat covered his body. He lowered her to the floor to continue pumping into her wet, tight canal. Her green plaid skirt wrapped around her waist, exposing her almost bare pussy. He groaned, viewing the naughty girl beneath him. "You're so hot, Jui. I could fuck you all night long."

"It's early. Do your best."

* * * * *

After a more unhurried lovemaking session on the living room couch, Jui led Rob to the shower. She washed his body, exploring its secrets and dimensions for the first time. *Very sexy, much sexier than his usual business suits led me to believe.*

"Do I pass?"

Jui giggled. "Busted." She wrapped her arms around him and kissed his blond-covered chest. "I was thinking I wish I'd discovered Rob Hawthorne a little sooner."

"Oh you do, do you?" he said, sounding pleased by her remark. "Well, I'm here now."

"Yes you are." Jui turned off the water and offered Rob a warm towel. She sauntered into her bedroom and returned with a man's bathrobe. "Here, this ought to keep you warm."

"Are we going somewhere?" he asked, exchanging the damp towel for the thick, long robe.

"On the roof. The stars are out and it's the most gorgeous sight." Jui cinched her blue and white-flowered robe and picked up a comforter. "Come on," she said, extending her hand to him.

Under the stars, Rob wrapped the blanket around his shoulders and Jui leaned against him, completing the circle of warmth.

For a brief moment, her breath floated like a cloud in front of her face and then evaporated in the chilly autumn air. "Isn't the sky beautiful?"

Rob kissed her temple. "Endless, full of possibilities—just like you."

A whimsical smile turned up her lips. "Yeah, definitely lots of possibilities."

* * * * *

Wade Kairos strutted into the lobby of The Peabody Memphis hotel on Union Street. Ornate, expansive, wood columns and beams supported the grand lobby design. The room's centerpiece was a large marble fountain, replete with the famous Peabody Ducks.

"My luggage is lost," Wade explained while checking in. "My bags will be sent to your FedEx office. Please deliver them to my room when they arrive."

"Absolutely, sir. You also have a message," the uniformed clerk said, sliding an envelope across the marble counter.

Wade stuffed the letter in his breast pocket. "Thank you."

He took the elevator to the third floor and slid the electronic key in his door. The room was chilly, as he'd requested. Wade took off his shoes and jacket while gazing around the well-appointed suite. A California king-sized bed, covered in peach and cream striped linens, looked just his size. He shut the heavy draperies and turned the air conditioning down as low as it could go before he undressed and stretched out his tired, sore body on top of the cool sheets. Teleporting himself across the Atlantic took tremendous concentration and energy. He replenished himself before arriving at the hotel, but he needed rest before he could help Christophe. "Effing boar. What was I thinking?" he muttered before dropping off to sleep.

After he rested and fed again, Wade relaxed on the chaise lounge with Christophe's message in hand. Hunting for Gerhardt was disgusting work, but Wade knew Christophe wouldn't quit until he exacted revenge with Gerhardt's life. Christophe's first years of vampirism were nightmarish so he made sure Wade's transition didn't follow suit. Wade accumulated wealth in his own right, working as he pleased in the many degreed professions on his resume. He traveled and lived with Christophe when it suited him but always appeared when Christophe went on a hunt for Gerhardt. Wade owed him that much.

Unlike Christophe, Wade accepted being a vampire as long as he kept human relationships at arm's length. When he got too close to a human, useless emotions and desires like morals, love, family, companionship, and the brevity of human existence tangled with his psyche. They filled him with remorse and self-loathing for his hedonistic, vampire lifestyle, which to a large extent he couldn't change. Knowing

Jui was trying to form a relationship with Rob filled him with emptiness and anger even though he urged her to move on. *I have to stay clear of her. I'm not human, Rob is.*

Wade sliced the envelope open, slid out the cream-colored linen paper, and read the missive. He scanned the list of vampires who could lead Christophe to Gerhardt. The vamps were the equivalent of police snitches and any human looking for them would find a dead end because the parasites had no real social existence. Wade paid them with blood and that was the worst part of hunting Gerhardt. These vampire cockroaches made sleazy demands, including kids and domestic animals. At times like these, Wade really wanted to tell Christophe to go fuck himself, but he didn't need Christophe as an enemy. At seventy years into vampirism, Wade still wore baby fangs.

He ran through his first three vamps on the list without any luck. His next informant, Leon, holed up near Graceland. Leon's reputation for drop and flop was legendary. He'd "drop" unsuspecting victims in the shadows and leave them flopping in near-death shudders after he damn near drained them. The old vamp was well connected and reliable.

Wade materialized on a residential street off Lehr Drive. Street lamps abounded, but Wade's ability to exist as a shadow made it easy for him to search for Leon. Moving through the area like a gentle breeze, Wade spotted a garden party. He raised his chin and cocked his head to the side, listening, and sniffing for Leon. *This is too damn easy.* He appeared near the carriage house and watched the well-dressed Leon working the crowd.

Wade telepathically approached the old vampire. *May I have a word with you?*

Leon snuggled up to a buxom woman at the party, letting his sexual pheromones snag every delicious pint he wanted. *Get away, I'm busy.*

Wade transmitted a high-pitched buzz into Leon's brain, distracting the crowd-pleasing vamp in disguise. *Now.*

"Please excuse me," he said, gazing at the beautiful blood bank clinging to his arms. Leon worked his way into the house and found a bathroom. His words were delivered to

Wade's brain with a snarl. *What the fuck do you want?*
I'm looking for Gerhardt Meuhler. I heard he's in town.
And if he is?
The familiar dance began.
There's a Sweet 16 party at the Weston on Beale tomorrow. Your name is on the guest list, Uncle Leon.
A smug grin lifted Leon's thin lips. *I can go to any party I want.*
But not for the entire evening. Where can I find Meuhler?
Leon took a moment to check Wade's thoughts. His bullshit detector never turned off. Finding no conflicting energy in Wade's gray matter, he communicated his reply. *There's a new production studio opening on Primacy Parkway. I hear Meuhler hired on as the host for their home shopping program. Suits him. Faggot.*
A scan of Leon's thoughts revealed no reason for Leon to lie. Wade placed the party credentials in Leon's smooth-skinned hand and disappeared.
Back in his hotel suite, Wade summoned Christophe. While he waited, Wade ordered dinner for two.
"It took you long enough," Christophe said after stabilizing. He took a seat in one of the soft cushioned chairs. "Are you healed?"
Wade snorted. "Almost. Wild boars are at the top of my list to avoid the next time I'm pissed." He lifted his black shirt to reveal an ugly wheal along his left ribs. "I can't imagine the damage that animal really did to my body." He shook his head. "I almost didn't make it across the Atlantic. I got here yesterday but laid low and rested."
Christophe got to the point. "What have you learned?"
"Leon said Meuhler is working at Carpathian Studios on Primacy."
"My source provided the same information. I've been keeping an eye on the place but I haven't seen him."
"Your source?"
"Blake," Christophe said.
"Blake is a vamp? Son of a bitch."
"You know him?"
"Actually I spoke to him a couple days ago. Jui--"

Christophe blew his cool. "Jui? What the hell has she got to do with this? Haven't you learned your lesson yet?"

"Keep your voice down. It was business. The studio had a problem she thought I might be able to solve. She referred me to Blake since he's the construction superintendent. Is he on our side or not?"

"Neutral."

"I handed over a bevy of 16-year-olds to that slimy bastard, Leon, for this information. Who knows how many will lose their virgin blood tomorrow night."

The remark didn't faze Christophe. "Hate his tactics, but he's reliable."

"I'll talk to Blake again tomorrow. Since he isn't aware of what I am, I'll see what I can learn on the phone. What's your plan for Meuhler?"

"I'd rather not tell you."

A knock sounded at the door.

"That must be dinner," Wade said.

A man in his middle twenties stood at Wade's door with a dining cart.

"Come in," Wade said, opening the door wider. The waiter pushed the cart in and a moment later, Wade grabbed him by the chin from behind and joined with his carotid.

Christophe waited for Wade to finish his quickie meal. "Hurry up, will you? You're giving me a hard on just watching."

Nurse him back to health and enjoy him, too. Maybe he'd get off on a serious romp with you — after he gets his strength back, of course. Wade filled Christophe's vampire brain with maniacal laughter. A satisfied smile curled his lips after he released the waiter.

The stunned man shuddered. "I'm sorry, were you saying something?"

"You look a little pale," Christophe said. "Perhaps you should take a seat."

The waiter wiped his sweaty brow with a crisp, white handkerchief. "Maybe I'm coming down with the flu." His cheeks flamed with embarrassment. "I'm sorry. I don't know why I said that. I'm fine — perfectly fine. If you'll sign for your room service, Mr. Kairos," he said, offering a pen and leather-bound folder with unsteady hands.

As soon as the flustered waiter left, Christophe's chortles filled Wade's head. *I think the guy would die of fright if either of us approached him again.*

Guess you'll have to find your fun somewhere else. "Getting back to business," Wade said aloud, "I'll contact Blake and see how the design corrections turned out and whether I can learn Meuhler's schedule."

"Keep Jui away. It's dangerous for her to be around."

Wade whirled around and snarled after the parochial comment. "I'll let you know when I learn something new. Get out."

After Christophe left, Wade dumped the beverages down the sink and flushed portions of their perfectly grilled tuna steaks down the toilet. Then he pushed the cart outside his door and hung the *Do Not Disturb* sign on the handle.

* * * * *

Even their combined body heat under the blanket couldn't keep Jui and Rob warm for long. The lure of nighttime beauty evaporated as shivers claimed them and so they returned to her living room. Jui turned on the fireplace and they pushed cushions near the windows to continue stargazing. Her cell phone buzzed on the kitchen countertop.

Rob shagged a thumb toward the noise. "You going to get that?"

"I'll just see who it is. We have a couple of problems at work. This might be one more." Jui padded over to the kitchen and picked up her phone. Her heart skipped a beat when she saw the name on caller ID.

Rob called to her. "Who is it?"

Jui shut her eyes and took a deep breath. "Nobody important. It can go to voicemail." Jui pressed *IGNORE* and put the phone down. Her relaxed mood turned melancholy as she stared at the electronic device blinking against the black granite surface.

"Coming?"

She gave Rob a pleasant smile that rose into her eyes. Settled back in his arms, she said, "That's better."

* * * * *

While Rob slept, Jui tossed and turned. Wade's waiting message tickled her curiosity, making it impossible for her to fall asleep. Exasperated, she got out of bed, put on her robe, and snuck downstairs to the kitchen to retrieve the ignored call.

"Jui, it's Wade. I'm sorry to interrupt your date with Rob, but I must speak to you. Call me no matter what time it is. What I need to tell you is important."

She erased the message. *How in the hell did he know I was on a date with Rob?* She glanced at the clock on the microwave. *Two o'clock.* Her gaze returned to the phone and her pulse quickened, knowing she had a bona fide reason, or at least the pretense of one, to speak to Wade. She went into the half-bath off the kitchen and shut the door to make the call.

"Good morning, Jui."

Jui's stomach quivered. "Hi, what's up?" she said, not wanting to sound too cheerful or too eager.

"I can understand why you didn't answer your phone earlier. I wouldn't tear myself out of your arms, either."

"That's a bold assumption."

"What? That you were in his arms or I wouldn't leave yours?"

Her throat tightened with sadness. "Why do you tease me and then push me away?" After a long pause, she asked, "Wade?"

"Jealousy I guess. Wanting what I can't have," he said in tones that didn't cover his emotional tracks very well.

"Your decision, not mine."

"And the right one, no matter how much I hate it."

"What's so important that it couldn't wait?"

"You couldn't sleep anyway."

"Damn it, how do you know these things about me— about my life?" Jui pressed her fingers across her forehead while she leaned against the cool, tiled wall. "I know something about you."

"Really?"

"The man my grandmother was engaged to was also named Wade Kairos. My father told me about him. Is he a relative?"

"Probably a distant one."

"Also a mathematician? My father's description of this other person is quite similar to the way you look."

"Coincidence — genetics, take your pick. We Kairoses have brilliant minds and striking good looks. Both are hereditary."

"Funny our paths crossed," she added, still not willing to let the subject drop.

"Kismet, six points of contact, or whatever that book said about people."

"What do you want?" she said, changing the subject before she lost her temper.

"Are you coming to Memphis?"

"I thought you and Blake got things under control."

"I'll call him again tomorrow to be sure the problems are solved."

"I am planning to attend the first tapings at Carpathian Studios."

"Promise you won't come here until you speak with me first."

Jui frowned at the unfounded demand. "What the hell for?"

"I can't explain, but my associate, Christophe, is well-connected here. Something is about to happen and I don't want you caught in the middle."

"Blake showed me around several times before. I'll be fine."

"You've met Blake — been with him?"

"What is your problem? Stop acting like some jealous lover, because you have no right, and I don't need a daddy."

"I don't mean to come off that way. I know things you don't and I'm asking you to trust me. Promise you won't come here without contacting me first."

Frustration bubbled in her brain. "What if you've already left the country? Don't you hear how ridiculous you sound?" Jui paused. Something in the sound of his voice made her want to give him the tiniest reassurance. "Let me know how it goes with Blake and when you're leaving America."

"You haven't given me your word."

"I won't. I don't have a reason to."

"Not even if I tell you, you could be in extreme danger?"

Jui didn't know whether he was telling the truth or he just didn't want to see her again. "Let me know when you're leaving."

"Not good enough!"

"Don't you dare shout at me! I promise not to come to Memphis when you're there and that's all I'll promise!"

"My concern isn't about staying apart, it's about staying alive."

"You have to be more specific and if you can't, then I don't have anything else to say. If I'm in some kind of danger, if you care about me, we should contact the police. Goodnight, Wade." Jui disconnected the call before he could say another word. *Every time we talk, you upset me. Who needs this shit?*

Jui placed her phone in the exact spot and position on the counter. Anger and frustration roiled in her mind and she wished she hadn't called him. *Now I won't be able to sleep for sure.*

She left her robe on her desk chair and slid back into bed with Rob.

"Where did you go?" he mumbled, sounding half-asleep.

"I couldn't remember if I locked the service door before we came up."

Rob drew her against his side. "Go back to sleep."

Easy for you to say.

* * * * *

Christophe was right. Wade didn't need a distraction like worrying over Jui. He chastised himself for wasting time on her when Christophe needed him focused. Wade paced his suite, trying to figure what to tell her without divulging his secrets. He arrived in her bedroom and hovered as a shadow against the wall. When he saw her lying naked in bed with Rob, jealousy soared through his body. The intimate scene urged him to drain Rob and leave the carrion for vultures. *I could do it, too.* Wade backed off. *I told Jui to work things out with the man.*

He went back into Jui's mind. He felt her conflicted emotions but he couldn't read her thoughts. *She's stronger than I thought.*

You're safe with Rob. Don't come to Memphis alone.

Her eyes flew open as Wade's voice trickled into her mind. She concentrated on his words, connecting with him. *Why do you do this to me? Why?*

I shouldn't, I know it. I can't help myself now, but I can help you.

Stop manipulating me. Get out of my head, out of my life.

You don't mean that.

Tears stung her eyelids. *You won't let me try. What hold do you have on me? I barely touched you and yet....*

He responded with a truth he knew Jui couldn't grasp. *You flow in my veins, too, minx.*

I don't want to. I don't want a man who doesn't want me.

His anger rose hot and quick. *That's a lie!*

What am I supposed to think? You say you want me but we can't be together. I'm tired of this circular argument. We get nowhere. I end up angry and depressed and you go your merry way.

Being apart hurts me, too. I'll be gone soon — I promise.

That should make me happy?

You'll have an easier time forming a real relationship with Rob once I am out of your life for good.

Jui glanced at the man sleeping next to her. *He deserves better.*

Stay with him; let him keep you safe from me, from Memphis.

I can't stay away from you. No matter where I am, somehow you find me, especially since you know I want you to. Just because you physically leave the States....

I'll leave you alone after Memphis, I promise, once I know you're safe.

Why can't you protect me yourself? Why aren't you here instead of Rob? Tears seeped onto her pillow and Jui wiped them away with the heel of her hand. *Stop tormenting me.* She tuned him out as surely as she shut off her phone.

* * * * *

Wade hit the streets of Memphis in a rage, attacking anyone in his path, only taking time to lick their wounds before he moved on to his next victim. He gorged on young and old, healthy and ill. He didn't care. He laughed, looking forward to tomorrow's headlines about people found mysteriously collapsed on the streets. There'd be no clues and no connections among the victims "...*who were found weak and near death but expected to live.*"

Two hours later, he materialized in his suite. Blood drunk, Wade stared at his reflection in the mirror. Traces of his victims covered his body. He burst into churlish laughter, letting his fangs extend, and his eyes dance with golden flames. *Rob can't save you from me, Jui. Only you can.*

Wade returned to Jui's bedroom as a moon shadow. He gazed over the entwined couple, studying them vampire-style. Jealous hunger coursed through him. Ideas of turning Jui snaked through his brain. *I want her so badly.* The scent of their lovemaking filled his nostrils and it sickened him to know Jui gave herself to this human. He leaned over Rob's prone body, trying to decide exactly which vein he ought to tap. Rob shifted to his back and rested his arm above his head. Wade's mouth watered. He licked his lips, preparing to bite down on Rob's subclavian artery, rich with oxygenated blood.

Jui stirred and her eyes fluttered.

In his shadowy state, it would be almost impossible for her to see him. He froze like a thief with his hand in the till.

"Wade?"

He vanished.

Chapter Seven

Jui awakened ill at ease the next morning. She lay in bed, recalling her phone conversation with Wade. Her dreams were confusing and frightening. *Did I really see him standing over Rob?* "*Rob can protect you from me, from Memphis,*" Wade said on the phone. *What did that mean?* Questions pummeled her brain. The way he seemed to enter her thoughts unnerved her. The hold he had on her was a mystery. *Maybe if I get things cleared up with Blake in Memphis, Wade will leave the States immediately. Rob and I can get on with our relationship and I can get on with my life.* She glanced at Rob, still asleep, and her heart softened. *He's a terrific guy. He deserves a fair chance or I ought to break it off now before he gets hurt over something he doesn't understand. Something I don't even understand.*

She rolled into a sitting position and jumped when she felt a hand on her hip. "Wade?" The name leapt from her lips before she had a chance to think. "I mean what the heck?" Jui put a happy smile on her face to frost the lie. She said to Rob, "You scared me!"

"You thought of Kairos the minute you woke up?"

Jui rolled back into bed and into Rob's arms. "No, I just misspoke. You startled me. I meant to say 'what' but it came out 'Wade'. But since you reminded me, I need to call him and Blake to see how things are going at Carpathian."

Skepticism shined in his blue eyes and Jui hoped to erase his doubts with a hot kiss.

Much later, Rob drank coffee while reading the newspaper in the living room.

Jui toasted bagels and cut up fresh fruit in the kitchen. "Come on," she called to her lover, signaling breakfast was ready. "We're already really late for work."

The newspaper crunched as Rob tossed it aside. He pulled up a chair at the table and bit into the toasted bread covered in honey walnut cream cheese.

"I think I'm going to work from home today. I don't have

a heavy schedule and I need to make some travel plans," he said between bites.

"If everything is straightened out in Memphis, I promised I'd come down for the first tapings. Want to come along?"

"Let me know when. If I can, sure."

"I'll probably find out from Blake this morning. I was thinking maybe from there we could hop over to Harkers Island for a long weekend."

"Where's Harkers Island?"

"North Carolina, kinda along the Crystal Coast. Our family has a house there. It's nothing fancy, but it's right on the water. We can walk the beaches, have bonfires on the shore, and sit on the big front porch watching the tide roll in." Jui gave him a bright smile. "Are you interested?"

"Sounds terrific—sure, I'm interested. Let's try to make it work." Rob picked up his plate and brought it to the kitchen counter. Coming back to the table, he gave her a gentle kiss. "Thanks for inviting me." While stroking the slender column of her neck with his thumb, he said, "If I didn't know better, I'd think you and I are building something special." He kissed her with more passion and Jui moaned softly.

"I'd better let you get to the office," he said in a husky voice, "while I still can."

* * * * *

Jui arrived in her office at 10:30 a.m. She came and went as she pleased, but arriving this late was unusual without a good reason.

Her administrative assistant, Maria, handed her a stack of messages.

Jui said thanks and walked into her office while still looking through the pink slips of paper. She set her briefcase on her walnut desk and dropped into her leather executive chair. While studying the message from Blake, she whispered, "Better be good news."

"Hi Blake, it's Jui," she said when he answered the phone. "What's up? Something good for a change, I hope."

"Yeah, actually that guy, Kairos, did the trick. The sound issues are fixed."

"Awesome. I'm so relieved to have that monkey off our backs. When will they begin production?"

"We should be able to turn over the building to the new owners next week. I guess I'd check with them to see what their plans are. Are you still coming down?"

"I'm going to try to be there. You're invited to the opening too, right?"

"I'm not sure I'll go after all the hassles we had with this building but I might if you ask me nicely."

Jui could hear the grin in his voice. She and Blake hit the town together twice on her previous visits and he was more fun than his somber-looking face let on. "I'm probably bringing Rob Hawthorne with me."

"Damn, beat out again. Lucky guy."

"Thanks for understanding, but I hope that doesn't mean you won't attend the celebration. I'd love to see you and we can have a drink together."

"Yeah, get me drunk, take advantage of me—please!"

His warm laughter filled Jui's ears and she giggled too. "I'll let you know my plans. Thanks for sticking with me on this project. We owe you one."

"No sweat. See you soon."

Their playful exchange left a smile on her face. Then Jui's smile faded into a disgruntled frown. "Might as well get this over with." She dialed the number.

"Good morning again, Jui." Wade's voice sounded rough, his tone edgy.

"Everything is fixed at Carpathian. You can leave."

Frigid anger furled through Wade's chest and into his voice. "Your impudence is astounding. Not even so much as a thank you or goodbye?" Wade tried to penetrate the thick wall surrounding her thoughts, but got nothing but barbed wire.

"Just a minute." Jui got up and shut her office door. She picked up the handset again and spoke in low tones. "I don't know what you want from me. You told me to stay away from you, to move on with Rob, and that you'd leave me alone after the situation in Memphis was fixed. What the hell else is there to say? You've made yourself abundantly clear and couldn't give two shits about what I have to say about our non-relationship. So get out of my head and get the hell out of my life." Jui slammed the receiver down and felt tears scalding her eyes. "Get out of my life," she said with a whimper.

* * * * *

A snarl ripped from Wade's throat. He was sick and tired of being pissed off all the time.

"That's what hanging around humans does to you." Christophe had materialized behind Wade, catching him off guard.

"Thanks for knocking, you blood-sucking ass."

Christophe's eyes narrowed at Wade. "She's going to destroy you. You know that." He picked up the newspaper from under Wade's door and showed the front page to him. "This your handy work? 'Mysterious Illness Hits Memphis Streets'?"

Wade dodged the question. "As soon as we're done with Meuhler, I'm leaving—putting her and all this human insanity behind me."

"That's the smartest thing I've heard you say in weeks. I hope you mean it. I want Meuhler this time."

"When are you going to tell me your plans?"

"That's why I'm here. I want you to monitor Meuhler—get his routine down. Now that Carpathian Studios is opening, he'll be going there to prepare for his new television show," Christophe said.

"What are you going to do?"

"I'm leaving town. Let me know when you have a reliable pattern to report. I'll organize my attack away from Memphis."

"But you're killing him here, right?"

"Yes, but maybe if he thinks I'm not seriously pursuing him, I'll have a better chance."

"I'm sure our snitch, Leon, went right to him and it's not like Meuhler doesn't know who I am or about my relationship with you."

"You have a legitimate reason for being here. You know

how to play it. Entertain the kiddies at the park for all I care, just let Meuhler continue thinking I'm out of the picture."

"The construction superintendent doesn't know I'm a vamp."

"And you can work that to your advantage. Just remember to keep Jui out of your head and away from Memphis."

"I already warned her."

Christophe raised his eyebrows and mocked him. "Oh, big fucking deal! I know what you're up to. Your body's twisted with human emotions that spell doom for her. If you fuck up my plans because of some human chick you have the hots for or whatever it is you think you have for her, your fiery gates of hell will open sooner than Meuhler's!" Christophe's eyes flamed with anger and determination. His voice became a menacing growl. "You owe me. I don't ask for anything but this. Get your head in *this* game."

* * * * *

Three days later, Wade paid a visit to Blake in his construction trailer. He hissed like a cobra at the sudden arrival of another vamp. "What do you want?"

"Don't go all gothic on me," Wade said, sounding a bit bored with Blake's drama.

"Who are you?" he asked, with eyes still blazing yellow and his teeth bared.

"Kairos."

"What are you doing popping in like this? Use the fucking door like everyone else."

"I'm not just 'everyone else' so put your attitude in a drawer. I came to talk."

Blake backed off but didn't let his vampire guard down completely. "I assume this hasn't got anything to do with Saint Claire Symphonic. What do you want?"

"I'm looking for Meuhler. I want to know his schedule and I'm certain you can give me the info."

Blake scoffed. "A five minute-old vamp could accomplish that feat." His wooden-legged chair creaked as he leaned backward and scanned Wade's thoughts. "What does Christophe Strasse have to do with this?"

"It's an old score but Strasse is finally letting it die."

"Two arch enemies want to play nice? What a crock of shit." Blake leaned forward, letting the front legs of the chair hit the floor with a solid thump. "I don't care what you two do. Keep me out of it. Meuhler has a driver through the studios. That's all I'll tell you."

"Good enough. One last thing."

Blake arched an eyebrow, listening.

"Jui Fabrice—stay away from her. If I find out you've drained one more drop of her blood, I'll take care of you myself. I'll laugh watching your vampire flesh blister and run from your ancient bones like wax dripping from a candle."

The warning amused Blake. "Why do you care who I feed on?"

Wade's body became a blur as he flashed in front of Blake and grabbed him by the shirtfront. Cold fire danced in his eyes and his voice became threatening. "Don't press your luck. Keep your teeth and everything else off her." With a forceful but controlled shove, Wade sent Blake to the floor. "She's mine."

Blake got on his feet and glared at Wade. "You got problems, Kairos. You're dangerous to us. Get the human out of your life before it's too late."

"Remember what I said. I'm going to be around for the opening at Carpathian. If I see you—"

Blake threw his hands up in mock surrender. "Whatever. In your spare time, maybe you ought to remind yourself you're a vampire and emotional relationships with humans never work. Humans have a tendency to be really pissed when they find out they've been turned, in case you've forgotten." He licked his lips. "Jui was, um, how shall I say it? Tasty." Deciding broad daylight offered him enough protection from an all-out vampire scuffle, Blake said, "And damn good in the sack. But I suppose you already know about her lover, Rob. Hell, Jui hinted I might get a little on the side when she comes down with him." He dug his talons a little deeper into Wade's psyche. "A threesome would be cool. I can share."

"Don't touch her. Your life is over if you do." An angry rush of wind scattered papers and chairs all over Blake's office as Wade vanished.

* * * * *

Meuhler's driver was a vamp, as were his closest associates. Wade wasn't surprised and thought the vampire entourage made his job a bit easier; he knew exactly what he was up against. *Plus, I don't have to worry about unpredictable humans and the families left behind.* The thought pricked his ire. *Useless fucking conscience.* For the sixth straight day, he perched on top of a five-story apartment building a half block south of Carpathian Studios. Wade blended in with the background while he waited for Meuhler's limo to arrive. Schedules. Wade loved them. *I wonder if Meuhler has any idea what an easy target he is.*

Meuhler's driver parked the white stretch in its designated spot. *How fucking pretentious can you get?* The cast grew as one vamp got out and opened the door for Meuhler. Two younger men hung on his arms and another man followed.

Wade dialed into their conversation. Even from this distance, he heard every word. The man following Meuhler was his personal secretary. *I guess he can get more pretentious.* Wade kept listening.

"Taping starts Tuesday at ten thirty," the male secretary said. "You meet with wardrobe this morning."

Wade didn't need any more details. He materialized in his hotel room and concentrated on Christophe. Wade stretched out on his bed to wait. The hotel staff gave him peculiar stares when they delivered his laundry or a meal and found the room frigid, but they were too smart and polite to ask questions. *I can't wait to get out of Memphis and back to normal life—free of scrutiny and pretense.* While he waited, he decided to go back to Moscow. Once winter arrived, the snowy forest surrounding his home along the Moskva River provided the perfect place to recline vampire style, away from prying eyes.

Christophe awakened Wade with a gruff, "What do you have for me?"

Wade cracked an eyelid and gave the old vampire a half-assed grin. "Taping starts Tuesday at ten thirty. He arrives by limo at eight every day and leaves at different times so your best chance is in the morning." The glee he expected to see in Christophe's eyes wasn't there. "Something wrong?"

Christophe's words were terse. "I'll take it from here. You can leave—do whatever the hell you please, just get lost."

Wade swung his feet to the floor. "Why? We've always worked together on a hunt."

"And they've always failed. This time I'll succeed. I have no doubt."

"So—I don't get to celebrate too? I've been hunting him for seventy years with you." Wade tuned into Christophe's thoughts and got a low vibration for his effort.

"I want you out. This is my moment."

"Dispense with the theatrics, will you? Why are you so anxious to get rid of me?" Wade pushed him a little more. "What have you got planned that you don't want me involved in? Your schemes better not include Jui."

Christophe roared with fury, seemingly unconcerned about the racket he created in the hotel. "It's not about you! Get the fuck out. Your preoccupation with her is a hazard. How many times do I have to say it before it gets through your thick skull?"

Wade slid into his shirt, glad he didn't have to watch Christophe fail again. *There'll be another chance, I'm certain. Vamps aren't easy to kill and despite Christophe's best attempts, Meuhler is proof of it.* "I'm headed to my *dacha* in Russia. See you when the snow flies." Wade disappeared without a backward glance.

Minutes later, he arrived in his log-framed *dacha* north of Moscow. September brought rich color to the landscape and comfortable daytime temperatures. Residual heat from the day warmed the pitch in the trees and mingled with the breeze, creating a warm pine scent. Wade filled his lungs, glad to be home, glad to reclaim his lifestyle.

He sensed Christophe's presence. *You'll know when it's*

over, he heard Christophe say. *Embrace it, you lucky bastard and know love changes everything.*

Wade shook his head at the uncharacteristic, obscure, romantic communication. He sent Christophe a head-full of laughter. *Are you high? How many have you drained?*

Christophe's warm voice returned. *You'll see. I just never told you. Chasing shadows is exhausting. Look at me.*

I'll keep a snow bank plowed for you. You'll come, right?

Sure.

Good luck with Gerhardt. Wade didn't receive a reply. Christophe's demeanor and words were a complete puzzle. *Something's up. Monday, I'm heading back to Memphis.*

Chapter Eight

While Wade got reacquainted with Russian blood, Jui and Rob made plans to go to Memphis.

"Vie is coming over tonight. I haven't talked to her since I went to Germany," Jui told Rob on the phone. "We're going to have pizza and beer and catch up."

"Sounds like a nice evening of girl talk." Rob audibly shuddered. "I think I'll go to bed early."

Jui chuckled. "Worn out, are you? We're going to have to work on your stamina," she said with another giggle.

"I think I'm coming down with something. I'll hit the hay and I'm sure I'll be in great shape tomorrow, if you're interested, that is."

A happy smile curled her lips and warmed her tone. "Sounds like a plan. You have to be well for our trip to Memphis and especially Harkers Island."

"I'm looking forward to all of it." After a long yawn, he said, "Whew, sorry to yawn in your ear. I'm beat."

"Get some rest and I'll talk to you tomorrow."

Jui's doorbell rang a minute after she hung up the phone.

A deliveryman dressed in a brown uniform stood outside the front door. "Jui Fabrice?"

"That's me."

"If you'll just sign here," he said, indicating the electronic signature line. "Where do you want them?" he asked while she signed.

"You can bring the boxes in the living room."

Afterward, Jui stared at the three cases of wine she'd paid a small fortune to ship from Germany. "It'll take me years to finish all this." She opened the three thick-padded boxes and examined their contents. Memories of that Sunday afternoon came flooding back. She couldn't help wondering what might have happened if the vineyard worker hadn't arrived at such an inopportune moment. Her passion rose as she recalled being in Wade's arms, the way his kiss turned her knees to butter. She remembered the sounds he made while she went down on him.

"Stop it, Jui!" she scolded. "It's over and done. Wade is gone."

She uncorked a slender brown bottle of the Riesling in the kitchen and poured a glass full. Raising the pale gold wine, she said, "Hope you feel better, Rob. North Carolina is gonna be awesome."

The semi-dry wine slipped down her throat and ended with a mellow apple flavor. Her thoughts meandered back to the vineyard cottage in Germany where she fantasized Wade carried her to the small back bedroom. The imaginary creak of the mattress springs as he laid her on the quilt-covered bed and the weight of his body on hers raised lust-filled goose bumps on her body. His tongue surged between her lips, possessing her mouth, and making her pussy burn for his cock. She gripped his shoulders, urging him on, moving her body with his in anticipation. The sound of alternate pounding and doorbell rings shattered Jui's lusty trance.

Vie stood in the doorway with a pizza in one hand and a six-pack in the other. "What took you so long? I was beginning to think you forgot about me."

"Sorry, I was upstairs on the phone and didn't hear you."

"Can I come in? Holy shit, Jui, what's up with you?"

Jui opened the door wide to let her sister pass. "Guess I'm just a little distracted. This week has been kinda tense."

Vie gave her a suspicious glance. "Tense? I can't wait to hear all about it."

Sylvia was three years younger than Jui. While Jui shared their mother's professional traits, Vie's talents were more like their Grandmother Claire's. Well, sort of. Vie played electric guitar and sang in a local rock band.

While sliding a slice of pizza with the works onto her plate, Vie asked, "What's his name?" She chose a bottle of autumn lager and walked into the living room.

Jui started the fireplace and they sat in front of it. "Rob."

"Hawthorne? The sales guy who has been asking you out for months?"

"Yeah. And he's the sales director not a sales guy. Anyway,

we went out one evening in Germany and had a nice time and one thing led to another."

"What score did he get?"

"Six," she admitted with a laugh.

Vie wrinkled her nose. "Six? And you went out with him again?" Vie took a sip of her beer. "He must have improved a lot on the second try."

"He did and he's a nice guy, Vie. We have a lot of fun together."

"But? I sense there's a 'but' in there."

Jui sighed. "I met this other guy in Germany—Wade Kairos. Talk about hot, smart, and mysterious."

Vie's eyebrows raised in curiosity. "And?"

"And nothing. We kept running into each other in the strangest places, in the strangest ways." Jui began to speak as though she was reliving, not relating, what actually happened. "Sometimes I swear he can read my mind, you know, talk to me telepathically. I'd be thinking about him and suddenly I'd hear him in my head. I still feel so connected to him. Kissing him was like an out of body experience. "A warm blush crept up her neck and covered her cheeks. "TMI?"

"Did you sleep with him?"

Jui shook her head. "Almost—a couple of times actually, but we were always interrupted. His body is amazing. Mine fits perfectly...."

"Why don't you go after him?"

Jui went from wistful to wooden. "He doesn't want me. He said it was dangerous for us to be together and told me to build a relationship with Rob." Jui's expression hardened. "And that's what I'm doing. Wade be damned, Rob is a great guy and I'm moving on."

"Sounds like it," Vie said, and then bit off another gob of pizza.

"What? Don't you believe me?"

"Not exactly. Sounds like this Wade guy is still in your head and maybe in your heart or at least in your jeans."

Jui thought for a moment. *What's the point of lying?* "I guess so. But it's stupid to chase after a man who reels you in and then tosses you away. It's a waste of time and emotional energy."

"Are you using Rob?"

"No! Not at all! I started a relationship with Rob before anything happened with Wade. I mean, I met Wade before I went out with Rob and we talked for a few minutes, but the guy's a playboy. He's always got women hanging on him, ogling him. It's no wonder he wants me to stay away. I'll probably ruin his reputation."

"Doesn't sound like your type. What's the attraction? Is he a 'bad boy'?"

Jui went to the kitchen and retrieved two more beers. "I don't know if he's a 'bad boy', but he sure is mysterious. The moment he spoke to me, I felt we connected — like he reached into my soul. It sounds so stupid, farcical even — like love at first sight. Who believes in that crap?" she asked with a shake of her head. "But when he kissed me, holy shit, I couldn't breathe. I thought my heart was going to stop, I've never had such an intense kiss."

"Go on."

Jui arched her brow, gazing suspiciously at her sister. "You living vicariously through me now?"

A smug grin made its home on Vie's lips. "Hey, if it helps to talk, I'm all ears."

"I thought he was going to make love to me." Jui closed her eyes as she spoke. "He was kissing my neck and I felt this rush of desire through me. It was so erotic, like nothing I've ever experienced. We could have been in a train station at rush hour and I'd have wanted him right then and there."

"But he didn't want you?"

"I know he did. There was no mistake about it." Jui gave her sister a sly wink. "He would have been an eleven."

Sylvia leaned back against her over-stuffed chair. Her face registered envy. "An eleven? Wow, maybe I should give him a call since he says the two of you are toast."

"Sylvia! For Christ's sakes, I'm serious. I can't get this guy out of my head and I might see him on Tuesday. If Rob sees the two of us together, he'll know right then and there and I'll never have a chance with Rob."

"So maybe you should hook up with Wade in Memphis. Sleep with him, get him out of your system."

"Are you serious? You're suggesting I just have casual sex with him because you think I'm caught up in the mystery of Wade Kairos and he makes me horny?"

"Please don't act so prissy, because I know you're not. The way I see it, you have two choices. Use Rob to push Wade out of your mind or find Wade and sleep with him. You'll know afterward who you should be with."

"What if it turns out I want Wade but he still doesn't want me?" Jui asked, intrigued by her sister's bold suggestion.

"Do you think he'd sleep with you, knowing you have feelings for him, if he didn't feel the same way?"

"Maybe. He's undoubtedly a playboy. Maybe I'd just stroke his ego, I don't know. I don't want to cheat on Rob. He's a great guy and he wants to be with me."

"Then run from Wade. They call guys like him 'man whores'. I'd take his advice and see how things go with Rob or somebody else."

Jui drew in a deep, shaky breath. "Wade and I could have been together somewhere else, uninterrupted, but he wouldn't do it. It was like he was protecting me somehow."

"Is he married?"

"He said he isn't."

"Are you sure?"

"How the hell can I be sure? I don't even know where he lives." She balled her fists and tapped her forehead over and over. "Oh! How did I get into this situation? What a freaking mess!"

* * * * *

Around midnight, Jui said goodbye to Vie, promising to keep her posted on her trip to Memphis and her trip to Harkers Island with Rob.

"Yeah, yeah, yeah, I'll share all the juicy details," she said as her sister walked down the steps to her car.

"Call me if you need me," Vie said over her shoulder and then turned. In the stillness of the Seattle night, her words came through sounding loving and concerned. "I mean it, Jui.

If you run into Wade in Memphis or you need help sorting this out, I'm here for you."

Jui rubbed her arms, shivering in the late evening air. The front lamp attracted a few moths and night insects. She shooed them away from her face and waved goodbye again. "Thanks, I'll call you if I need you. 'Night!"

Jui locked the front door, switched off the outside lights, and listened to the silence. The fireplace glow reflected on the living room wall and the horrifying vision of Wade standing over Rob replayed in her mind. Wade's eyes danced with golden flames, like the fireplace, on the face of an inhuman being. She shuddered. *How did I come up with such a creepy, horror-flick image?*

The open bottle of Riesling sat on the kitchen counter and Jui refilled her glass. Lights flickered on the water from houses along the lake. She inhaled slowly, feeling so restless and unsure about her relationship with Rob and her feelings for Wade. "Why did we have to meet?" she wondered aloud. She forced herself to concentrate on how she felt when she and Rob were together. *Satisfying. Comfortable. Easy. Genuine. Sounds like a recipe for boredom.* She wondered if Wade would keep his word and stay away from her in Memphis. *I know it's best if we don't see each other. Damn it, since when do I usually do what's good for me?* She flung her half-filled glass against the stone fireplace. Shards of glass and spatters of wine deflected off the stones, onto the window, and slid down.

* * * * *

The next morning, Rob phoned Jui.

"You sound awful!" she told him.

Rob voice sounded like a croak. "I've got a plugged nose and sore throat so I'm just going to stay home. If we're going to Memphis on Monday, I need to kick this thing. I'm sure if I stay in bed and rest, I'll be fine."

Jui listened to his optimistic words and doubted every one of them. "Do you need anything? Can I get you some cold medicine or something?" Rob's dry cough made Jui's heart sink. "Maybe you should go into urgent care and see if you have the flu."

"I've been sick before; I'll be fine. I already went to the pharmacy and stocked up on stuff for colds," he said through sniffles and more coughs.

"You don't sound good at all. I'd sure hate for you to miss Harkers Island. I mean, I don't really care if you come to Memphis...." Her voice trailed as she remembered Vie's suggestion to find Wade.

"I know, and that's why I'm just going to stay home. Don't come over here. I don't want you catching this. Even if I have to cancel Memphis on Monday, I can fly down to North Carolina on Tuesday night or Wednesday morning at the latest." Rob excused himself to blow his nose. "I'm sure I'll be better in four or five days."

"You're probably right," Jui said, wanting to hope for the best. "Get some rest. You sound like you could nod off right now."

"Going to the store really wore me out," he said.

"Oh geez. If you're worse tomorrow, you have to see a doctor, okay?"

"Yeah, yeah."

"I'll let you get some rest." Jui hung up the phone and muttered under her breath." I sure hope our vacation plans aren't shot to hell, too. Shit."

* * * * *

On Sunday, Rob was a lot worse. At Jui's insistence, he went to urgent care and was diagnosed with the flu.

Jui moaned, disappointed. "You gotta be kidding. I don't mean to sound selfish but dang, I was so looking forward to our trip."

"I'm really bummed, too. Are you still going to Harkers Island?"

"I don't know. It won't be any fun now if you aren't coming."

"If you decide to go, let me know. If I'm better, maybe I

can still catch up with you there."

"Maybe," she said, still bummed. "I'll see how it goes in Memphis. I was looking forward to a few days away and I really need some time off."

"Call me from Memphis. Maybe the prescription I got will clear this up sooner than we think."

* * * * *

Jui dropped five bucks in the bellman's hand and shut the hotel door behind her. She wasn't looking forward to the taping tomorrow or anything else since Rob was sick. She packed to go to Harkers Island just in case Rob could join her there in few days, but she wasn't optimistic.

While she unpacked her overnight bag, her cell phone rang and Jui answered it. "Hey you!"

"You made it," Blake said. "What are you up to?"

"I just got in. I was going to order room service."

"Room service in Memphis?" Blake let out a hearty laugh. "We're going out. Beale Street is open and we're going to have some fun. What do you say?"

"Can we go to B.B. King's again?"

"I'll be there in five. Watch for me in the lobby."

A playful smile flittered onto Jui's face. Blake was always a lot of fun. She changed into something dressier for the evening and brushed her hair. As she dabbed on fresh lipstick, she remembered Wade's warning not to come to Memphis alone. *Blake can keep an eye on me and I'll be gone before Wade knows it.* Jui couldn't help wondering if Wade was still in town. The idea made her nervous with anticipation or dread, she wasn't sure which.

* * * * *

Blake watched her push her meal around her plate, barely touching the spicy carbonara she ordered. "Would you like something else?"

"I'm sorry, it's delicious," Jui answered, pushing a few pieces of ziti pasta round her plate for the hundredth time. She gave him a weak smile. "I think I'm just disappointed Rob got sick and can't be here."

Blake tuned into Jui's thoughts and confirmed the truth. "Sorry to hear it."

She chortled at the remark. "Like hell. You couldn't be happier he's not here."

Blake raised an eyebrow at the remark. "Can't blame a guy for trying."

"Long distance relationships suck, Blake. Believe me. I don't want to get tangled up with a guy half way across the world again."

"I'm not half way across the world and the next job could be closer to Seattle."

"You know what I mean."

The long distance lover's name flickered through Jui's mind and Blake picked up on it. "I'm not interested in a long-term commitment. I just like having a little fun. By the way," he said, digging into the heart of her distraction, "is Kairos coming tomorrow?"

Jui's voice registered her surprise. "Why do you ask?"

"He was rather instrumental in solving our sound issues down here. I thought—"

"You thought wrong. I mean, I don't know," she said.

All evening long, he noticed she had surreptitiously watched the restaurant's entrance and scanned the crowd.

"Did he call you?"

Suspicion filled Jui's eyes. "Why do you care? Did he say something to you about me I should know?"

Blake returned the serious gaze, starting a mind game of his own with her. Wade's very clear instructions to stay away from Jui or risk death by fire seemed like a suggestion at the moment. "He seemed, how should I say—very protective of you. What's up with you two?" Blake could barely contain the glee in his voice, sensing her discomfort over the subject and his line of nosey questions. "Did you two have a thing?"

"I don't think that's any of your business. But for the record, no, we did not have a fling or a thing. I don't even think he's still in the country." Her voice sounded huffy and her body language conveyed nervousness.

"Oh, he's around. I promise you. He hasn't called you, huh?"

"Haven't heard a word."

"I'm surprised, very surprised."

Later, as Blake pulled his sedan in front of Jui's hotel, he noticed her furtively glancing around. Just because she hadn't heard from the illusive vampire, didn't mean Wade wasn't lurking. Her behavior put Blake in the mood for danger. He put the car in park and turned toward her. "I hope I didn't make you angry earlier, asking so many questions about Kairos."

"No harm done."

"I just like to know who my competition is."

"I'm trying to build something with Rob, not Wade, not that there ever was something between Wade and I. I'm sorry Blake, but I really can't imagine anything but casual friendship between you and me, either."

Blake did his best to act disappointed. "I understand. Well, I'll say goodnight."

"I really did have a nice time tonight and I apologize for not being better company this time around." Jui moved to hug Blake.

He threw caution to the wind. *One little sip was worth the risk.* Her hair smelled fresh and he brushed it aside, drawing her closer. He suppressed a victorious laugh as his fangs neared her throbbing carotid. Through the passenger window, Blake saw a flash of Wade Kairos with eyes blazing and fangs bared. A serpent's hiss burrowed into Blake's consciousness. Blake released Jui.

She studied his disappointed face. "Something wrong?"

He gave her a quick kiss on the cheek. "Nothing. See you tomorrow."

Chapter Nine

Long after midnight, Christophe materialized in the parking garage where Gerhardt Meuhler's limousine sat for the night. A few security guards pretending to monitor video surveillance huddled in an office far from the parking spot. *Not much of a challenge for a vamp.* Glancing around for intruders and keeping his ears attuned to any unusual sounds, he waited, but nothing hit his vamp radar. *Coast is clear.*

He opened his small duffle bag next to the rear wheel of the limo and gently extracted about a pound and a half of C-4 explosives. There was no time for anticipation, glee, or anxiety. The last thing Christophe needed was to blow himself up and let Meuhler roam the Earth unfettered for all eternity. *Three hundred years is long enough.* Pressing the plastique into the wheel well took only a few moments. Then he used a battery-operated drill to make a small hole inside the well.

Using vampire stealth, Christophe materialized inside the car and removed the interior door panel with the drill. *Now for the tricky part.* He secured the electric blasting cap inside the door panel with double-backed tape and then attached the firing wire to it. *One last connection to make.* Christophe wired the sensitive microswitch into the door's electronics. After the door's interior panel was back in place, Christophe polished the rigged panel clean of fingerprints.

Back outside, he crouched low again—even a vampire could be videotaped—and savored the blood scent of revenge while he wiped down the rear quarter panel until it gleamed. *This time I won't fail.* With a satisfied grin on his face, Christophe picked up his bag and vanished.

* * * * *

At seven-thirty the next morning, Gerhardt Meuhler and his entourage climbed into their studio-supplied limousine.

Meuhler's spirits soared, filling the vampire with giddy anticipation over his new television career and his most-desired reward—fame.

His secretary rattled off the daylong schedule of tapings, interviews, and parties. He listed the names of special guests expected in the audience, which included the studio owners, investors, the contractor's top brass, and a few loyal fans who won exclusive seats to the first taping. Overall, Meuhler couldn't have been more pleased with this new chapter in his eternal life.

The car left I-240 and turned west onto Park Avenue. The Saint Francis Hospital came into view and after a few more blocks, they turned south onto Ridgeway Road.

Christophe materialized in the limo to the surprise of all its occupants.

Meuhler and his secretary bared their fangs and hissed. Meuhler's boy toys did their level best to disappear into the upholstery at the unholy sight in front of them.

Christophe greeted the group in a smug tone. "Good morning, Gerhardt, I came to extend my best wishes for your new television career."

Meuhler's head bounced on his neck like a cobra ready to strike.

"Not a friendly welcome at all," Christophe said. He gazed at the humans cowering on both sides of Gerhardt. "You mean he didn't tell you he was a vampire?" A sarcastic grin spread Christophe's lips. "Tsk, tsk. All this time you've been fucking each other and he didn't have the courtesy to tell you he's been draining your blood, too?"

The wide-eyed men seemed too stunned to speak.

"Terrible manners," Christophe concluded with a cluck of his tongue.

Gerhardt said, "What do you want Strasse? Your little Halloween tricks aren't amusing."

Reddish-orange flames flickered in Christophe's eyes. "It's been a long time."

"Get to your point," Gerhardt demanded. "We're almost to the studio and I have damage control, no thanks to you."

Christophe sneered. "Worried about your reputation?"

"I can take care of this mess," Gerhardt's secretary volunteered while pointing at Christophe.

Christophe gave him a cold, feral gaze. In an instant, the secretary's head left his neck, dropped to the seat, and rolled to the floor like a rotted melon. The dead vamp's open eyes registered surprise.

The two humans on either side of Gerhardt came unglued, pressing themselves into the seat corners and trying to avoid the razor-sharp blade still dripping in Christophe's palm.

"Let me out," one pleaded. "I won't say a word. Just let me go."

"This can't be happening," said the other man over and over.

"Maybe we just need some air to clear our heads," Christophe said. He trained his gaze on Gerhardt. "What do you say? Shall we have some fresh air, for the sake of our long-standing friendship?"

"You're insane! Get out of here," Gerhardt commanded but made no move to force Christophe's hand.

"A little air and we'll all be thinking much clearer." Christophe rested his thumb on the window control. "I told you I'd repay you someday." The flick of the window switch detonated the C-4, blowing the limo and everyone in it to smithereens.

* * * * *

Jui received a phone call from Blake but she had already heard the news. Coverage of the shocking event cannibalized all other broadcasting.

"Meuhler is dead for sure. He was in the car with his secretary, two companions, plus the driver," Blake told her. "I got the information from the studio manager."

"My God, who would do such a thing?"

"Meuhler was a pretty flamboyant creature on screen but otherwise quite anemic, if you ask me."

"Should I come to the studio?" Jui asked.

"The blast happened just as they turned onto the parkway

so the area is cordoned off. You couldn't get near here if you wanted to."

Jui sat in stunned silence on the corner of her unmade bed. "You there?"

"Yeah, I'm just in shock. The project has been rife with problems and delays and finally everything is straightened out and now this. I can't believe somebody would blow up his car."

"Not much left from what I hear," Blake said. "You might as well head home. There won't be any taping or celebrations today."

"I guess I'll make a few calls in case people down here need to reach me for some reason."

"You going to call Kairos?"

"I don't know. What's there to say?"

"He can find you if he wants to anyway."

"Yes, he can. Thanks for calling me, Blake. I sure wish things had turned out differently." Jui ended the call, shaking her head. "Holy shit."

* * * * *

Wade hovered like dust particles at the crime scene. There was no sign of Christophe and no communication from him either. Ever since he heard about the explosion, Wade remained at the scene, expecting to hear Christophe's triumphant laughter. *Where are you?* A new idea struck him. He materialized in the passenger seat of Blake's company-issued F-150.

"You are so fucking annoying," Blake said by way of greeting.

"Like I give a shit? Where's Christophe?"

Blake sneered while continuing to drive. "Not worried about Jui this time?"

"Don't push me. I'll deal with your inability to follow simple directions later. Right now I want to know if you heard from Christophe Strasse."

"Don't even know him. Who does he work for?"

Faster than a heartbeat, Wade was at Blake's throat with a

hooked knife blade. "Answer."

In a tight voice, Blake said, "Don't know him. Don't care."

Wade sliced the tender skin on Blake's throat from his Adam's apple to his right ear. "A reminder I'll finish the job if I ever find you near Jui again."

With the truck cab now passenger-free, Blake spit heavily into his hand and rubbed his sliced open neck. "That's what you think, Kairos. Next time it'll be you."

* * * * *

Wade returned to the crime scene. He stayed out of sight and used his keen sense of hearing to eavesdrop on police conversations. No bodies were found. Video from the parking garage showed the driver plus Gerhardt, his secretary, and two companions getting into the limo just as planned. Surveillance overnight and right up to the moment the car left the garage indicated nothing unusual. The police were checking into stalkers.

The reality hit Wade as hard as a second explosion. *Christophe died in the car. He didn't want me around so I wouldn't be killed, too. "This is my moment," he'd said.* Wade didn't know whether to be angry or grateful Christophe excluded him from this last attempt. For more than seventy years, Christophe had been Wade's companion. He'd made becoming a vampire and living the solitary, vagabond lifestyle bearable. They'd lived and worked together at times. They'd traveled the Earth in one hundred-percent, self-indulgent, vampire style.

Wade left the crime scene and materialized in an alley. Trashcans overflowed with stinking, rotting garbage. Potholes and litter. Human discards. Rundown houses with broken windows and broken occupants. There was no beauty, no joy, no vitality. Wade looked around and never felt so soulless and alone in all his dead years. He watched a rat scurry to its next conquest. The despised creature illustrated Wade's vampire existence — secretive, feared, and predatory. *What do I do now?*

Wade had to be sure. He hunted for Christophe, hoping he was wrong, knowing he wasn't.

* * * * *

Jui phoned Rob from the Greenville airport. Glancing at her watch, she figured it was only four p.m. in Seattle. The phone rang until Rob's machine answered.

"Hey, it's me," she said after the beep. "I'm in Greenville and headed to Harkers. You must be asleep. I'm sure you heard what happened to Meuhler and his entourage. I wish I could talk to you about the disaster." She spoke in halting sentences while walking down the marble-tiled hallway. "I hope you're resting and getting better. I wish you were here with me. I'll be in the car for awhile if you want to call me." Jui paused, hoping Rob might pick up the phone. "I miss you. Feel better."

The sun hung low in the western sky by the time Jui drove out of Greenville in her rental car. She opened the sunroof. The day's unsettling events still crowded her mind and she wondered how Rob was doing and whether he'd be well enough to join her. Scanning the satellite radio stations, she found something loud to listen to and drove southeast toward the ocean.

The closer she got, the more she looked forward to feeling the sand under her feet, hearing the gulls and the waves rolling in, and smelling the fish and the salt spray. As children, Jui and her sister spent many happy summers playing on the beach, digging for clams, and picking up the sea creatures washed ashore. The memories restored lightness to her spirit and Jui decided to invite Vie to spend the weekend with her if Rob couldn't make it. She pressed the gas pedal harder now, anticipating her arrival rather than just accepting it.

The late September offshore breeze wrapped its arms around Jui the second she got out of the car. Shivering, she hustled into the house and turned on the kitchen lights. Her purse and travel bag rested on the slate floor while Jui went to the refrigerator, took out a bottle of Guava juice, and poured a tall glass full. The house had been cleaned and stocked with her grocery requests.

In the large master bedroom upstairs, windows filled

the curved outer wall, providing spectacular north to south ocean views. She cranked open one of the windows and filled her lungs with the cool sea breeze. "I just gotta go for a walk," she said to the waiting Atlantic. She changed into jeans, and put on a long-sleeved shirt with a hoodie over it. Then she hustled downstairs to the closet to find her beach shoes. She slid into them, eager to hit the sand.

Brilliant stars filled the moonless sky, unfettered by light pollution. While she walked the vacant shoreline, Jui searched for familiar constellations and kept a lookout for falling stars. In a few hours, the tide would go out, but right now she stayed clear of the lapping waves. Jui wished she could feel the sand squishing between her feet, giving her soles a gentle exfoliation while she walked. *Too cold.* She stuffed her hands into the front pocket of her thick hoodie and ambled, not paying too much attention to where she went. Harkers Island was like a second home.

On impulse, she took out her cell phone, hoping to catch Rob. Her spirits deflated when she got voicemail again.

"I hope you're resting—or maybe on your way here to surprise me," she said. Warmth filled her. "It would be so cool to come back tonight and find you waiting for me. I'm walking along the beach. The stars are out and it's so romantic. You'd love it. If you're on your way, the back door is open. Bring your stuff upstairs. You'll know which room. Build a fire if you're chilled, but I'll keep you warm." She paused, again hoping he'd pick up the phone. "Talk to you soon."

Lightning illuminated the offshore clouds like celestial lamps. An anticipatory smile lifted Jui's lips. She loved storms—hurricanes, not so much—but a great thunderstorm excited her, especially when she was ensconced in the master bedroom watching. *Better head back. It's too cold to be caught in the rain.* Jui turned and realized just how far she'd wandered. Her hair blew around her face with tendrils catching on the wind like Medusa's snakes. She grabbed at the locks, tucking them into her collar. Cracks of thunder sounded and jagged lightning rippled through the sky as the storm came ashore. She picked up the pace, jogging for home. The first droplets splattered on the sand, large and noisy. Jui knew she'd be drenched before long and dug into the sand in an all-out sprint.

A tall, slender person walked toward her, not appearing to be in any hurry or concerned about getting sopping wet. The shoulder panels of the person's oilskin duster flapped in the breeze. Jui didn't recognize the stranger. She slowed, not wanting to rudely race past, even if it was raining hard. Her steps sputtered to a halt and Jui brushed rain-drenched strands of hair out of her face.

"Hi, I'm Jui Fab—" The words died in her throat. Lightning illuminated an anguished man's face. His lips were drawn into a flat, grim line and his hard gaze pierced her. Lighting flashed again. "What are you doing here?"

He waited with his fists stuffed deep in the coat pockets. He wore no shoes and his jeans were soaked to mid-calf. Long and loose around his shoulders, his hair turned wavy and unruly in the rain.

"Answer me."

Wade shrugged, his voice sounded deep and hollow like a bottomless well. "I wanted to see you."

"How did you even find me? Nobody knew I was here except family and Rob."

"Do you really have to ask? Can't I find you if you want me, no matter where you are, no matter where I am?"

A brilliant flash of lightning let Jui see the pain on his face.

"I should go." He turned away.

"Wait!" she called after him. "Aren't you going to tell me why you wanted to see me?"

Wade kept walking, leaving barefoot prints in the sand that the rain began scrubbing away immediately.

Jui jogged after him and grabbed his arm, turning him toward her. "Tell me!" she shouted over the thunder. She gazed into his troubled eyes and asked in a more gentle voice, "What's the matter? Why did you come here?"

Wade drew her against his rain-soaked body and captured her lips in a desperate kiss. He cradled her head in his hand, while his lips twisted against hers. When her body sagged against his, a low moan left his throat and he opened his jaw. His tongue explored her mouth, teasing her, tasting her like a man dying of hunger.

Jui put both hands on his muscled chest and shoved him away. Wiping her mouth with the back of her hand, she asked between gasping breaths, "What the hell do you think you're doing?"

Wade's eyes smoldered. Jui couldn't tell if she saw passion or anger, both were so close. She could have sworn she saw flickers of gold dance in his eyes. The rain fell harder. She was drenched. "Why do you do this to me? You know I want—"

"Want what? To send me away or for me to take you to bed?"

Jui screamed. "Shut up! You have no right. You set all the rules and you break them, not me!" She spun on her heel, preparing to leave him behind, but this time Wade stopped her.

"You don't want me to leave any more than I do."

"That's what you think, you arrogant son of a bitch." Her fury over being used no longer remained hidden and she mocked him. "Jui, stay away from me. Jui, I'm dangerous. Jui, build a relationship with Rob." Her nerves crackled with anger. "But you won't let me go and you don't want me. I'm not a toy." She yanked her arm free and ran to the stairs without looking back. Tears of frustration and resentment coursed down her cheeks. She slammed the front door behind her and turned the lock. Wade stood desolate in the pouring rain, right where she left him.

After stripping off her sopping wet hoodie, Jui tossed the sodden garment into the kitchen sink. She kicked her shoes off, letting them sail and smack the wall with a sandy smudge. If she'd misjudged him, Wade would be pounding on the door... but rain was the only thing pounding on the door.

The light flickered, the fridge stopped running, and the microwave beeped. With a groan, Jui walked through the lightning-lit kitchen to get the lanterns stored in the pantry. The chilly autumn rain made her teeth chatter. With one lantern in each hand, she checked the door locks and went upstairs to take a hot bath.

* * * * *

Impervious to the cold and the rain, Wade watched the lanterns disappear from the first floor to the second. He cursed himself, Christophe, and Jui for making him feel like a man, something he wasn't any more. With the threatening huff and growl of a lowland gorilla, he disappeared into the rainy night.

Conflicted and hungry, he prowled the streets of Morehead City. The storm hadn't arrived there yet, so Wade had no trouble finding dinner. He waited in the city park for dessert, contemplating what Jui said. He had been unfair to her, trifling with her life and emotions. *Am I strong enough to be with her even one time and not turn her? What about feeding on her?* The very thought disgusted him. *I don't want to be alone tonight.* Emptiness ripped through him like an arctic blizzard.

* * * * *

Hurricane lamps containing thick candles glowed in the bathroom while Jui filled the soaking tub and added scented oils. Her anger at Wade transposed into depression. She wished Rob were there to protect her from him and remind her who she really wanted to be with.

She hung her robe over the vanity chair and dipped a toe into the steaming water. *Ah,* her soul whispered as she slid into the perfectly heated water. Jui closed her eyes and listened to the storm. Wind gusts drove the rain against the windowpanes in syncopated rhythms. Thunder rumbled across the sky chasing after lightning. Her mind returned to Wade and their kiss. She was glad she kept her self-respect and pushed him away, but it hurt. *He treats me like a yo-yo, bouncing in and out of my life at his will. Why did you come tonight of all nights? And why didn't you come after me?*

"I did."

His low, soft voice startled Jui. She drew her knees to her chest and glared at him. "How did you get in here?"

Wade stood in the bathroom doorway with a white cotton towel slung low around his hips. His hair was drawn back in its customary ponytail. The mink-soft fur Jui fantasized about so often lightly covered his chest, organized itself into a thin line down his midsection, trailed below his naval, and disappeared beneath his towel. His body looked well defined and muscular, even in the flickering candlelight.

"You wanted me. I'm here." He took a few steps toward the tub. "I won't hurt you."

Her mouth turned to dust seeing him this close and so vulnerable. "You keep telling me you're dangerous. You have the stealth of a panther. I dreamed—"

He interrupted her fearful confabulation. "A fruitful imagination, I assure you, nothing more."

Uncertainty still filled her. "Where did you go?"

Wade let out a tired-sounding sigh, seeming to gather his thoughts. "I had to think. My best friend died today. I've known him my whole life and then...." Wade snapped his fingers. "He was gone, killed in the limousine explosion in Memphis."

An incredulous frown knitted her eyebrows. "He was in the car? He knew Meuhler?"

"Yes to both questions. They knew each other for eons."

"I'm sorry. I didn't even know Mr. Meuhler. What was your friend's name?"

"Christophe, Christophe Strasse. He was a mathematician like me. In fact, I studied under him at the University of Heidelberg at one time."

"Why did you come here?" she asked in a soft voice. "If you can't give me an honest answer, you need to leave."

Wade scanned her thoughts and got nothing "You're infuriating, you know."

"Don't change the subject."

"I'm not," he said stepping close enough to the tub for Jui to see the caramel-colored scruff on his face. "You know I have a gift for reading one's thoughts."

Jui raised an eyebrow at the absurd admission.

"But you have the unique ability to shield me from yours, especially when you're angry. I can find out the most bizarre things about you. Right now you're wondering if I'm trying to derail you from what you want to know."

"That's no gift, that's obvious. Any half-intelligent person could deduce that," she said. Jui lifted a handful of fragrant water and let it slip through her fingers onto her knees.

"Yes, I like the scent. It's not too feminine."

Her head shot up at his remark. She narrowed her eyes at him. "One last time, Kairos, why did you come here? My bath is getting cold."

"For you."

A lump formed in Jui's throat and she felt tears well in her eyes as she studied Wade's inscrutable expression. Her gaze held his while Wade's towel dropped to the floor.

Jui slid forward in the tub and Wade settled her between his legs. Her lungs seemed to forget how to breathe. Her mind scurried to collect enough information to form a coherent thought.

"Shh," he whispered into her ear as he pulled her close. "It's what you want—it's what we've both wanted since the moment we met." He nibbled the rim of her ear and then relaxed against the tub with her in his arms.

The tepid bathwater gurgled as Jui scooped it into her hands, letting it fall on her shoulders. Silence yawned as though a five-gallon pail of awkward had doused her. She'd lusted after Wade Kairos from the moment she heard his voice and saw him kissing that trollop at the German café. The times they kissed were branded on her psyche with "sizzling hot" stamped on the images. He never seemed to be far from her thoughts and now she was naked in a bathtub with him.

Wade brushed her hair away from shoulder and kissed the soft skin along her collarbone. "Relax, I'm here, but we don't have to make love. We can just enjoy each other's company and get to know each other better."

Jui barely heard another word after "make love." The suggestion sent an erotic jolt through her body. His voice warmed her. She reached for his long fingers and kissed them, beginning to feel aroused by her initiative. She turned his hand over and kissed his palm, leaving a sensual trail with her tongue.

Jui couldn't suppress a giggle. "Are you purring?"

The soft rumbling stopped and a gentle chuckle replaced it. "I suppose I am. Another one of my gifts—animal sounds. Does it bother you?"

"I think it depends on the sound. I hate snakes."

Wade pressed a soft kiss on her temple. "I'll try to remember."

"The water's getting cold."

"I hadn't noticed," he said, wrapping his arm across her shoulders. "I'm actually quite comfortable."

"I thought you'd be freezing after standing in the rain so long."

"Things weighed on my mind."

"I'm cold. I need to get out of the tub before I shrivel up. You first," Jui said, suddenly feeling modest.

Wade hoisted himself out of the tub and reached for his towel.

"There are more in the cupboard," Jui said, while her gaze raked over his naked body.

He held her bathrobe wide open for her. His mouth watered and his teeth ached while watching her sleek, wet body emerge from the tub. Muscular and lean, she embodied a goddess. *There are so many delicious places I could bite. I don't know if I can do this without feeding on her.* He growled low, commanding himself to exercise the utmost self-control.

Jui's gaze snapped toward Wade.

"Don't be afraid of me."

"I'm trying not to. You're so unusual. There are things...."

"Shh," he said, pressing a finger to her lips. "Not tonight. Tonight is for us. I'll be gone in the morning and out of your life."

Jui's face crumbled. "Why?"

"I didn't want be alone tonight." He studied her sad eyes. "You care about me. As much as you try to deny it, I know you do."

"Stay. We can work through these things you worry about."

Wade approached her with the gentleness of a breeze. Their lips met like a breath first drawn after resuscitation, deep and life sustaining.

"Make love to me, Wade."

He gazed into her emerald-green eyes. He saw certainty and wished he felt the same. He wanted to be with Jui as a man, not a vampire. *Is it possible?* His desire lay confused between vampire bloodlust and human passion. Christophe's warning rang in his mind. *"Relationships between humans and vampires are doomed."* In his seventy years as a vampire, Wade had always heeded the warning. Until Jui.

Lightning flashed and thunder barked in response while he lifted her into his arms, carried her into the bedroom, and laid her on the bed. He did not intend to bring up Rob's name, but he needed to ask. "Are you sure?"

She ran her well-manicured forefinger under his chin. As Wade leaned forward to kiss her, she pulled him with her against the downy-soft comforter. "Tonight is for us. I want to make love with you and forget about everything else."

Wade's forearms bulged as he held himself inches above her. His breathing became deeper as the long-repressed passion of a man soared though his inhuman body. "Jui, the beautiful green-eyed, flower," he whispered. His dead heart drummed in his chest like the rain pummeling the windows. He kissed her again. The kiss wasn't one of bold seduction made to make her knees buckle and her heart stop. Nor was it a kiss to devour the soul and imprison the heart in one fell swoop. He wanted this kiss to beckon and coax Jui's body and soul to come to him with joy.

Jui peeked at him from under her lashes and relaxed in his embrace, a soft moan slipping from her throat.

His body reacted to the sound with an imperceptible tightening of his torso muscles. Wade broke from the kiss. He gazed into green eyes filled with awakening passion. Her cheeks were flush, her lips moist and pouting with anticipation.

He kissed her until he couldn't resist tasting more of her. His tongue brushed her lips, asking her wordlessly to welcome him nearer. Jui's lips parted and he felt the warmth of her tongue against his. The repartee began as he stroked her tongue and retreated, making her tongue follow into his mouth.

She reached behind his head and slid her fingers into his hair, releasing his mane from its leather tie.

Her breasts, so warm and enticing, rose and fell against his bare chest. This exquisite torture threatened his self-control. *How long can I hang on before I can't stop from showing her what I am?* The idea made him shudder.

"What's the matter?" she said, concern filling her voice.

Wade rolled onto his back and put an arm over his eyes. He swallowed hard, feeling the line blur even more between vampire bloodlust and human passion.

She leaned over him and nibbled his lower lip before kissing him hungrily, effectively sapping every other thought from his mind. Wade wound his fingers through her hair, cupping her head as the kiss deepened. His body sung with vampire tension but his gentler kiss belied the strength of it. Unable to control his tempo any longer, he opened his mouth wide and his tongue darted into her mouth.

Wade.

His name sounded like a whisper from the past. He acquiesced to a memory from a lifetime ago and became determined to act like a human with Jui if only for tonight. He would give her everything she wanted from him and take the surreal memories with him tomorrow. His lips twisted on hers, tasting her tender mouth, letting her draw him into a web of sweet madness.

Jui's hands moved up his arms and shoulders, exploring, seeming to relish each corded muscle beneath her fingers. She pushed onto her hip and untied the sash of her robe.

Wade sat up and pushed the plush material off her shoulders and down her arms, until it pooled around her naked body. He traced the outline of her breast with his forefinger and watched Jui's nipples ripen before him. They beckoned his lips and he leaned in to capture one, but Jui gave him a gentle shove backwards.

"I think," she said in a smoky voice, "you deserve a little punishment for making me wait so long — for playing games."

Wade lay against the pillows and folded his arms behind his head. "Punished?" He watched her walk around to his side of the bed. His mouth watered, reacting to the prize approaching him. He shoved the vampire behavior into his black soul and focused on her. *I like the way you think.* A smile curled his lips.

"You know what I'm planning?" she asked, seeing his smirk.

"I told you I am telepathic. I'm all yours." Wade extended his hands to her.

Jui pulled the tie from her robe and wrapped his wrists with the soft strip of cloth. Straddling his chest, she secured his bound hands to the headboard. She let her passionate floodwaters loose. Running her fingertips down the inside of his muscled arms and to his chest, she watched his reaction to the sensations she wanted to illicit.

"I'm not ticklish."

Jui scratched him and a grin curled his lips. Wade raised his knees behind her, and she moaned as his erection tapped against her ass.

"Remember, minx, I'll get my turn. So have your fun, have your way with me, please, but turnabout's fair play." A naughty grin left his lips and rose into his eyes.

Jui leaned forward and nibbled his chest, leaving faint red marks. She caught one of his nipples between her teeth and held it, flicking the tender nub with her tongue.

He drew in a sharp breath.

"Like that?" she asked.

"You know I do."

Jui bit down on his lip and tugged it.

Wade managed to turn his head before Jui drew blood. "Don't. Don't draw blood. That's all I ask."

"Enough foreplay."

Slick, warm wetness from her body spread across his lower stomach as her hips moved in an undulating motion against him. "Do you want to make love to me?" she whispered against his mouth. "Slide your cock deep inside me until I come?" She kissed him, using her tongue to illustrate her point.

Wade raised his knees, lifting his hips under her. His cock rode hot and powerful against her pussy.

She reached back, wrapped her hand around the base of his shaft, and squeezed hard.

A cry of erotic pain tore from his throat. "Ahh!" Wade's stomach muscles rippled with the sudden desire to protect himself. He tugged against the plush tie holding his hands above his head, struggling to get loose. "Jui, minx, let me have you."

Disregarding his demand, Jui threw back her head and cupped her full breasts in her hands. "What do you want?" she asked with a provocative smile. "Something like this?" She applied more pressure against his rod, now slick with her private lubricant. Her body felt like molten lava against his shaft.

Wade closed his eyes, on the verge of using vampire skills to get free and take what he wanted. He wanted her, all of her. He squeezed his eyes tighter to hide the flames dancing there, proclaiming his true identity. His mind raced; he needed to calm down and separate his emotions, but before he could, Jui grasped his rock-hard cock in her hand and started a slow, delicious descent. His eyes flew open at the new sensation filling him. He'd fucked *a lot* of women in the past seventy years; he'd made love to none.

"Let me free, please," he said. "You have to trust me on this, untie me now."

Groggy passion covered Jui's face. Her brow furrowed in concentration.

Reading her discomfort, he whispered, "Open, open for me." Wade felt her walls strain from the unaccustomed pressure of a cock so large. "Open, Jui, relax. Let me love you."

Mechanically, she reached up and untied the sash binding his hands. As soon as she freed him, he brought his hands to her hips.

"Gently," he whispered while flexing his hips, firming up his base. His sexual pheromones released in full force to seduce her and ease his penetration.

She groaned and gazed at him with uncertainty.

"You're not ready." Wade pulled out and rolled her beneath him. Spreading her thighs, he blew against her swollen, glistening labia. The action made her flinch. With the pad of his thumb, he rolled her erect clitoris. Jui's head thrashed left and right and her hips bucked wildly.

As a generous drop of his spittle landed on her clit, she cried out, "Holy shit!" She moaned through clenched teeth. "I want you. I want you."

Her scent filled his nostrils and Wade's body prepared to join with her. He clenched his eyes shut, dousing the flames

121

he knew were obvious, and focused on her body not her blood. He concentrated on her pleasure, not his selfish needs. His teeth stopped aching. His dark side was under control.

Wade caressed her with a wide, flat tongue — soft strokes starting at her tight puckered ass and ending at her clit. He suckled her clit and swirled his fingers inside her drenched pussy, intending to take her to a new level of passion. Her hips bucked against his face while his fingers made their way into her tight ass as well. Loud cries of approval filled his ears, and her scent made him crazy with desire. The first pulses of her orgasm gripped his fingers and he finger fucked her even faster until she screamed his name with ragged, monosyllabic sounds. *She's ready.*

Wade pulled her hips backward and began mounting her. Jui gripped his forearms with unnatural strength, encouraging him. His cock throbbed in a way he hadn't experienced since becoming a vampire.

"Relax. You're so wet but so tight."

"You're so big," she moaned. "I don't know...."

Wade leaned forward and whispered as he took her lips, "Taste yourself, as I have." He tweaked her raised nipples while they kissed and was rewarded with a flood of moisture around his throbbing shaft. He inched forward, feeling her accommodate him. "That's it," he said. Gaze locked with hers, he sunk his cock in all the way to his balls, and her breath left her body in a hiss.

"Are you okay?" he asked between ragged breaths. Vampires are unable to orgasm, but sublime sensations damn close to an orgasm were surging through Wade.

She nodded. "Go slow, but make love to me. I want you, all of you."

His strokes were precisely as she asked — slow all the way in and then all the way out. When his rigid length left her hot body, he stroked her clit, keeping her wet and hungry for more of him. In a few minutes, she joined his rhythm with a tentative rock of her hips. His penetrations became more fluid and she raised her legs to encircle his lean waist.

"That's it, Jui, ride me. Let me love you until you've had enough."

Jui gasped, as his words seemed to break through her impassioned fog.

"I want you to come so hard your teeth gnash and you think your heart is going to stop." He reached behind her shoulders and lifted her into a sitting position. The pressure made Jui come instantly, sending gushes of warm, silky wetness around his tumescent cock.

Jui clung to his back, biting and scratching his shoulders. "Come with me, Wade."

His movements stilled. "I can't, minx."

Confusion ruled her half-lidded gaze. "What do you mean, 'you can't'?"

"I simply can't." The awkwardness of the moment came to bear on Wade's psyche. In all his vampire years, he had never explained this one. When he wanted to participate in sex, he cognitively controlled his penis to achieve erection. He made appropriate sounds to fool his human partners into thinking he'd achieved orgasm. By this time, however, he'd always be fully engaged in feeding and the human was so distracted by the sensation of a love bite they didn't care about the truth.

"You can't orgasm?"

"Right, I can't orgasm."

"You just haven't been with the right woman then," she said, resuming her gyrations against him. "You have the most amazing cock. Our bodies fit together perfectly," she said between light kisses. "I've never felt anything like you in my life."

"Nor I, you," he admitted, rejoining her thrusting motions.

"I can make you come. It'll be a moment you'll never forget."

Wade rested his forehead in the soft curve of her shoulder. "Please don't test me. Take my word for it." He lifted his head and gazed into her puzzled eyes. "I can pleasure you as long as you want, but I can't orgasm."

Her body stilled. "Don't I turn you on?"

"You do. Never doubt it." He kissed her with loving tenderness. "It's another one of those unique things about me." He studied her face, penetrating her thoughts. "Tonight isn't for questions. You're a passionate, desirable woman. You feel wonderful, and I haven't been this happy in years. Please accept those truths."

Wade distracted her with a devastating kiss. His hands moved down her body to her hips and he lifted her to resume thrusting. His keen senses told him she couldn't enjoy this first lovemaking session too much longer. Her body was unaccustomed to a man his size. Cradling her lower back, he rocked against her. "Come again, minx, and then you can rest. Your body needs this release. Let me feel your sweet pussy release its secrets."

Smudges of lust dotted Jui's cheeks. She dug her heels into the soft mattress and leaned back on one arm. Her jaw clenched while she pummeled his shaft, taking everything Wade could give her. Sweat curled the locks around her face and a sheen of perspiration covered her body.

Her strangled cries told Wade she was at the precipice of another powerful orgasm. He supported her body and slowed his strokes while she came again. His lips instinctively found her neck; his tongue flickered against her soft skin. The desire to taste her blood overwhelmed him. Her heartbeat thundered in his ears and he listened to her blood moving through her veins. He smelled the elixir of life. *No, no, no!* Without warning, he laid her against the pillows, swung his legs off the bed, and hid his face in his hands.

Her gentle hand on his shoulder startled him, but he couldn't face her yet. She could too easily see what he was.

She asked in a soft voice, "Are you okay?"

He nodded but still didn't face her. "Are you?"

"I'd be better if you were lying next to me."

He'd fed before he took Jui to bed so he wasn't hungry. Instinctive vampire behaviors were just surfacing. Wade took a few more deep breaths. With his darkness concealed, he rolled over and pulled Jui back into his arms. He kissed her temple, damp from their energetic lovemaking. The steady pulse beneath his lips threatened his composure again.

"Sleep now, minx. You must be exhausted."

Jui let her fingers wander through the crisp curls on his chest. *They're dry and so is his skin.*

"Jui, don't," he cautioned her, addressing the question

before she asked.

"I don't know what to think. I feel and probably look like I've just run a marathon."

"Don't ask me to explain. Tonight isn't for questions."

He tuned in to the feeling of dread that crept into her heart, so he wasn't surprised when she asked, "Are you sick? Is that why you can't come and you don't sweat?"

He let out a long breath. "In a way." He picked up a lock of her hair and caressed the strands between his fingers. "Can we drop the subject?"

Jui lay in his arms, doing her best to remember — tonight, she wanted to be blind to the truth about Wade. She promised herself she'd get to the bottom of his secrets tomorrow.

A few minutes later, Wade's body shook with laughter.

Jui propped up on her elbow and gazed into his face. "What's so funny?"

"A twelve? I scored a twelve on your sex card and you can't wait to tell Vie?" He clucked his tongue at her. "I told you I'm telepathic. Now do you believe me?"

She felt the heat from fifteen shades of red coloring her face. "Well at least I hold the record."

Jui raised an eyebrow and gave him a half-grin. "Maybe we should make sure I scored it properly."

* * * * *

After they made love again, Jui lay in Wade's arms, running her fingers up and down his side. She traced the outlines of his ribs with her fingernails, hoping to find a ticklish spot, but found none. "I need a shower. Care to join me?"

"I'm dying of thirst. I'll join you in a few minutes, all right?"

She gave him a quick kiss. "Don't be long."

Wade let out a long, appreciative whistle when she walked away. Jui winked at him over her shoulder and disappeared into the bathroom. He had no time to waste. Wade slid into his jeans, hustled downstairs, and then made some kitchen noises just in case his inquisitive lover followed him. He couldn't stay with Jui much longer. Questions about him pounded in her brain and Wade could read them all. He opened and shut the cupboards looking for a glass, splashed some juice in one, and then pitched the rest into the sink before disappearing into the pre-dawn darkness.

A heavy mist fell and the temperature dropped to the mid-forties. Even without his shoes and shirt, Wade was comfortable. Concealed in darkness, he canvassed Morehead City. His teeth throbbed and blood hunger filled him with anxiety.

A middle-aged deliveryman became his first victim. Wade dragged the unwitting guy back inside the bread van and paralyzed him with a surgical bite to the carotid. The blood reenergized Wade as soon as it hit his system. After licking the bite wounds clean, he let the paunchy fellow slide to the bakery truck floor.

Next, he tuned into the early morning street sounds. *Solitary footsteps.* Wade followed in the shadows, hunting for the owner of the hard-heeled clicks on the pavement. He spotted a woman heading toward a diner. *It's time for breakfast, in more ways than one.* The dark-haired woman was nearly as tall as he was. Her firm body rested against his bare chest and shoulder while he fed. The scent of the brunette's fresh, clean hair and skin filled his nostrils. Another time Wade might have seduced the woman too, but sex didn't interest him at all this morning. The revelation surprised him. *Was he in a hurry or not interested?* He put the questions to the test.

The woman moaned when his seductive pheromones reached her olfactory lobe. She turned in his arms until her dazed gaze met his. Raising her lips toward his, she asked, "Where did you come from? You're a pleasant surprise this morning."

Her body pressed against Wade's, letting him feel all her soft curves while they kissed. Her passion left him disinterested. "I have to go," he said.

* * * * *

A warm shower soothed Jui's tender muscles. Her night with Wade exceeded every sexual experience and erotic fantasy she'd ever had. No other man ever possessed the tools or the stamina to make love to her the way Wade had. Regret and guilt jabbed at her conscience. *Certainly not Rob.* While she washed her hair, Jui wondered if she'd been using Rob to forget Wade. *Writing off this night as a wanton sexcapade and calling it 'over' will be impossible.* Questions about Wade bubbled in her brain and she didn't know how she would get the answers unless Wade came clean. *What are you hiding from me?*

Suds ran down her legs and water splashed between her toes as she rinsed her hair. *How did you get in my house? Why can't you orgasm? Why don't you sweat? Why does blood freak you out?* Jui wondered if he was a hemophiliac or had some other blood disorder. *But what about his telepathy?* The ghoulish image of him standing over Rob resurfaced. She shuddered, recalling the vision of Wade's golden-flamed pupils in stark contrast to his paper-white skin. He held Rob's arm against his face. *Why?*

Lost in thought, she didn't hear the shower door open and jumped when Wade snuggled against her body.

"Oh, you scared me!" She faced Wade with guilt and fear playing hide-and-seek in her brain.

"I'm sorry; I thought you were expecting me." He probed her thoughts to get the truth but only heard water splashing in the shower. "What's the matter? And please don't tell me it's because you didn't hear me arrive."

"You feel chilled, come and stand under the warm water."

Trading places under the stream, Wade tipped his head back, letting the water run over his hair.

"May I wash your hair? I've never washed a man's long hair before and yours is so beautiful."

Wade penetrated her thoughts while she spread the shampoo and worked it into a rich lather. *You're turning me on, Jui. Do you know how happy that makes me?* He observed her puzzled face as the words left his mind and entered hers.

She slid her arms over his soap-covered shoulders and kissed him. Wade's erection pressed against her mons and

Jui's body responded with a firm desire of its own. Their languid kiss built steam under the shower. She wove her fingers in his hair and brought her leg around his hip.

Wade reached down to guide his entry. *You're so wet. No woman has ever made me want her the way I want you. I didn't think it was possible.* He flexed his knees and entered her in one brazen stroke.

Jui gasped in pleasure and surprise. "The way you feel. I've never...."

Wade smiled. "I want to satisfy you in every way tonight."

"You have to stay with me," she whispered against his neck while he rocked deep within her. "I won't give you up."

Wade's black heart lurched at her declaration. He let his seductive pheromones loose, lifted her onto his hips, and then pressed her back against the smooth shower wall. His jerky, powerful penetrations made Jui's breath leave her body in grunts.

"Come on, minx, give it up. I want to feel your pussy gripping my shaft when you come."

Jui concentrated on the pressure and pleasure Wade's enormous cock created in her. Her nails dug into his back, scraping his skin and leaving wheals behind. Another flare of lust burst in her. Jui assaulted Wade's mouth, stabbing his tongue with hers and nipping at his lips. She scraped her teeth along his jaw line, leaving behind nothing but her moans of uncontrolled ecstasy.

"Harder, harder," she pleaded.

"I can't, I'll hurt you," he replied without skipping a beat.

"Put me down." Jui slid from his hips and leaned against the shower wall, presenting her back to him. "Finish it—now."

Her pussy glistened even under the shower. Wade shut his eyes, teetering on disaster. Her heartbeat pulsed in his ears. The warm water and their lovemaking raised her body temperature. Wade's mouth watered at the opportunity in his arms. *Her blood would taste so sweet.* He took deep breaths while reminding himself he didn't need to feed. He'd never denied himself anything since becoming a vamp—until now. *You can't feed on Jui. You can't feed on someone you care about.*

He swirled his bulbous tip in her wet pussy and plunged

in all the way to his hips. Wade steadied her while he thrust vigorously into her welcoming body. Every fiber of his vampire being shouted at him to sample her luscious blood. He had to end this fast before he caved in. After slowing his thrusts, Wade ran his tongue along her spine.

"Oh yeah," she whimpered, again and again, as the tremors of her release began. She rose on her toes as he delivered the last few strokes into her shaking body and caught her under the arms as her knees gave out.

He lowered Jui to the shower floor. "Are you okay?" he asked. He turned off the water and then gave the shower door a shove. He dried her face with a towel and gazed into her passion-fogged eyes. "Did I hurt you?"

She pulled his mouth to hers for a tender, post-coital kiss. "That was beyond amazing," she said between shallow pants. "I've never, ever felt this way before."

Wade chuckled. "You scared me. I've never had a woman collapse on me before — at least not while making love."

"Just give me a minute to catch my breath."

Wade stepped out and wrapped a towel around his hips before returning to help Jui up and out of the shower.

"I'm starving, aren't you?" she asked while they walked to the bedroom.

"I hadn't thought about it."

"I've gotta eat something before I faint, for real," she said with a laugh. She slipped into her robe and glanced back at Wade, who was pulling up his jeans. "I'll see you downstairs."

"In a minute. I'm not in the habit of midnight feedings."

"It's hardly midnight — more like dawn."

Wade glanced out the window. *Our time is so short.*

"What's the matter?"

A smile flittered across his lips. "Nothing. I'll dry my hair and see you downstairs."

* * * * *

Jui scrambled eggs, toasted English muffins, and cut fresh melon. Coffee brewed and melded with the other kitchen aromas to make the house smell like a diner.

Wade sauntered into the kitchen and poured a cup of coffee.

"Help yourself," she said while heaping scrambled eggs onto her plate.

He slid into a chair opposite Jui. "I'm allergic to eggs. I'll just have a piece of this melon." Wade stabbed a small piece and stared at the sweet fruit perched on the end of his fork.

Observing his hesitation, Jui said, "It's not going to bite you." She watched while Wade masticated the tender fruit to death. "I can get you something else or feel free to look in the fridge...."

"I'm not very hungry. Please enjoy your meal and I'll wait for you in the living room."

Jui's good mood evaporated along with her appetite.

* * * * *

The sun turned the sky to gray moments before dawn. Wade watched the transformation feeling utterly alone. *Yesterday Christophe died and I spent the night in the arms of a human being, acting like a man not a vampire. Today I have to leave her.* He felt desolate and aimless except for his work. *Looking forward to work more than feeding frenzies and whoring around is as ridiculous as wearing a bathing suit in a snowstorm.*

Jui slid her arms around his bare waist and rested her cheek against his back. "What are you thinking about?"

Wade let out a long breath. "I need to leave soon. I have to take care of Christophe's affairs."

"Tell me about him — about your friendship."

Wade led her by the hand to the couch and drew her against him. While stroking her soft, dark hair, the humanness of the situation floored him. *I'm behaving like a man in a relationship. I'm leading her on.* Guilt shook him hard and filled him with a terrible urge to escape.

Jui twisted in his arms and gazed into his face. "Where are you? You seem so preoccupied."

The lies fell off his tongue so easily. "It's a difficult time for me. I don't want to think about settling Christophe's affairs. He doesn't have any family."

"That's sad to hear. Were you very close?"

Wade nodded. "My family lived in Europe most of my life and I met him in Germany."

"Is that why you have a German accent, because you grew up there?"

"Germany isn't the only place I lived, but I've lived there longest and Christophe and I always spoke German."

"Tell me about him."

"He was a brilliant scientist, and had many other talents. He was a ladies' man. Women flocked to Christophe."

"The waitress at the café in Heidelberg said the same thing about you."

Wade harrumphed softly. "Not true," he said while pressing a kiss on her temple and snuggling her nearer. "Christophe was renowned for his sexual prowess and generosity toward women—and sometimes men."

Wade waited for Jui's reaction. Scanning her thoughts he added, "No, he and I weren't lovers—ever." Tension left her body and he continued. "But we were close. We traveled together, I studied under him at times, and we worked together occasionally. We understood each other and never interfered in each other's lives. I guess if one were to describe our relationship, we truly were blood brothers."

"Do you have family?"

He shook his head. "No, not any more. Christophe's death was so unexpected and I am alone. It makes living so much more difficult now."

Jui laced her fingers between his and kissed the onyx and silver ring on his index finger. "I'm here."

"I wish I could stay or take you with me."

Tears welled in Jui's eyes.

"You make me happy. I can't remember the last time I said that or even thought about being happy again. I guess Christophe and I rather existed, doing whatever the urge brought us. He was wealthy—I have no financial concerns, and we did what we pleased. I gave up on finding someone to share my life years ago. Now we've met and as much as I wish it weren't so, I can't change my destiny. You can't change yours."

"Isn't it possible our destiny is to be together?"

Wade closed his eyes while human sorrow strangled him. His voice became a hoarse whisper. "You don't know what you're saying. I can't offer you the life you envision or one you'd even want."

"Can't we try to see where this," she said, wagging her finger between them, "takes us and let me decide? Last night was fantastic. You make me feel so desired, so safe. Maybe you're the man I've been searching for."

A frown drew his brows together and Wade's jaw flexed with tension. He studied her while wondering whether she would run away screaming in fear if he told her what he was. *Vampires are supposed to live with vampires, solitary lives of leisure and self-gratifying pleasure. Humans screw that up. It would cost Jui her life. The price is too high for both of us.*

A blush crept up her neck and into her face. "I'm sorry, I thought you—"

"Shh," he said. "You take away the loneliness and restlessness I've felt for more years than I can recall. You're so intelligent and so sexy." He glanced away, allowing his face to become a hard mask. "Still, the timing is all wrong."

"You mean because you have to take care of Christophe's affairs? That won't take forever. We can talk to each other, see each—"

"I can't, Jui, I told you before." Wade abruptly got off the couch and stared at the early morning sky. Waves pummeled the shoreline at high tide and the seagulls called out. "I'm on my way to Moscow. The way I live...you'd have to give up everything. I can't ask you to do it; you'd hate me."

"Stop talking in riddles! What is so horrible about you? I know you have unique talents but those are gifts." She came to his side and turned him toward her. "Are you dying? Is that why you behave so weird sometimes and talk so cryptically?"

"I died a long time ago, minx. Now I'm just waiting for it to actually happen." He brushed away the tears rolling down her cheeks. "Don't cry. You've made me so happy these past hours, but I have to leave. You need to make a life for yourself.

Choose Rob if he can make you happy, but don't wait for me."

"Won't I see you again?" she asked through her tears.

"Your soul and mine are irrevocably intertwined. If you need me, I'll know it and I'll find you."

She lifted her chin in defiance. "Then you'll go insane with knowing I want you in my life. Here. Next to me."

"So be it, but I promise a day won't pass when I won't wish the situation between us could be different." Wade lowered his head, his lips a breath away from hers. "I wish it could be different."

Their lips slid in Jui's salty tears, in a long kiss of farewell. Her heart ached, but she resolved to enjoy the last minutes she shared with Wade. *They might have to last me a lifetime.*

* * * * *

After they made love again, Jui lay on her back and stared at the highlights in Wade's hair while his hand moved slowly up her calf and higher to her thigh.

"What are you doing?"

"I'm memorizing you."

Jui's stomach flip-flopped.

Sensing her unhappy thoughts, Wade gazed into her eyes. He traced the line of her jaw, the shape of her brow, and the soft curve of her ear. "I want to remember your body, your scent, the sound of your voice, the little cleft in your chin, the way you mischievously wiggle one eyebrow at me." He traced the contour of her quivering lips. "Your mouth—whether it calls my name, moans in desire, or pleasures my body." He kissed her gently and Jui's tears fell in earnest.

"I'm glad we were together, but I'm pissed you won't be honest with me. I chose to be with you and maybe...."

"Wishing won't change anything," he whispered. "Go on with your life. Remember distance means nothing to the soul. I'll always hold you here," he said while tapping his heart.

Jui rested her cheek on his chest. A few moments later, her head popped up. "I can't hear your heartbeat!"

Wade rolled away and sat with his back to her. Pushing

his hair out of his face with both hands, he let out a deep sigh. When he gazed back at Jui, fear and shock registered in her eyes—already an all-too familiar sight. "You're mistaken. Of course I have a heartbeat."

Her face was ghostly pale. "Can I listen again?"

Wade jerked his jeans over his hips. "I'd be dead, wouldn't I?" Glancing at Jui one last time, he entered her consciousness. *I don't regret a minute I spent with you. You made me happy.*

She took his leather hair tie from the nightstand and fastened it around her slender wrist. "I'll stay here. I can't watch you leave."

Chapter Ten

The back door shut with a soft rattle. Though unnerved by their heartbeat conversation, Jui still entertained the idea of running after him and begging him to stay. The thought lasted half a minute. Being unable to convince Wade to work things out frustrated and angered her, but their relationship was too new to consider groveling. *Maybe time apart will force Wade to realize we have something special.* She refused to think of their relationship in the past tense. *Moscow. That's half way around the freaking world.* Farewell tears continued dripping from her chin, but self-respect reigned and she didn't give chase to Wade, the man without the balls to stay and fight for her.

She pulled herself together and went for a walk on the beach. Her relationship with Rob weighed on her mind while she left sodden footprints in the sand. *Should I tell him what happened last night?* The seagulls mocked her with their ceaseless, hawking cries and the stiff Atlantic breeze chilled her.

Jui came back to the house and retrieved her cell phone. She discovered three messages: one from Vie and two from Rob. She tried not to be angry because Wade hadn't called. *I'd better get used to it.*

Jui dialed her sister's number. "Hey you," she said when Vie answered.

"Hey yourself! How's it going at Harkers Island? Are you and Rob having an awesome time? Details, sister!" Vie demanded in a cheerful tone.

Jui exhaled a long breath. "Got a minute?"

"Sure," Vie said. "What's up?"

"Well first of all, Rob isn't here. He came down with the flu and I haven't spoken to him for a couple days. Every time I call, I get his voicemail."

"Yeah, so?"

Jui blurted out the truth. "Wade was here."

"The sexy German guy we talked about? How in the hell did that happen?" Her voice gurgled with salacious excitement.

"It's so confusing, Vie. We met on the beach here. I haven't a clue how he even knew I was here." Jui gave her sister the lowdown on the past twenty-four hours. "Did I tell you he's telepathic?"

"No way."

"Yeah. I mean, I thought I was losing it the way he'd kind of pop into my head and know what I was thinking. And sometimes when I would be thinking about him—" Her voice dropped low. "Missing him, actually, I'd hear him in my thoughts. I didn't believe him at first, but after spending this time together, it's true."

"That would creep me out," Vie said with a laugh. "I don't want anybody digging around in my head."

"That's not all. Somehow he got into the house and surprised me when I was taking a bath."

"He attacked you? Oh my god, are you okay?"

"I'm fine, it ended up being so hot, but I can't figure out how he got into the house. When I came inside, he was standing on the beach in the pouring rain and I locked the door behind me. And another thing—he doesn't eat or drink hardly at all. I was half-starved this morning and he barely bit into a piece of fruit. He freaked out when I was going to bite him. Like he was afraid to bleed or of blood...I'm not sure which."

"So the guy has a sensitive stomach and is squeamish about blood. So what?"

"The strangest thing is I couldn't hear his heartbeat."

"What? What do you mean, 'you couldn't hear his heartbeat'?"

"Exactly that. I put my ear on his chest and I heard—nothing."

"You're mistaken, Jui—stressed out and emotional. It's just not possible. That's just crazy talk."

"Maybe you're right, but there are things about him that don't add up. He won't tell me why we can't have a relationship when we both are really into each other. He keeps saying he can't give me the things I expect and he won't ask me to make terrible sacrifices to be together." Jui rubbed her forehead tiredly. "I don't know, maybe he's got cancer or some kind of blood disorder. Maybe he has AIDS and he's dying." The sentence rattled Jui's heart to a stop. "Oh god, what if he has AIDS? We had unprotected sex!"

"Oh shit, come on, it can't be AIDS. I mean, you've gotta go get the test now, but do you think he'd really put you at risk? If he won't ask you to give up 'everything', whatever 'everything' is, why would he infect you with AIDS, which could *take* everything, including your life?"

Jui's mouth turned to dust and she felt sick to her stomach. "I'll kill him. I'll hunt him down in Moscow."

"That's where he went?"

"Yes, to settle his friend's estate. But now that I think about it, there were a couple more strange things about him. Wade couldn't come and he didn't sweat. He was so amazing in bed—I've never been with a man like him. What he could do with his cock—you'd faint. I nearly did a couple times. But I looked like I'd run a marathon after we made love and he hadn't even broken a sweat. He could perform like you wouldn't believe but he never had an orgasm—he said he couldn't. When I asked him why, he wouldn't answer."

"AIDS isn't the problem."

"You're probably right, but I'm still going to get the test to be sure." She paused for a moment, recalling how tender and playful Wade was with her. "I really don't think he'd deliberately harm me. He felt terrible about leaving me. He kept saying he shouldn't have even come here, but he couldn't stay away. He said he cared about me and knew I cared about him."

"I'd get the test to be the safe side and for Rob's sake, too."

Jui met Vie's statement with a long silence.

"What are you going tell Rob?" her sister asked after a moment.

"He left two messages. I need to call him back."

"And? Are you going come clean with him?"

Jui let out another nervous sigh. "I have to. I was never sure about my feelings for either man, but now I am. I took your damn advice and now I'm in a mess. My heart is tangled up with some weird guy continents away and a really nice guy is going to get stepped on. I hate romantic drama."

"So you're just going to break it off with Rob?"

"After I tell him I slept with Wade and have deep feelings for the man there won't be much choice. Even if it's one of those sappy unrequited love situations, the feeling are real for me, Vie. I think Rob has always known there was someone between us. Now the 'someone' has a name."

"Wade Kairos, world traveler, man of strange gifts, mysterious habits, and no heartbeat. Jesus, do you realize how bizarre all this sounds?"

"It wasn't a dream," Jui said while twisting Wade's leather tie around her wrist. "He was here. Last night was real and now I have to deal with the consequences."

"What can I do to help? Do you want me to come with you when you talk to Rob?"

Jui chuckled. "No, it's not like we are married or I missed my curfew. I'll talk to Rob about it when I get home. I'm not going to do it on the phone, but you can do me a favor."

"Name it."

"Ask Dad if he has any pictures of Grandma Claire before she and Grandpa Claude got married. I know he has a bunch of her photos and stuff. I want to take a look at them."

"What are you looking for?"

"Grandma Claire was engaged to a man named Wade Kairos and he died before they could get married. Dad described the Wade in the pictures he'd seen, and the Wade who just left looks a lot like the man Dad described. When I mentioned the similarities, my Wade brushed it off as coincidence and genetics. He told me they were probably relatives, but that's all he'd say."

"You're not giving up on him, are you?"

"You know me, I don't take no for an answer very well. I'm going to look around and see if I can satisfy my curiosity. He sure doesn't add up."

"I don't want you to take this wrong but you're sounding a little bit desperate. Why don't you just let the guy go and leave things alone?"

"Maybe I could if we hadn't spent the night together. I felt connected to him before but now it's stronger than ever, different than I've ever felt. Before last night, I was deluding myself about Rob, too."

"Are you in love with Wade?"

"I don't know. I have to find out why he's pushing me away. When I do, maybe I'll run."

"Which way? To him or from him?"

"That's a damn good question."

* * * * *

"Hi, Jui!" Rob said in a nasal voice. "I'm glad to hear your voice instead of your messages for a change."

"It's good to hear your voice, too, even if you still sound like hell."

"I'm better but there's no way I'm getting on a plane this weekend. I'm really sorry."

"I'm disappointed too. I had great plans for us and after the explosion in Memphis, I really wanted to get away."

"Are you going to stay the weekend?"

"I'm not sure yet. The past few days have really given me a lot to think about, and it's not like I'd come over and catch whatever horrid flu bug you've got."

"Chicken. Nah, I wouldn't want to inflict you with this. The last week has been over the top nasty. I can't remember the last time I got so sick."

"Well, I'm glad you're feeling better. It's pretty chilly here. It rained last night and I have a fire going."

"I wish I was there to warm you up. I doubt we'd need the fire."

The guilt knife twisted in Jui's chest but this wasn't the time to make the announcement about her indiscretion. "I'm sure we wouldn't—you have a fever." She chuckled over the tiny joke.

"Oh, make jokes at my expense, thanks a heap. I'll get you, Jui Fabrice. Wait 'til I'm back on my feet."

"Thanks for the warning. Get some rest. I'll call you when

I'm back in town."

Jui hung up the phone and cursed her sister for advising her to test the waters with Wade. *Yeah, blame it on somebody else, Jui, atta girl. Like Vie was here forcing you into his arms.* Her breath stalled in her lungs, as thoughts of her and Wade's frenzied lovemaking filled her head. *Where are you, Wade? Certainly not where you belong.*

She flipped open her laptop and Googled "Wade Kairos." The search turned up zip about the Wade Kairos she was looking for. Jui dug a little deeper and found a reference to him on the Carpathian Studios project. A scan for info about him on Heart Strings Cove in Heidelberg only produced some puffery from Martin Wergen, the publicity director. Typing his name and "Heidelberg, Germany" delivered nada. She didn't know whether Wade even lived in Germany. Drilling his name with all kinds of subjects manufactured blank screens.

"Wade Kairos Moscow" retrieved a short article with a picture of him in front of his *dacha*. Jui hoped the translation was accurate as she read the ten year-old story. According to the article, Wade's house featured the architectural mastery of a native Russian named Kirill Vadik. She wondered how Wade came up with the money to hire someone with Vadik's credentials. The article described the house's amenities and some of its costs. Jui ran a ruble-to-dollar converter. Her eyes bugged out of her head when the result appeared. Squinting at the screen, she calculated Wade must have been in his very early twenties at the time. From what she could see, he hadn't aged a day. Christophe Strasse was in the photo as well. *At least now I know what Christophe looked like.*

Jui poured a glass of wine and then created a file on Wade. In it, she developed a list of questions and then cut and pasted her Internet findings. So far, the questions outnumbered the answers.

* * * * *

Wade materialized in his sprawling *dacha* in Moscow. He

walked onto the balcony and stared deep into the forest. The autumn breeze rustled pine boughs and dying summer leaves. Moments ago, Jui was in his arms, alive and loving. A lion's roar ripped from his throat followed by a series of aggressive snarls. The chasm of emptiness created by Christophe's death and leaving Jui besieged him.

Wade needed a powerful distraction. He assumed another persona, howling to his nocturnal brethren in the soulful cry of the Russian wolf. Feeling the golden flames leaping in his eyes and baring his long fangs, Wade bounded over his balcony railing and dashed into the forest. He barked into the wilderness, calling and hunting the wolf pack that roamed nearby. He found them feasting on a moose. The alpha male raised its tail straight in the air and rigidly wagged it, signaling to Wade that he must wait to feed along with the other subordinates.

Recalling his recent battle with the wild boar, Wade chose another tactic. He raised his head, sniffing and listening for humans. With their voices in his ears and their scent filling his nostrils, Wade became the hunter.

He materialized behind two men out for a late afternoon walk. The fact they were armed meant nothing to Wade. He attacked the first man, dragging him off the gravel road and into the eerie forest to the shocked amazement of his companion. Wade greedily feasted on the younger man's blood and then dropped his limp body to the ground.

Then Wade trained his evil sites on the older man, who glanced over his shoulder while screaming in fear and running for his life.

A sinister smile curled Wade's lips, still tainted with warm blood. He materialized in front of the scared man.

The horror-struck soul skidded to a halt. While shouting in Russian to leave him alone or he'd shoot, the man aimed at Wade and fired both barrels.

The shotgun blast barely slowed Wade, who dismissed the injury as if it were a mosquito bite. "You'll pay for that." Wade opened his throat and cried the metallic-sounding warning of a cougar.

The startled man reloaded and fired again while backing

141

up. His spirit bore a resolute expression of "do or die."

Wade didn't falter when some of the lead shot penetrated his body. He looked at the rips in his torso and then leveled a death stare at the terrified man. Repeating the cougar's extended growl, Wade stalked nearer. Looking petrified, the man stumbled and almost fell backwards.

Wade laughed at the human's sad predicament. "*It's pointless to run. Come to me or I'll let the wolves feast on you.*" Wade could see the Russian was in excellent shape and probably outweighed him. After reading his thoughts, Wade said in Russian, "Your shotgun blasts did nothing. Do you seriously think your fists can harm me?"

The man glared at Wade before making the sign of the cross and stammering, "I won't come willingly. My brother never had a chance."

Wade laughed at the proud man standing in front of him. "But your brother will live — if the wolves are full after they're finished with you!" He leapt at his victim, slicing into his plump carotid before the doomed man could blink.

Paralyzed by the blistering heat on his neck, Wade's prey was left to listen to his heartbeat fading and the wolves lurking nearer.

Afterward, Wade dragged the back of his hand across his bloody lips and chin before dropping the unconscious man into the dirt. The Russian was still alive but Wade couldn't care less what the wolves did to him next. He let out a long, soulless howl and disappeared.

* * * * *

Jui tossed and turned in the guest room that night. The thought of sleeping in the same bed she and Wade shared left her desolate. She dreamed of him holding her again, of their bodies moving together. She balled her fists and pounded the mattress in frustration when she awakened. Her upcoming conversation with Rob wasn't going to be easy either.

"How did I get everything so damn screwed up?" she asked over and over again.

She yanked on her robe and went downstairs to her laptop. After responding to her e-mails, she started investigating diseases that might prevent a person from sweating, ejaculating, cause loss of appetite, and any of the other symptoms and strange behaviors she observed Wade to have. She ended up learning about sexual dysfunction and childhood illnesses, looked through numerous cancer websites and treatments, and still had no specific diagnosis. In fact, she didn't have a clue. She sent Rob a brief e-mail telling him she'd be home sometime tomorrow and shut the laptop.

With another frustrated huff, she went back upstairs to bed. As she walked down the hallway, the bed she'd shared with Wade beckoned her. Jui slipped off her robe and slid under the covers. Heaviness filled her soul. She fingered the braided leather on her wrist that used to encircle Wade's soft mane. *Why did you leave?* In the recesses of her mind, she heard a wolf howling and the surf pounding on the shore. "Distance means nothing to the soul? What a crock," she grumped before turning over and hugging the pillow.

* * * * *

Wade materialized in his lodge after his feeding frenzy and gazed at his reflection in the bathroom mirror. As his hair fell onto his forehead in unruly shocks, covering his eyes and shoulders, he remembered Jui had kept his leather hair tie. The haggard look on his face reflected the bruised condition of his soul. Blood spatter dotted his shirtfront, and his chin and lips told a similar tale. Indomitable self-loathing filled him.

"Is this the life you would give her?" he shouted at his reflection. "One of bloodlust and shadows? An eternity of hunting and hiding? She deserves life, you idiot!" He roared with frustration. The cords of his neck stood out, seeming to want to burst through his skin as he screamed her name. "Jui!"

His chin dropped to his chest in defeat. Blood-drunk, Wade dragged himself into the shower and afterward, went to bed alone.

* * * * *

In the morning, the local newspaper headlines described a horrific wolf attack on two brothers out for a peaceful, afternoon walk. Family members began searching when the two men didn't return after nightfall. They were armed and their shotgun, found near the remains of one brother, had been fired. Wolves devoured the older brother on a rural gravel road north of Moscow. Searchers found the critically injured younger brother nearby. He was hospitalized and clinging to life in a near-catatonic state. The incoherent ranting of the surviving man couldn't be trusted, the reporter wrote. Local authorities were hunting for the wolves, which now were considered a menace to humans.

Wade flung the paper to the floor. *Christophe was right. My preoccupation with Jui will lead to disaster.* Wade went through his address book and dialed the number.

"*Das Büro von Herrn Lamburg,*" the secretary answered politely.

"*Herr Lamburg, bitte,*" Wade said.

"Who shall I tell him is calling?"

"Wade Kairos." He waited for the call to be transferred.

"Good morning, Mr. Kairos," Urs Lamburg said. "What can I do for you?"

"I'm calling on behalf of Christophe Strasse. He died suddenly and as executor of his will, I am asking you to release the legal mechanisms to settle his estate."

"This news is quite a shock. The last time we spoke, Mr. Strasse was in excellent health; in fact, he never seems to age."

"Excellent genetics, I'm sure."

"It will take some time for me to assemble the proper team of associates. His estate is large and spans several continents."

"I'm aware of that, but you are paid handsomely to take swift action." Wade's tone was hollow with grief. "I'm coming to Munich. You'll need my signature on certain documents."

"This is true; this is quite true," the lawyer said. "Will you provide a death certificate tomorrow, as well?"

"He died three days ago while on a trip to America. I'm

not sure how long it'll take me to get the proper paperwork but I am investigating the certificate."

"I can't settle—"

Perturbed by the lawyer's attitude, Wade said, "I'm perfectly aware you cannot settle the estate until I provide the proper document—the death certificate—but you can begin. Is that too much to ask? You're going to be a very rich man when this is over, Herr Lamburg. I'd think you'd be happy."

"I'm just following the letter of the law. I am an honorable man, Mr. Kairos."

"I'll be at your office at 9:00 a.m. the day after tomorrow. Good day," Wade said and hung up on the lawyer.

Wade spent the next twenty-four hours visiting Christophe's estates in Seoul, Helsinki, Madrid, and Rome. At each home, Wade chose one or two personal artifacts and arranged with the estate caretakers to have them shipped to his home in Bucharest. Wade didn't know where he'd be living for the next few years, but after last night, he couldn't stay in Moscow and he didn't want Jui to find him either. Unassuming Romania was as fine a place as any to disappear.

His meeting in Munich with Christophe's lawyer was short and professional. The whisk of his pen on the proper documents set the wheels in motion to assess Christophe's fortunes and dispose of them.

"I can't sell or transfer anything until I have a death certificate," Herr Lamburg reminded Wade.

"You'll have it in a day or two." Wade extended his hand to the aging lawyer. "Thank you for your services. I'll contact you soon."

The lawyer gazed at Wade over his reading glasses. His silvery hair was thinning at the top and his moustache was slightly yellowed around the corners of his mouth from heavy smoking. "Is there some way to reach you, Mr. Kairos? I'm sure to have questions and will need to advise you about progress once we begin."

At that moment, Wade wanted to abandon the whole process and leave everything Christophe owned to the rats and his human playmates. The generous vamp let many of his human friends live on his estates while he was jaunting about the globe, fucking and feasting on whomever he pleased. Wade let out a long, tired breath and gave the lawyer his business card. "My cell phone number is on the card. I'll be working with the authorities in Memphis, Tennessee."

"Why Memphis?" Urs Lamburg licked a finger as he sifted through the stack of documents in Christophe's dossier. "I don't recall Mr. Strasse having any property in America."

"He died in Memphis but he has apartments in New York City."

"Ah, I see." The lawyer paused, huffing out his cheeks, "I'm sorry for your loss. You were very close?"

"Yes. Good day."

* * * * *

The worn, wooden floors of Ladislav Husek's office in Brno, Czech Republic, echoed the hollow sound of Wade's heels. Wade never met the ancient vampire but all vampires knew where to find Ladislav, who kept *The Book*. When vampires died, their passing into a different kind of eternity was scribed into the records Husek kept. *A sort of mortician for the undead.* Wade smirked at the analogy and then remembered his mission.

Husek hunched in front of his computer. Perennially in his fifties, the vampire was actually older than anyone really knew. He'd come to Brno in the 18th Century at the advent of the industrial revolution there.

"Kairos," he said in a strong voice, "I've been expecting you." The man lifted his gaze to Wade. "Strasse?"

Wade nodded affirmatively.

Ladislav Husek reached to his printer and handed Wade an official death certificate resembling one from the Memphis coroner's department. "You're clear about what must be done with his estate?"

"I began the process this morning with Christophe's lawyer in Munich. It'll take some time to settle his affairs." Wade cleared his throat and said, "I'm concerned about people — humans checking into his death."

Husek crooked a thick, dark eyebrow at him. "Because?"

"You know what a social and generous vamp Christophe was. I don't know if he told anyone where he was going or what his plans were."

"If memory serves correct, Strasse frequently reminded you of that problematic behavior. Are you certain it's not your own wagging tongue you're concerned about?" Husek drilled and Wade couldn't stop the invasion into his gray matter. "I thought so—Fabrice." Husek's feral gaze bore into Wade. "Consider yourself warned, Kairos. We'll hunt you down and dispose of you if you don't bury your tracks and stay out of her life. I won't let you risk the safety of our society." He steepled his fingers in front of his chin. "Do I make myself clear?"

Even as Wade teleported himself back to Romania, he heard the warning again from Husek. "We protect our own, Kairos. Either turn Jui Fabrice or make sure she never finds you again."

"I can't," Wade communicated back to the Ancient One.

"Can't what? Turn her or leave her?"

"Both."

"I'll prepare your entry in *The Book*. Your days are numbered."

Wade's form was still a shadowy state when he received the last of Husek's warning. He gazed around his empty home in Bucharest. He had no desire for anything. He faxed the manufactured death certificate to Christophe's lawyer and thought about getting his own affairs in order. *My days are numbered. Like I give a flying fuck.*

147

Chapter Eleven

Jui put her car in park and sat in the driver's seat for a few moments to collect her thoughts. *This week has been a total nightmare. Here I thought I'd be coming back with Rob, and we'd be happy and really solid in our relationship after Harkers. Instead....* She let out a disappointed sigh, took out her cell phone, and dialed Rob's number.

"Hey, you're home," he said in a cheerful and healthier voice.

"Yeah, I just drove into the garage. You sound much better."

"Not one hundred percent yet, but definitely improved. I'm going back to work on Monday. Did you have a good trip?"

A pregnant pause filled the connection.

"Jui?"

"Yeah, sorry, yeah, I had a smooth flight."

"What's the matter? You're not coming down with the flu, are you?"

"No, not at all." Her body filled with tension and her thoughts scattered like mice. "The past week just wasn't anything like I thought it would be."

"What do they say? 'Life is what happens while you're making other plans'?"

"I'll say. Look, when you're not contagious anymore, I'll come over. We need to talk."

"I hope you mean talk about rescheduling a weekend away together."

Jui couldn't resist rolling her eyes at his suggestion. *This sucks.* "We'll talk when you're feeling better, okay? Give me a shout."

"Let's plan something. I'm going back to work on Monday, so how about dinner on Saturday evening? We can spend Sunday together getting reacquainted, too."

Jui could picture the twinkle in his eyes and the mischievous grin on his face. She felt flush as guilt raced through her body and she hated the idea of shattering his happy bubble. "Dinner it is. Would you like to come here since your place is probably still riddled with flu germs?"

Rob glanced around the living room. Cold medicine bottles, boxes of tissues, books, and extra pillows and blankets littered the room. "Probably a good idea if you want to stay healthy. I'll look forward to it. What time?"

"Six-thirty okay? And don't bother with the wine; I have cases here."

"See you then."

* * * * *

Jui went to the market on Saturday morning to shop for her dinner with Rob. Appetizers were the only thing on the menu. *He probably won't stick around once I give him the news.*

He arrived on time, looking a bit thinner for his ordeal but still boyishly handsome.

Jui's heart sank. *Damn girl, how could you let this one get away?* "You don't look much worse for the wear," she said with a smile on her face.

Rob presented her with a bouquet of autumn flowers and kissed her. "I missed you."

"Come in," she said, leaving his embrace. "I'll put these in water. Would you like a glass of wine? Something stronger?"

"White wine. I'd hate to fall asleep on you during dinner." He followed her into the kitchen where she found a gold ceramic vase for the flowers. He reached around her waist and nuzzled her neck while she filled the vase with water. "I can think of lots of ways to fall asleep together *after* dinner."

"A week on your back has done nasty things to your mind," she teased without turning to face him.

"Can dinner wait? Because I can't." Rob turned Jui in his arms and kissed her again.

The force of his passion took her breath away and for a few long moments, she got caught up in his seduction. "Whew," she said, breaking from the hot kiss. "I'll say you've recovered."

"And then some," he whispered before devouring her lips

once again. Rob unbuttoned her jeans while he kissed her.

Jui pressed her hands against his chest. "Whoa, how about we have a glass of wine and talk first?"

"Wine can wait, I want you," he said, making another move to bring her into the seduction mode.

"Rob, please, let's talk," she said in a gentle, yet firm voice.

He studied her green eyes and guessed there was more to her request than taking the evening slower.

"Let's go in the living room."

Rob followed her without another word. He'd been in this spot before and only needed to hear the words. He accepted a glass of wine and sat at the opposite end of the couch. "What's up?"

"Something happened at Harkers Island." When Rob said nothing, she continued. "I was running home in the rain on Tuesday evening and...."

"And?"

"The most peculiar thing happened. I never in a million years would have expected this to happen."

"Spit it out, Jui. What happened?"

"Out of nowhere I met—Wade Kairos appeared."

"Kairos, the guy in Germany, the one who kept popping up, who had his hands all over you on the balcony?"

"Yeah, I have no idea how he knew where I was. He knew I was going to Memphis, but I told him you were coming along. I swear I didn't say a word about going to Harkers."

"So he was there," Rob said, as the bottom dropped out of his gut.

"I accused him of stalking me. I mean, there was no way he could have known where I was or that I was alone."

Confusion furrowed Rob's eyebrows. "So he showed up—did he hurt you? What are you trying to tell me?"

"We argued and I told him to get lost—for good." She dropped her gaze and fiddled with the leather band on her wrist.

"But he didn't—he didn't get lost, did he?"

"No."

In no mood to let her off easy, Rob pushed her to spell it out. "What happened between you?"

She leveled her gaze to his. "He spent the night."

Rob studied her, as half a dozen reactions zipped through his mind. "So now what? You told me about your sordid, hot, little affair. What do you want from me now except the address to which you should mail your *Dear John* letter?"

"I'm sorry. This thing between me and Wade—"

"Oh, so it's you and Wade? You're a couple. Where is the lucky guy? Hiding upstairs somewhere?" Rob rose from the couch and walked toward the stairs calling, "Kairos, come on down. Cat's out of the bag. Show your cowardly face."

"Stop it, he's not here. He didn't come back with me. He's not going to either."

"You slept with him and he dumped you?" Rob pressed the back of his hand across his lips, laughing as the irony of the situation became clear. "He used you. How does it feel?" He laughed at her again and then narrowed his eyes, and injected an accusatory note in his voice. "I knew from the moment I saw you together there was something going on. You just couldn't leave it alone, could you? I wasn't enough." He walked to the front door. "He dumped you." Rob uttered another cruel bout of laughter as he left, slamming the front door behind him. Outside, he leaned against the doorpost and sobered up emotionally. "Your loss, Kairos. Mine, too," he said in a hoarse whisper.

* * * * *

"How'd it go?" Vie asked when Jui called her a little later. "Do you want me to come over?"

"He laughed at me. He knows Wade dumped me."

"That bastard! He's got balls."

"Ah, he was hurt. I can't blame him. At least knowing Wade dumped me will help him get over his rejection a little faster. God, Vie, I felt so damn stupid telling him. When I think about Wade and the time we spent together, it's so magical and sad, but I never saw it through Rob's eyes. He thought I got my just desserts."

"Jerk. Now what?"

"I suppose it'll be awkward for awhile at work. I just hope we don't have to travel anywhere together soon." Jui huffed out her breath. "This is why I always avoid office romances. They're a disaster waiting to happen. I'm such an idiot. How could I let myself fall into something as dumb as unrequited love?"

"Are you telling me you love this guy?"

The impact of Vie's words hit Jui in the forehead like a sledgehammer.

"Jui?"

"Maybe you should come over. I have a ton of appetizers and wine. We can yack and get drunk. I just wanna forget this night happened."

"I'll be there within the hour."

"By the way, did you get a chance to ask Dad about the pictures—the ones of Grandma Claire and Wade?" Just saying his name made her feel like a dolt all over again.

"I did. He gave me what he had."

"Bring them along, will you? One way or the other I have to get to the bottom of his secrets." Jui hung up the phone and typed Rob a brief e-mail apologizing again for the way things turned out. *I'm skipping the whole "I hope we can be friends" bullshit, because that's all these little missives ever are—bullshit.* Those were the words she wanted to type. Instead, she wrote a bland paragraph:

I hope we can maintain a professional relationship in the office. I admire your talent. You are an asset to the company. Sorry things didn't work out. Jui

She shut her laptop with a frustrated groan thinking how lame the note read. Then an idea occurred to her. She fired up the computer again and began searching through news headlines in Memphis to see what she could learn about Christophe Strasse. Surprisingly, there was no mention of him in the papers or news feeds. *That's odd.* She sent a note to her contact at the Memphis P.D. inquiring about Strasse. *How could the guy get in the car without anyone knowing?*

She found her cell phone and called Blake next.

"Blake, it's Jui."

"How are you? Are you still on vacation?"

"No, I'm home, but I have a question for you."
"Shoot."
"Did anyone come up with information about that guy Christophe Strasse? Wade said he died in the car along with the others."
"Perhaps you should let sleeping dogs lie."
The sudden chill in Blake's voice puzzled her. "Did I say something wrong?"
"No, I'm sorry. I didn't mean to be rude. I haven't heard a thing," he said in a friendlier sounding tone.
"I sent a note to the lead detective."
Blake cautioned her again. "I really think you ought to stay clear of the investigation. You could get burned."
"What's up with you? A guy dies and nobody knows about it."
"Don't be so sure. Like I said, let it go. I have another call. Take care."
Blake hung up and Jui stared at her cell phone wondering why he behaved so strangely. After refilling her wineglass, she returned to her laptop. Looking through more news feeds, one headline caught her eye. She squinted at the monitor, reading a "believe it or not" story from Moscow about two men attacked by wolves.

The younger brother clings to life by a thread. During more lucid moments, he describes his assailant as a long-haired, younger man with long, fang-like teeth and crazy-looking eyes filled with flames. The victim claims he was dragged into the forest but doesn't remember what happened next. When he awakened afterward, the victim said he heard wolves howling and his brother's pitiful screams while wolves killed him. Gunfire saved the surviving man from the same fate. The man's condition is critical. His identity is being kept secret while the case is being investigated.

Jui sat back in her chair. The story disturbed her beyond the horror the brothers endured. *The flames, the fangs.* She remembered her dream about Wade with Rob's arm near his face. She shuddered and then slammed the laptop shut, forcing the image and the questions out of her mind.

Vie arrived a short time later, armed with emotional support and the pictures from their father. "Could I get in the house before you tear them out of my hands?" she said to Jui.

"Come in, shut the door," Jui said while opening the brown paper envelope her sister brought. "Did you look at these?"

"Not really. Dad said some of them have notes on the back but they're pretty faded. Mind if I help myself?" she asked, pointing to the wine and appetizers.

"Go right ahead." Jui thumbed through the pictures, looking for one of Wade. The picture wasn't good quality nor was it a close-up, but it was Wade. "Holy shit."

"What?" Vie asked, walking to her sister's side.

Jui held up the photo for Vie to see. "It's him. This is Wade Kairos with Grandma Claire."

"*The* Wade Kairos?"

"*My* Wade Kairos." Jui stared at the image, stunned and baffled. "How can this be? I mean, he looks just like my Wade. This isn't genetics. This can't just be genetics." She gazed at her sister. "Can it?"

* * * * *

Running into Rob at work was awkward, just as Jui expected. The chill between them was palpable as they sat across from each other in the conference room at Saint Claire Symphonic.

"The new, year-round concert hall and amphitheatre at Powder Ridge opens in a few weeks and we're invited to the grand opening celebration," Terry Fabrice told his assembled staff. "Mark your calendars for the November twelfth party." He turned his attention to Jui and said, "Your mom is coming along and we invited Vie. We thought we'd stay the weekend and enjoy some skiing and relax. Can you plan to stay on?"

Jui flipped through her calendar. "I'll be there," she said without enthusiasm. "Is the entire staff staying, too?" she asked without glancing up.

Terry replied, "You all can do as you wish. The company will pay for your flights to and from Boise, and two night's lodging and meals. Everything else is at your own discretion. It's a bit of a drive from Boise so plan accordingly. I think that's about it. My assistant will provide the details about the trip as soon as possible," he said to the small group. "Thanks for a great job at Powder Ridge, by the way. The client is ecstatic with the results." As the staff rose to leave, Terry said, "Jui, would you mind hanging back for a few minutes?"

After the room cleared, Jui said, "What's up?"

"Did something happen between you and Rob? You could cut the air in here with a knife."

"We broke up."

"I see. Is it a permanent kind of breakup or—?"

"Please don't play matchmaker, Dad. I'm not desperate. I know you like Rob and vice versa but this is personal, not business, so please kinda butt out, would you?"

Terry studied his daughter. "What else happened?"

"Why do you insist on prying? You never have before."

"Vie asked for the pictures of my mom and that Kairos guy. Does your breakup have something to do with any of that? You talked about Kairos a few weeks ago and sounded smitten."

Jui rolled her eyes, vexed at her father's parental nosiness. "Smitten?" She picked up her paperwork and expected to drop the subject like a rock.

"I like Rob. He's a real asset to this company," her father said.

"Don't you dare meddle in my personal life for the sake of this company."

"Your mom and I want you to be happy."

"I know. Rob is a great guy and I screwed up. I'm not writing him off completely, but it's a real long-shot considering how I hurt him."

"There's somebody else?"

"Maybe. I don't know for sure, but I'll tell you one thing, I won't stay in a relationship with anyone because it suits Saint Claire Construction." She picked up her paperwork and strutted out of the room.

*****

While driving home from work a few days later, Jui thought about the e-mail she sent to the lead investigator in

Memphis. The police detective replied, curious as hell about the mysterious sixth occupant in the limo. He asked her to phone him. Jui nibbled the corner of her lip trying to figure out what to do. *Blake said I could get burned. Wade warned me to stay away from Memphis — not to get in the middle of something dangerous.* Jui broke out in a sweat, wondering if she'd made a huge mistake by digging into Strasse's death. *What if Wade is implicated somehow? Nah, that couldn't be the reason Wade wanted me to stay out of Memphis. He was devastated over his friend's death.* She hadn't responded to the detective's request and hoped she wouldn't have to.

A group of adults dressed in Halloween costumes waited at the cross light. Dracula approached her car when the light changed. He fanned his black cape like in an old horror flick. White makeup covered his face and the fake vamp hissed at her, exposing fanged teeth between ruby-red-painted lips.

Jui screamed in surprise and then got totally pissed. Lowering her window, she called out, "Asshole! I should run you over. Grow up!"

She peeled away from the stoplight, leaving the costumed group behind. Her stomach did back flips all the way home. She pulled into the stall, turned off the ignition, and shut the garage door. Panic had a firm grip on her. Sobs wracked her body, which shook and shuddered with every breath Jui took. Eventually the garage light flicked off, leaving her in total darkness. Jui panicked again and turned on the car's lights. She'd never been so creeped-out in her life.

With her bearings restored, Jui went inside. She poured a tall, cold glass of water and drank it while leaning against the kitchen sink. Her blouse clung to her, sticky with perspiration. She dried her tear-sodden face with the back of her hand and took a couple of deep, cleansing breaths. *What was that all about?*

Setting the empty glass on the counter, Jui decided to call it a night. Before she undressed for her shower, she took a few minutes to gaze into the mid-autumn sky. Stars twinkled and a brilliant crescent moon rose against an inky backdrop. She wished Wade was there to share the beautiful night with her, and to help make sense of her irrational behavior tonight.

157

Where are you? She caressed the braided leather tie on her wrist. Despite the humiliating scene with Rob, she hadn't taken the band off since that morning in North Carolina, when Wade left. A tear dripped down her cheek.

Jui squeezed her eyes shut and concentrated on Wade, calling to him with her mind. "Come on you telepathic bastard," she moaned when he didn't communicate with her. She relaxed and remembered their night together, hoping a less confrontational approach would bring him to her. Frustration and deafening silence were her rewards.

* * * * *

Meanwhile, two voluptuous women hung on Wade in a cozy Bucharest café. A mid-morning snack of two eager women was just what he needed to re-energize his body and get his mind off Husek's ominous threats.

"Let's go somewhere a bit more private," he suggested to the women, using their native Romanian language.

One of the women replied in a silky voice, "My apartment is just around the corner."

Wade tossed down enough lei to cover the check and with a scrape of their chairs, escorted the women out. They barely arrived at the apartment when Wade experienced a now all too familiar ache. Jui was reaching out to him telepathically.

Determined to ignore the ceaseless questions and demands, Wade latched onto one playmate's carotid in a swift, precise motion. With his other hand, he unzipped the other woman's chocolate brown sheath and prepared for a long, satisfying morning of fornication and bloodlust. *This is how vampires live.*

Wade purred while the woman's blood flowed down his throat, warming and nourishing his body. When he couldn't drink any more without risking her life, he released his bite and licked the wounds clean to heal.

"You are positively delicious," he said. Focusing on the other companion, he said, "And now your turn."

The naked woman wasted no time stripping Wade and

then led him to the bed. She kneeled and gazed over her shoulder as he positioned himself between her shapely legs.

Jui's soft pleas moved through his brain like waves to the shore. The more he tried to ignore her, the louder and clearer her voice became. The past few weeks exhausted Wade as he tried tuning her out.

With a frustrated shake of his head he said, "Fuck! I have to leave."

The surprise on the woman's face turned to irritation. "What do you mean, leave?"

Wade jerked his clothing back on. "I can't explain. Another time."

Back at home, Wade paced. He wanted to comfort Jui and feel her reassuring presence, but Husek's warnings pummeled his yearnings to a pulp. *Husek is deadly serious. I've seen his work.*

* * * * *

Early Monday morning, Memphis Police Detective Ambrose phoned Jui. "I'm curious to know why you think a sixth individual was in the limo that exploded. We reviewed the tapes of those getting into the car and no one saw a sixth person. The driver didn't make any stops, scheduled or otherwise," he reported.

Jui's heart strummed with anxiety. She felt cornered. *Blake was right. I should have kept my nose out of this — or at least kept my ideas to myself.* "An acquaintance told me his friend died in the car," she told the detective. "Maybe I misunderstood."

"What is the friend's name?"

Jui could hear him scribbling on a piece of paper.

"Ms. Fabrice?"

"Yeah, which friend?" she asked, stalling the conversation. "The guy who supposedly died?"

"That is why we're talking, isn't it?" the officer said, sounding a bit irritated.

I have to lie. "Carl Spafford."

"Can you spell Spafford?"

"Your guess is as good as mine."

"What's the friend's name? The guy who told you about this death."

She continued fibbing her way through the conversation. "Kevin Marks, but he doesn't live here. He's kind of a wandering soul."

The officer pressed for more information. "Any way to reach the elusive Mr. Marks?"

"He contacts me when he's in the States—every once in a blue moon."

"We'll look into this Carl Spafford fellow, see if anything comes up. If Mr. Marks contacts you again, make sure you tell him I want to speak to him."

"Sure, sure I will." Jui disconnected the call and swallowed hard. She sincerely hoped she'd pointed the dogs in the wrong direction, at least until she knew whether she should sic them on Wade. The very idea of sending the authorities after Wade made her heart lurch. *What the hell is the matter with you, Jui? You lie for the guy but you still keep digging. Either you believe him or you don't!*

In Bucharest, Wade caught hold of Jui's stream of consciousness. Fury burned in his chest. *Traitor!*

Chapter Twelve

After the last call from the cops, Jui covered her tracks by using a laptop at the public library for searches about Wade. The microfilmed engagement photo of Claire and Wade looked a bit sharper than her print, but it didn't matter; the man in the photo and the man in her heart could have been identical twins. But how was that possible?

Wade's death announcement provided his parents' names and the sad details about the burial. *I can't image how devastated Grandma Claire must have been.* Jui didn't dare discuss the subject with her father. Talking about her grandmother would only raise more suspicions she didn't have answers to.

She also spent a weekend in Chicago and visited his gravesite in Westley Gardens. The manager gave her directions to Wade's plot. Her toes edged the imaginary boundaries of the burial site that held a small, sunken headstone. Lichen grew on the pale gray marker and the letters were etched in black from age and mold.

Wade Kairos
Born May 15, 1911
Died September 2, 1941

Her eyes welled with tears. Jui wasn't sure if she cried for her grandmother's lost love or her own misery over the man with the same name. After placing a sunflower on the marker and making the sign of the cross, she whispered, "Rest in peace."

Cold November winds stung her face as Jui hurried back to her car. Once inside, she fired the engine and cranked up the heat. She'd reached a lot of dead-ends in Chicago. Wade's family was dead, the people who knew him were dead, those who buried him were dead, and his life seemed quite ordinary.

Her brain plucked an uncomfortable recollection: she

couldn't hear his heartbeat. *It's not possible for him to be walking around.* The confluence of fact and fantasy gave her a headache. She huffed out her cheeks while jotting information her small notebook, filled with the odds and ends of her mysterious search. "What am I searching for?" she kept asking.

A knuckle-knock on her window made her jump. "You okay, miss?" asked a stranger.

"Yes, thank you," she said through the glass. She put the car in drive and with a wave of her hand toward the stranger, pulled away from the curb, leaving behind the gravesite of Wade Kairos.

* * * * *

On November 11, Jui packed for her early afternoon flight and then loaded her trunk. As luck would have it, her car wouldn't start. Checking her watch, Jui saw she had plenty of time to catch her flight so she called for a tow.

"I'll have to take a cab," she told Vie on the phone. "My car won't start so they're coming to get it. I'll be there, don't worry." She unloaded her car. Looking at the heap of ski gear and luggage jogged loose a memory of another time in the Alps. Jui stomped on the humiliating recollection, more determined than ever to have a fun weekend.

The moment the tow truck arrived, she called for a cab, but nobody seemed to be on time this morning. Halfway to the airport, Jui knew she was going to miss her flight. She called the office and asked them to reschedule her for a later departure and then phoned Vie.

"Where are you?" Vie asked.

"I'm still in a cab. I'm not going to make the flight. I'm booked on the three-ten. I'll just be a couple hours late. Save me a beer, will you?"

"Dang—now I'll have to talk to Mom the whole time. You know how she likes to pry," Vie said.

"Better you than me. Dad's been nagging on me about Rob."

"I thought he gave up."

"I wish. I could have smacked him the other day. He

actually told me to play nice with Rob tomorrow night. And he said he had the same conversation with Rob!"

Vie chuckled. "No shit? I'd have liked to been there for that dumb move. What's up with him?"

"I really think he wanted me and Rob to stay together."

Vie groaned. "Like married? Cripe sakes. I gotta go, they're calling our seats. I'll see you there. Call the minute you land."

"I will. Have a good flight and get Mom all talked out so she'll leave me alone."

Vie laughed again. "I'll try. Bye!"

* * * * *

Jui's flight left on time and she landed in Boise just after five in the evening. She climbed into her rented SUV and took off for Powder Ridge, about 125 miles north of Boise. An earlier snowfall turned the roads slushy near the airport but the highways were decent and she settled back for the drive with a tall cup of coffee.

After a brief stop, Jui got back in the driver's seat for the last leg of the trip. She left a voice message for her sister.

"Hey Vie, it's about seven-thirty. I'm about fifty miles away. I had to stop to pee before I died." Jui giggled and continued. "I got a bite to eat, too, and I figure I should be there within the hour. Don't have too much fun without me."

Leaving the freeway, she turned onto the two-lane road to Powder Ridge. Temperatures hovered around the freezing mark and she groaned, knowing they would dip when she climbed through the canyons. A patch of ice caught her wheels and sent her fishtailing into the oncoming lane. She let off the gas and gently steered back into her own lane, breathing a sigh of relief once her truck was back under control.

Snowflakes dotted her windshield. "Come on, I have thirty miles to go. Can't this just hold off a little longer?" she grumbled.

The snow fell harder. The thermostat in the dash showed the temperature had dipped a few degrees below freezing. Jui slowed and turned on her fog lights. Squinting at the asphalt for trouble and creeping through the snow squall, she hoped the weather would clear soon.

Her heart worked overtime. She gripped the wheel, concentrated on keeping her vehicle safely on the road. A second later, the front end slid left and then right on a patch of black ice. The truck's rear end veered around toward the ditch. Jui let off the gas and guided the truck back toward her lane, hoping to drive out of the skid, but her front end swung back around too far. Snow along the shoulder snagged her front tire and the truck went over the embankment.

Jui screamed. An enormous pine tree stood ten yards in front of her. The antilock brakes pounded rapid-fire beneath her foot as the runaway SUV slid down the uneven terrain gathering speed. The truck glanced off the tree and collided with a boulder, taking out the headlights. The cab went pitch black.

White-hot pain engulfed Jui's chest when she slammed against the steering wheel. Her head snapped forward and back with the force of the impact.

The truck jolted left and right, continued blindly on its destructive path. With a metallic, crashing groan, the vehicle tipped onto its side. Another boulder popped through the door's window, and fireworks exploded in Jui's head.

* * * * *

Olivia Fabrice dialed her daughter's cell phone again. "Still no answer," she told her husband. "I'm worried. Jui should have been here by now."

Terry Fabrice gazed out the window. The snow stopped as abruptly as it had begun. "She probably has no service through the mountains and with the weather being bad. I'm sure she'll be here any minute."

Liv Fabrice asked Vie, "How long ago did she call?"

"I already told you a hundred times, Mom, around seven-thirty."

Liv glanced at her watch. "I think we should call the highway patrol or somebody. It's nine-thirty. Maybe she had car trouble."

Vie stood and volunteered to check into the matter. She was happy to do something productive and her mother's fretting didn't calm matters.

Downstairs, Vie quizzed the front desk clerk. "My sister called a few hours ago and still hasn't arrived. We're getting worried," she told the evening attendant. "Is there somebody we can call to check this last stretch — to make sure she hasn't had car trouble or an accident?"

"We have a police scanner and I haven't heard anything, but I'll call in and let you know. What's your sister driving?" the clerk asked.

"Some kind of SUV. It's a rental from the Boise airport," Vie said, now as concerned as her mother.

"Try not to worry. The squall could have slowed her down. Maybe she pulled off until it cleared. I'll let you know the moment we hear anything."

Vie tapped her fingers on the wood desk. "Thanks, we'll be in my parents' room — Terrance and Olivia Fabrice — four-forty-two."

* * * * *

Near dawn, Wade slumbered alone in his king-sized bed. Sharp, tearing pains in his chest awakened him violently. He sat up, coughing and sputtering, trying to catch his breath. He gripped his chest and panted as agony radiated through his body. *What the hell's the matter with me? Vampires don't get sick.* He lay back against his pillows; excruciating pains stabbed him with every breath he took.

An intense, low-pitched buzz sounding similar to an electrical transformer filled his brain, making his skull pound. Gripping both sides of his head, Wade rolled out of bed and tried to focus on the powerful sounds. He wondered if Ladislav Husek, the Ancient One, and his black-hearted Prophets were exterminating him. Wade expected the experience to be ghastly but this was utter torture. A blip in the sound pattern relieved a bit of the horrific buzz. He drew shallow breaths to alleviate the agonizing chest pain.

"Wade, help...me."

His head shot up as the words, weak but clear, floated into his mind. Wade sprang to his feet and immediately crumbled to his knees. He sank to the floor, his world turning black.

* * * * *

The Idaho State Patrol crept up the mountain, using searchlights to scan the roadsides and gullies for Jui. During their journey, the officers called tows for three other stranded motorists. Her skid marks through a low snow bank marked her exit from the highway. The patrol officer pulled off and shined a search light down the embankment and caught a glimpse of an SUV resting on its driver's side about fifty yards below. He radioed for an ambulance and another tow while his partner descended the steep incline to investigate the situation.

The officer's feet skidded on the slippery terrain while he cautiously worked his way to the truck. Looking through the broken windshield, the officer saw a lifeless body strapped in the seat. Blood matted the side of the woman's face and head.

"Jui Fabrice! Jui Fabrice!" he called, hoping to learn whether the woman inside was dead or alive. "Hang on, Miss, help is on the way." Without a secure towline on the truck, the officer couldn't risk climbing aboard. The ground could release its perilous grip on the vehicle, sending it farther down the snow-covered slope.

At the roadside, another police officer called Powder Ridge to give Terry and Liv Fabrice an update. From the description the officer relayed, it sounded like the woman they'd found was Jui. The officer assured the anxious parents an ambulance and tow were on the way and he would call back with a status report.

Hanging up the phone, Terry said to Liv, "Get your coat. We're going down there."

* * * * *

At the crash site, a sheriff's deputy stood near lit flares and watched the plow truck clear away slush and lay down precious sand and deicer for the rescue vehicles. The deputy pointed to the safest place for the drivers to park once the plow left the scene.

An EMT asked the officer, "Any idea how long she's been down there?"

The deputy looked at his watch. "My guess? Several hours. She called her sister around seven-thirty and expected to arrive at Powder Ridge an hour later. I haven't seen her move a muscle. I talked to her through the window but she's done nothing to make me think she's still alive."

The EMT shined his flashlight into the cab and shouted. "We're going to get you out of there, Ms. Fabrice." He turned back to the officer. "She's pale, but not dead pale."

"The vehicle's secure!" hollered the tow operator and then he climbed aboard the tipped-over truck and busted the front window. Bits of safety glass fell onto Jui's motionless body while he peeled back the windshield.

Afterward, the EMT climbed into the cab and checked her pulse. "She's alive. Barely, but still alive."

Jui's family waited near the ambulance while the EMTs brought Jui up.

Liv gazed at her injured daughter. Her voice shaking, she asked, "How is she?"

The lead EMT told them as much as he could without giving false hope. "Alive. We don't know the extent of her injuries yet. She's been unconscious for hours and she's hypothermic. We're headed to Boise General."

Inside the ambulance, the lead EMT said to the other paramedic, "We need an intraosseous tap. With this cervical collar on and her head injuries, a jugular IV isn't going to work."

"I'll handle it," the assisting medic said. After cutting open Jui's jeans, he pressed the large-gauge needle into her leg until it penetrated her tibia and rested in the marrow. "The IO's in," he said. "Starting the warm saline drip."

* * * * *

In Bucharest, Wade laid on the carpet, groaning in pain. Thunderous noises in his skull made it impossible to focus. His vision remained blurred. Every now and then, he would hear a whimper or his name. Fractured and weak, the sounds let him know Jui needed him. A new assault, this time on his left leg, made him scream in agony. Invisible forces paralyzed him like a voodoo doll writhing at the mercy of its spell caster.

* * * * *

An hour later, the attending emergency room physician at Boise General Hospital came to speak to Jui's family. "Why don't we sit down," Doctor Lee told them. Once seated, he said, "Your daughter's condition is quite serious."

"What does that mean?" Jui's mother asked in a quivering voice.

"Your daughter's airbag may have failed," the doctor said. "As a result, she has a number of obvious injuries—cuts and bruises—from the rollover, but we're also getting a CT done on her head, chest and pelvis. She's still unconscious."

"Oh God," Jui's sister said.

"Fortunately her seatbelt held, but her left collarbone is broken, probably from the seatbelt or the rollover or both." Doctor Lee paused to let the information sink in. "Her body struck with such force the steering wheel cracked."

Jui's father put his arm around his wife's shoulder.

Dr. Lee continued, using a gentle voice to keep the situation calm. "Three of her ribs are fractured and one rib collapsed her lung. Your daughter's pulse is quite weak."

"Is she going to be okay?" Mr. Fabrice asked. "Can we see her?"

"She's unconscious, probably due to the head injury. We're giving her drugs to reduce brain swelling and she also has a chest tube in to re-inflate her lung." The physician gazed into the frightened eyes of Jui's family. "I know this a lot to take in. The good news is her unconscious state helped her remain calm and not feel the pain or worry of her injuries. The cold temperatures helped control the swelling in her brain. Those are positive things."

"But?" Mr. Fabrice said.

"But we don't know the extent of her head injury. Right now we're monitoring her condition to see if the Mannitol we gave her helps bring her around."

"When will you know more?" Jui's sister asked in a tight voice.

"She'll tell us. She was dressed warmly so she doesn't have significant signs of frostbite, but we're keeping an eye open for the aftereffects. We're continually reassessing her other injuries. When her condition stabilizes, she should start waking up."

"When?" Mrs. Fabrice asked.

"We don't know."

Her husband asked again, "Can we see her?"

"Yes, can we see our child?" Mrs. Fabrice asked.

Doctor Lee rose. "We're moving her to intensive care. After she's settled, someone will come to get you," he said. "It's going to be awhile. Perhaps you want to make some hotel arrangements."

* * * * *

At 3:30 a.m., a nurse brought Jui's family to her room in ICU. Olivia's stomach lurched at the sight of her daughter.

"She's obviously very bruised. Fortunately, her seatbelt held or she'd probably be in much more dire straits. Don't stay too long," the nurse said and then left.

Olivia's heart ached for her daughter, whose forehead and eyes were black and blue as though she'd been the loser in a boxing match. A sling encased Jui's left arm and near the top of the C-collar, Olivia noticed terrible looking burn marks and blood-red streaks. Jui's heart monitor made quiet blips on the screen.

Olivia took her daughter's right hand and kissed it. "Jui,

it's Mom. Dad and Vie are here, too. You're going to be okay. You've been in a car wreck." She stifled a sob and continued in a shaky voice. "You're in the hospital in Boise and we're right here. We're not leaving until you're better."

"Your mom's right, Jui," Terry said. "We're right here. You're going to be fine."

Olivia pointed to the leather-braided band around her daughter's slender wrist."Do you know what this is for?"

"No," Vie said.

"I never noticed it before," her father said.

"What an odd thing. Maybe I should untie it and keep it until she's better," Olivia said.

Vie shrugged. "Why do you care about a leather bracelet right now?"

Liv tried to untie the band and Jui's cardiac monitor blipped faster.

"Just leave it, Liv," Terry said. "It's not hurting anything."

Olivia watched the monitor settle down.

* * * * *

Eighteen hours passed before Wade's vision cleared and he could stand. He felt weak as a baby because he needed to feed and his body was going through a hellish ordeal. *First things first.* He needed to re-energize and that meant blood. He found a robust, middle-aged man walking his German shepherd on the outskirts of Bucharest. The dog growled, sensing Wade before its unwitting master did, and the dog ran off once Wade physically appeared.

Feeling steadier afterwards but still weak, Wade helped himself to a pint from a cross-country skier. A nagging headache and heaviness in his chest remained and now his stomach throbbed with worsening pain whenever he touched the tender area. Because he couldn't possibly be sick, the only logical conclusion for his physical problems was Jui.

Back at home, Wade tuned into Jui's thoughts and heard nothing. Over the next hours, he contacted her telepathically many times and received only emptiness. He called her cell phone and her house. It was the middle of the night in Seattle and Saint Claire's offices were closed for the weekend. He warred with himself, knowing he must stay away or risk his own death. *If Husek and his exterminators come after me, so be it. Jui needs me.*

He teleported himself to her home in Seattle and found the condo empty. Dawn's red and orange streaks painted the horizon. He snarled, thinking she might be with Rob. *She'll face my wrath if she dragged me across the world to walk into their love nest.*

He found one of Rob's business cards and materialized in the man's apartment. It, too, was vacant. Wade sat in the middle of Rob's living room floor and concentrated on Jui. *Where are you?* More hours passed and then he heard her.

Wade.

Jui, where are you? He heard nothing more. Wade sensed her ominous situation, but had no idea where to find her. He returned, once more, to her condo and scrounged around, looking for clues. A pair of ski gloves and hat lay on the storage room floor and he found her calendar with "Powder Ridge" written on it. There were eighteen Powder Ridges listed on the Internet. He searched through them for clues about which one she might be at and found the grand opening announcement for the Powder Ridge north of Boise. His gaze moved quickly across the screen. He'd already wasted two days.

Wade called Powder Ridge Lodge and asked for Jui's room. The desk clerk evaded his questions so he asked to speak to the manager.

He lied to the resort manager. "I got a message from Ms. Fabrice while I was traveling. I haven't been able to locate her and I'm concerned something is wrong."

"I can't give you any information. What did you say your name was?" the manager said.

Wade dodged the question. "Her message sounded like she was in trouble. Is there someone else I may speak to?"

"I'm sorry, no."

"Can I leave a message for her at the lodge?"

Wade heard the manager deeply inhale before saying, "I'm sorry, she never arrived. That's all I can tell you. Goodbye."

Wade reached out to Jui telepathically again. *Jui, I'm looking for you. Help me find you.* He repeated the message again and again. Finally, he heard the tiniest whimper from her. *I hear you, minx. Help me find you. I'm in Seattle looking for you.* Sudden pain soared through Wade's body, making him double over and sink to his knees.

* * * * *

Jui's doctor grew concerned as he listened to the nurse describe Jui's condition. "How long have her blood pressure and heart rate been up?"

The nurse checked Jui's chart. "About fifteen minutes."

"Give it another fifteen minutes. If they haven't gone back down, let me know," Doctor Lee said.

Fifteen minutes later, he rechecked Jui's blood pressure and heart rate. "They're still up. Let's get a blood draw, stat," he said to the nurse.

A little while later, the computer blipped softly with every mouse click Dr. Lee made. He paged through Jui's lab results, scanning for vital information about what was happening to his new patient.

The doctor approached Jui's family in the family lounge.

"Is Jui better?" Olivia asked.

"Actually no," Doctor Lee said. "We're prepping her for emergency surgery so I only have a few minutes."

"Surgery!" Terry said. "What the hell happened?"

"When I examined her about a half hour ago, her blood pressure and heart rate were up. Her upper stomach is somewhat distended and she has no bowel sounds. She probably has a laceration in her gut from the accident and we're concerned about peritonitis."

"The stomach stuff is serious, isn't it," Vie said.

"Her condition is very serious. She also has a bit of a temperature and slightly elevated white blood count."

"Infection," Olivia said.

"Likely. We're treating the fever with antibiotics and we'll remove her chest tube during the surgery to reduce the chance of infection. Hopefully doing those things will level her out. We have to wait and see, but right now I need to get a look inside and make sure we take care of any trouble brewing there." The doctor stood and shook Terry and Olivia's hands. "I'll see you after the surgery."

Her face covered with agony, Olivia nodded.

* * * * *

When the pain in his body subsided, Wade called Rob Hawthorne.

"What the hell do you want?" Rob demanded.

"I'm looking for Jui," Wade said in an icy tone.

"Her life is none of your business. You slept with her and then dumped her."

Wade's fury rose but he tamped it down, needing Rob's information. "I won't discuss my personal life or relationships with you. Jui tried to reach me." Wade followed a string of vulgar epitaphs in Rob's mind, until he got the information he needed. Rob was just launching into more of his lecture when Wade hung up.

* * * * *

Doctor Lee pulled his blue surgical cap off his head as he came to speak to Jui's family.

"How is she?" Olivia asked while rising to her feet.

"She's out of surgery. We repaired a small intestinal tear and gave her some blood."

"When can we see her?" Terry asked.

"She's still in recovery. Right now, we're doing everything we can for her and we just have to wait," Doctor Lee said.

"Is there any improvement with her head injury?" Terry asked.

"The swelling hasn't increased so that's good."

"But it hasn't gone down either?" Vie asked.

"Not significantly enough to say she's out of the woods or for us to get a good assessment of her injuries long-term. She's been through a lot and the intestinal injury didn't help matters. We're still monitoring for infection."

"Is she going to be okay? Is my daughter going to make it?" Liv sounded like she was going to burst into tears.

Doctor Lee put his hands on his hips and observed the tormented mother in front of him. He'd never met a person who appreciated hearing, "I don't know" when their loved one was in critical condition. He focused on the positives. "The swelling hasn't worsened and she's young and strong. Those all work in her favor so let's just focus on the positives for now and let your daughter rest. We're keeping a very close eye on her."

* * * * *

During the hours following her surgery, Jui's temperature spiked to 103 degrees and her white counts soared. "Staph infection set in," Doctor Lee told her family.

Wade hovered in a shadow state on the floor, blending in with the changing daylight and shadows in her room. He watched Olivia collapse in tears in her husband's arms. He'd never seen Terry, the son of his beloved Claire, until that moment. A million thoughts and emotions ran through him. *Terry could have been my son had I lived. Had I lived? In a way, I am alive. But is this life? Would Jui want to give up her family to live with me as a vampire?* He didn't know. He'd never given her a chance to decide.

He saw Jui's resemblance to her mother and Sylvia's uncanny resemblance to Claire. He felt protective of Jui and not at all conflicted by his past love for Claire. He realized his affection for Jui was different. She wanted him physically the way Claire had, but Jui needed him, reached out, and relied on him in ways Claire hadn't. Claire was much more self-centered than Jui, Wade concluded. *And I pushed her away to protect her.*

He continued watching the family agonize over her

precarious situation and wondered what to do. *I'm not a man. I'm not human. Even the passion we shared in bed would be different if Jui became a vampire. Sex would be a pastime, not something we shared emotionally. Vampires don't need sex. We get pleasure from the gift flowing in our victim's veins, not from the intimacy of lovemaking. And children aren't a possibility.*

He watched Terry comfort Jui's sister and observed the family clinging to each other in fear and love. *Could I deny Jui a lifetime of tenderness, commitment, family, and joy by turning her into a soulless creature of death?*

Wade hovered in her room as a shadow, listening to every word from Jui's post-surgical team. He communicated with her telepathically. "Hang on, Jui, I'm here. I'm going to help you."

When her fever reached 105 degrees, Doctor Lee called the family back to the hospital to break the bad news.

"Jui's condition has been downgraded to grave. I'm afraid she might not survive," he told them. "Her surgery, internal injuries, and the infection are stacking the odds against her. She's still unconscious."

Tears slid down Olivia's cheeks. Kissing her daughter's cheek, she whispered, "Jui, sweetheart, it's Mom. You have to fight. We're here and love you so much. Please keep fighting. I love you, Jui, I love you...." She broke down sobbing next to Jui's battered face, burying her tears in the white-encased pillow. "Fight Jui, fight with everything you've got. You have to live. You're my girl."

Still invisible, Wade watched Terry take his wife's narrow shoulders in his large hands and draw her into his embrace. "Come on Jui, hang in there," he whispered brokenly. "You're tough. I love you so much. Fight honey, you have to fight."

Vie approached her sister's bed and held Jui's slender hand. Her lips quivered in a frown. "You're the best, Jui. I need you, too," she whispered. "Who's going to rank the guys with me if you don't make it?" She teased through her tears. "You know all my secrets and I know yours...I...who will I talk to?" She gave her mom a half-hearted smile and said, "Mom would *never* get it. And what about Wade?" Vie touched the slender tie on Jui's wrist. "You still have to figure out how you

175

feel about him. You have to get better, Jui. You just have to."

"Let's let her rest," the nurse said in a soft voice. "We'll call you if there's any change."

"We're not leaving the hospital. We'll be in the family lounge," Terry said.

With her room finally empty—at least for the moment—Wade physically appeared. Human emotions roiled in him, finally making him understand the deep and binding ways his soul and Jui's were connected. He touched her wrist, tracing the leather hair tie with his finger, and whispered into her brain, *Jui, I'm going to help you, I promise.*

Her index finger twitched.

Noticing the tiny movement, he communicated again. *Rest. You need your energy to heal.*

Wade left the hospital to feed before appearing in a medical supply room at Boise General. Digging through the various plastic drawers, he found syringes and large gauge needles. After he stuffed the supplies in his breast pocket, he returned to Jui's room and waited in a near-molecular state for the nurses to finish their work.

When they left, he materialized. *Jui, I'm going to help you now.*

He screwed one of the long, large needles onto a syringe. Opening his jaw as wide as he could, he took a deep breath and guided the needle backward. A painful jolt went through his throat as the instrument found his large salivary gland. Drawing the plunger, he extracted saliva from one side. He withdrew the needle and then shuddered from the unpleasant sensations. He repeated the procedure on the other gland until the syringe contained about a tablespoon of life-saving saliva.

He was poised to inject the saliva into her IV when a nurse pressed against Jui's door. Wade became a shadow and anxiously waited for him to leave. The fluid loss dehydrated Wade and compromised his ability to stay out of sight for very long. After the nurse left, Wade reappeared, shaky but focused. He injected the vampire spit into her IV port. *Let my body heal you, minx. It's the least I can do for causing you so much pain.* Afterward, he gently touched her warm cheek with the back of his hand. *I'll be back. Rest, Jui.*

Wade didn't go far from the hospital. He didn't know how many injections it would take before Jui's body was strong enough to take over the healing process. He spotted a custodian leaving a supply room and the man became Wade's first victim. He had nearly finished feeding when the door suddenly opened and a redheaded woman walked in.

She flicked on the light and startled to find the men in what appeared to be an intimate embrace. "Excuse me...I...I had no...never mind."

Wade couldn't waste time. He let the dazed man sag to the floor and pulled the woman into a lethal embrace. She struggled only until his bite struck her plump carotid. Afterward, he settled the redhead's limp body next to the custodian. *The two of them can sort out the uncomfortable questions and answers together later.*

Back in Jui's room, Wade hovered against the wall, flat and transparent, waiting to learn whether her condition improved.

"Did you take the empty syringe to the lab?" one nurse asked the other.

"Yeah, they're testing it. I can't believe somebody got in here unnoticed."

"It's a lawsuit waiting to be filed no matter what."

The nurse making notes on Jui's whiteboard finished writing and snapped the dry marker cap back on. "Got that right."

In his haste, Wade left the syringe behind. He couldn't believe his blunder.

"Her temperature has dropped just a little bit," said the note-taking nurse.

"That's good news I'm sure her family will be glad to hear," replied the other and then the door softly shut behind them.

Wade brushed his hand across Jui's bruised cheek. *I'm here.* This time he withdrew even more saliva. His throat ached from the needle and the uncomfortable suction that left him jittery afterward. If somebody interrupted him now, he didn't know how long he could stay invisible. *Too late.* Terry

Fabrice arrived and Wade had no choice but to vanish.

"Honey, they said your fever is down a little bit. Hang in there. Your mom's asleep. She's exhausted, but I had to come by and cheer you on. You're as tough as they come, Jui. Fight."

A nurse arrived again to take Jui's vitals. "Her temp is 101. Still high, but coming down and that's good," the nurse told him.

"Keep fighting, Jui," her dad said.

"Let's let her rest; you look like death warmed over yourself, Mr. Fabrice. Come on, let's call it a night. We'll tell you if there's any change."

Terry gazed at his daughter's still body. "I'll be back tomorrow, honey. Rest now. We love you."

* * * * *

An hour later, Wade returned. He removed the syringe from his pocket and didn't waste a second before injecting his saliva into Jui's IV port. Knowing their time was limited, Wade sat on the bed and held her hand while he communicated with her. *You should feel better very soon, minx.* He gazed at her battered face. *I know you won't believe it, but I felt your pain on the other side of the world. Distance means nothing to the soul, minx. Remember that. Your soul cried out and brought me here to help you.*

Jui squeezed Wade's hand ever so slightly.

You're feeling better. Good. I promise I'll be back.

* * * * *

When Jui's family returned in the morning, Doctor Lee greeted them with the good news her fever had disappeared and her brain activity had increased.

Olivia's face filled with joy. "She's getting better!"

"I'd say her condition is still guarded, but she is definitely improved," Dr. Lee said. "We've put her in a coma now to make sure she rests and doesn't feel any pain, but you can go in and see her. Keep things calm. She's a long way from recovered, but she's improved and that's what's important."

"But you think she's going to be okay?" Olivia asked.

"We won't know what we're facing until she wakes up."

Wade hovered, listening to every word and then communicated to Jui. *Can you hear me, minx?* He heard a whimper, weak but immediate. *I'll be back tonight after everyone leaves.*

He teleported himself to his hotel room to wait until night fell and the hospital quieted. He'd need to prepare another massive dose of saliva tonight. Luckily, there were plenty of people around for the Thanksgiving holiday and Wade wouldn't have trouble finding his victims.

Around 1:00 a.m., he reappeared with another large injection for Jui. He gazed at her swollen, discolored features. *I'm here, minx. I'm going to help you.* He injected the saliva and then waited to see if there was any change.

Jui groaned out loud.

He took her hand. *Shh. If you make sounds, I'll have to leave. Tell me with your mind.* He tuned into her thoughts and got pictures and mixed up words he thought might be memories. *Take your time.*

Hold me.

Her battered body couldn't be moved, so taking her in his arms was impossible. He leaned over her right side and rested his head in the crux of her shoulder, barely touching her. *I can't get any closer. Your body is too broken.*

Thank you.

He didn't know if she'd remember any of this and he couldn't risk sticking around until she woke up to find out. He'd be exposed just like Christophe warned and that couldn't happen. He hadn't forgotten about Husek's extermination threat either. His fingers curled around hers. *I care about you so much, minx. Be well.* With a brief brush of his lips on hers, Wade disappeared.

* * * * *

Forty-eight hours later, Jui's condition improved enough to bring her out of the induced coma.

Vie asked Doctor Lee, "Is she okay? She keeps talking about people who weren't here and reaching for imaginary things."

Olivia frowned and asked, "Why does she keep talking about this Wade person? She acts like he was here."

"Hallucinations are common for people recovering from a brain injury," Doctor Lee explained. "Try not to get upset or participate. Just speak to her in a calm voice and bring her into the present."

When Doctor Lee had left, Vie tried to explain to her mother about Jui's complicated relationship with Wade Kairos. "I don't know how they left things, Mom," Sylvia said. "I know they were together at Harkers Island and that's why Jui broke it off with Rob. I'm guessing she's reliving memories from their time together. She didn't want him to leave."

"Where is this man if he is so important to my daughter?" Olivia asked.

Vie shrugged. "Last I heard, he was going to Moscow. I don't know if he is even aware of what happened—or if it matters."

"Clearly it matters to my daughter," Olivia said. "Perhaps you can find him. Maybe seeing him would help your sister's recovery."

"I don't think that's a good idea." Rob Hawthorne stepped into Jui's room.

Liv frowned at him. "Why? Do you know something we don't?"

"He used Jui. They were together and then he dumped her. She told me she has deep feelings for him but apparently that didn't matter much to Kairos. He flew off to Moscow and told Jui to get on with her life," Rob said with a sneer in his voice. "He called me last week saying Jui contacted him and he was worried about her. He wanted to know where she was."

"What did you tell him?" Sylvia asked.

"Jack. I didn't tell him jack. She's better off without him."

Liv crossed her arms over her chest, not liking the way this former boyfriend was making decisions for Jui. "Isn't that rather presumptuous of you? It's possible they have spoken since they were last together. Perhaps Jui wanted him to meet us at Powder Ridge."

"Do you know if he's in the States?" Vie asked.

"Not a clue," Rob replied, still sounding bitter.

"Why did you come here?" Liv asked.

Rob's mouth formed a thin, angry line. "I care about Jui, despite the crappy way she treated me."

"And?" Olivia said.

"And nothing. I came to see how she is. I think this is hardly the time to pitch myself as a better choice than Kairos."

"I'll say," Vie whispered.

"But you want to be here for my daughter during her recovery?"

"Kairos screwed with her head. If he stays out of the picture, maybe Jui and I can work things out." He walked closer to the bed. "This was his," he said, pointing to the leather tie on Jui's wrist.

"What was?" Olivia asked.

The bitter tone in his voice came back loud and clear. "The tie, I recognize it. Kairos wore it in his hair. He has long hair." Rob tried to remove the hair band and Jui twisted her hand away. A look of disgust covered Rob's face.

"Just leave it alone," Vie said. "Every time somebody touches it, she gets upset. The band must mean something important to my sister."

"I agree," Liv said. "And I don't want to argue. Vie, would you please try to find this elusive Mr. Kairos? If what Rob says is true, he should know how seriously injured Jui is. If he says he's sorry but has moved on, at least we know what to tell Jui when she starts thinking more clearly. But if he loves her, he'll come. Nothing could keep him away."

A weak voice came from the bed. "Mom?"

Olivia rushed to her daughter's side. "I'm right here, Jui; save your strength." Jui moaned and Olivia instructed Vie to get a nurse. "Shh, you're going to be all right. You're going to be just fine."

Jui's eyes opened and Liv saw her daughter's confusion. "Remember you're in the hospital. You had a terrible car accident and you've been unconscious for a week."

Jui attempted to lick her lips. Her tongue felt thick and uncoordinated. Her brain wasn't firing on all cylinders yet, but she knew her body was badly beaten. She raised her hand toward her shoulder.

"You broke your collarbone in the accident. Remember?" Liv said. "You have other injuries and you've had surgery. Rob is here," she said with a smile.

Rob moved into Jui's view. "You gave us quite a scare. I'm glad to see you're getting better." Squeezing her hand gently, he said, "I'll come by another time. Take care."

Jui's gaze followed him out of the room and then she croaked, "Wade, where's Wade?"

Liv came close again. "You mean Wade Kairos?"

She whispered, "Yes. He was here."

"No sweetie, I think you are imagining things. The doctors said you might be kind of mixed up for awhile. You have a nasty bump on your head."

"Wade," Jui insisted.

"He hasn't been here but I asked Vie to find him for you. He called Rob last week."

Jui squeezed her eyes shut, confused and exhausted.

* * * * *

After her discharge a week later, Jui went to her parents' home to recuperate. She couldn't shake a nagging feeling Wade visited her several times when she was in the hospital. Alone in her old bedroom, she recalled him saying he was going to help her. *Let me heal you with my body, minx,* or some such words. *But how in the hell could he heal me? There's no way I could have improved this quickly without help. Even the doctors are surprised. But why didn't he stay? Where are you?*

Vie told her she'd left a message for Wade but he hadn't returned her call.

That bit of news sent Olivia's temper into orbit. She promptly pronounced the man worse than pond scum and declared her daughter better off without him.

* * * * *

Winter had Bucharest in its clutches—cold, desolate, and bleak. The sun appeared only a few hours a day and late December snowdrifts covered the landscape. Below freezing temperatures suited Wade just fine.

He became a recluse since returning from Seattle and only left his home to feed. Jui's ceaseless pleas to contact her filled his consciousness. He was glad she was recovering and happier still he'd helped her, yet Wade was certain Ladislav Husek couldn't be far away. Once Husek found out Wade ignored his edict to stay clear of Jui, Wade's punishment would be swift. Each time he closed his eyes to sleep, he never expected them to open again.

The evening wind whistled through the frozen pine trees surrounding the house. Wolves joined in song, beckoning him with their plaintive calls, but Wade ignored the carnivorous beasts. Jui's voice resounded in his mind. His emotions ricocheted between the Elysian memories of their night together, and the inexorable ache of loneliness and regret the memories left behind. Wade cursed himself for giving into the baser pleasures and emotions of the human kind. He'd made the biggest mistake of his vampire life.

Ladislav Husek, the Ancient One, seemed to appear on cue. He brought the acrid scent of death with him, apparently not bothering to cloak it from his fellow vampire. The stench pervaded the room as an ominous sign.

"I've been expecting you," Wade said without getting out of his chair.

Husek's long, black coat hung open. With his hands on his hips, Husek gazed at Wade. "I heard about your escapades. You openly disregarded my warning."

"I couldn't just let her die."

"Why not? Humans do it all the time."

"She asked for my help."

The Ancient One moved in a blur, reached for Wade's collar, and dragged him from his comfortable leather chair. "You're not the Red Cross." Cold fire danced in Husek's eyes as he physically illustrated the definition of a vampire. His neck twisted in an unnatural, inhuman way while he sneered at Wade. "She didn't ask because she knew you could help. She asked because she's a besotted woman. Vampires take, we manipulate, we prey. Christophe coddled you like a favorite child and this is the sickening result."

"Leave him out of this," Wade answered in a deep, hollow voice. He teleported himself to the other side of the room. "She didn't see me. Nobody knew I was there or that I helped her."

In a flash of movement, Husek was back in Wade's face. "So that excuses your behavior? You weren't discovered, but what about the syringe or her memories? Your myopic behavior brings undesirable attention to all of us. Tell me she's not looking for you now and hasn't been looking for you since your sickening little tryst in America." Husek's volume rose to a deafening level. "Tell me she's not digging around, asking questions, and trying to figure out what you are or what your motives are for being a fucking coward!"

Wade gazed at the menacing vampire. "Do what you will. I knew the consequences. Jui deserved to live and I—"

"Made all her dreams come true?" Husek hissed like a snake ready to strike. "Drivel, utter fucking drivel." He spat in disgust.

Wade shoved Husek away and straightened his shirt collar. "No one would choose this life. I wasn't going to force Jui into it out of selfishness."

"Then you should have let her die. You should have stayed away from her and let nature take its course, you sanctimonious fool." Husek cocked his head to the side, mechanically sizing up Wade. A sinister grin curled his lips, exposing his fangs. "But then you'd lose your playmate and couldn't keep pretending you're a man."

Wade turned away, convicted. "What do you want?"

"Don't leave this place," he said through a clenched jaw. "Once Strasse's estate is settled, you're of no use to the planet. You've been an embarrassment to us for months. Feed and come right back here," he ordered, pointing to the floor to emphasize his point. "Go to her again and I'll turn her. She'll spend eternity with me." Husek's body shook with intense, depraved laughter. His eyes rolled back in glee, and his fanged teeth jutted from his jaw, razor sharp and ready. His cold, gray tongue slid across his blue-tinged lips. "Maybe I won't wait."

"You may be a vampire, old man, but you can die just like the rest of us."

Husek kept laughing, seemingly amused, with Wade's show of bravado. He shoved Wade across the large room like a toy. Wade slammed against a bookcase, emptying the shelves around him in a comedy of destruction. Before Wade could even react, Husek was at him again with a surgically sharp blade in his hand. His voice resounded from hell. "I can kill you this instant and claim your beloved Jui. There'd be nothing you could do then. Or I can let you live and claim her as my plaything and there'll still be nothing you can do but watch."

Wade glared at Husek.

"You'll be my puppet until I decide," he said, sending high-pitched sound waves blaring into Wade's brain.

Wade grabbed his skull and forced himself to his feet. His eyes felt like they were bursting out of his head and his face contorted with pain. "I'll kill her myself if you turn her. I'll get revenge on you, have no doubt," he declared through gritted teeth.

Husek gripped Wade by the shoulders. His cool breath slapped Wade's face with each word he spoke. "You'll never get past the Prophets. You're a bigger fool than I thought. How Strasse put up with your juvenile ways is beyond me. Grow the fuck up. You're a vampire and there's no turning back."

"You're wrong." He groaned while the vibrations and noise in his brain raged so powerfully Wade thought his head would explode.

Husek gave him a pitying glance. "Don't test me. You're no match."

Wade's knees buckled and he writhed on the floor, screaming in pain as Husek turned up the volume.

"Still want to play games, Kairos?"

Incapacitated by the carnage in his head, Wade could do nothing but curl into a fetal position and wait until Husek finished making his point.

Chapter Thirteen

By late January, Jui could spend a few hours a day at the office. Her shoulder still hadn't completely healed and she tired easily, but it felt good to resume some of her old routines.

"How you holding up?" Rob asked while leaning against her door.

Jui lifted her left arm a little. "It'll be a lot easier once I get this sling out of my life. What a pain in the rear."

Rob's gentle chuckle warmed the frosty air that almost always filled the space between them. "Feel like grabbing some lunch before you leave?"

Jui looked at her watch. "Man, the morning sure flies when you're only working part time." She let out a tired sigh. "I'll be glad when my strength is back and I can get through the day without a couple of naps."

"You went through a lot."

"Yeah, but I'm almost a couch potato compared to my life before the accident." She shut her laptop. "Anyway...if you could manhandle this thing into my case, I'd appreciate it and then we can take off."

Rob came around to pack up her laptop.

"It goes so much faster with two hands. I can't tell you how many times I've tried to wiggle it into the case with mostly one hand and dropped it."

Rob laughed. "Good thing you're the boss's daughter."

Jui snorted. "He'd still chew me out."

They lunched at a nearby café and made small talk, ignoring the subject they needed to discuss until Jui finally dove in. "I want to apologize again for what happened between us."

Silence accepted her apology.

"You're a terrific guy and I really thought we were going to have something special. At least I thought we were headed that way."

"What is it about Kairos that's so irresistible, besides being absent from your life, I mean."

The sarcastic jab stung. "We made this instant connection in Heidelberg." Jui fiddled with the leather tie on her wrist and then looked up at Rob. Anger smoldered in his eyes. She shook her head. "It's hard to explain. He's not here and I don't know where he is but still...."

"You're hung up on him."

"Yeah, I guess so."

"You're wasting your life," Rob said.

"It seems ridiculous to be caught up in unrequited love."

"Your words, not mine."

"And I'm not even sure that's what it is. Wade is full of mysteries." She had no reason to say his name aloud for so long and the music of his name warmed her spirit. She said it again. "Wade is full of mysteries."

"Halloween's suspense is long gone, Jui. Isn't it time you moved on?"

"I respect you and I still care about you. I just can't move on until I answer the questions I have about him."

"What questions?" Rob shot back. "Like what kind of asshole sleeps with a beautiful, intelligent, exciting woman and then drops her like Monday's dry cleaning?"

"He didn't want to leave. He wanted to stay as much as I wanted him to."

"Did it ever occur to you that maybe the guy has a wife and a family? Maybe he's an even bigger jerk than you realize."

"I'm looking into all of that." She leaned forward on her elbow and continued in a soft voice. "It's more than figuring out why he dumped me. There are things about him that just don't make sense."

Rob snorted with laughter. "Seems he did you a favor. Can't you just be happy he's gone and forget about him?"

"Move on with you?" Her gaze softened along with her voice. "Are you asking me to give us another try?"

He studied her, wanting to say yes, knowing he should say no.

"Rob?"

"You'd have to decide he's not worth it."

"Worth what?"

"Any of it—not one more second of thought or energy. Can you do that?"

She shook her head. "I'm sorry, but I have to figure this out first. I don't know if he and I would ever be a couple. Hell, I don't even know where he is or if we'll ever see each other again. I just have to know. After that...."

"How long do you expect me to wait?"

"I don't. I mean that sincerely. You don't need to waste your life, too. When I get this figured out, I'll let you know. I promise. You can decide then."

* * * * *

Jui knocked on her father's office door.

He waved her in while he continued his phone conversation. "The tests were inconclusive again? How can that be? Just what the hell am I supposed to make of that?" he shouted. "I don't suppose anyone ever checked my daughter's IV ports to see if she was injected with that fluid." Terry listened again. "I'll ask her and let you know. Goodbye."

When he hung up, Jui asked, "What was that all about?"

Terry shook his head. "When you were in the hospital they found this huge syringe by your bed one night. The hospital and an outside lab have tested and retested the contents but they can't figure out what was in the syringe. They've concluded it's water-based and contains some animal compounds. There were no fingerprints either so nobody knows where the syringe came from."

"Do they think I was injected with whatever was in the syringe?"

"I don't know," he said. "The nurse found it next to your bed the night you had such a high fever. We didn't think you were going to pull through. There were lots of hospital personnel going in and out of your room but visitors were restricted to family only. They've gone through the surveillance tapes and didn't find anything. The only other thing they know for sure is one of the supply rooms was missing some needles and syringes the same size as the one found in your room."

"Who was on the phone?"

"The hospital's lawyer."

"Are you suing?"

"I don't know. I mean you're fine but what if you'd died? They can't figure out what was in that damn syringe. If you were injected with whatever was in it and you died, who would be accountable?"

Wade's words zipped through Jui's memory. *Let me heal you with my body.* Giving her father her full attention again, Jui said, "What were you supposed to ask me?"

"The lawyer wants you to have tests to see if any trace elements are in your body."

"It's been months, Dad."

"I know. What do you think?"

"I think we should just drop it. I'm fully recovered. Maybe you could insist on some procedural review or security increases but beyond that, I guess I got off lucky."

* * * * *

Jui sat on her bed and sorted through the files of leads and dead ends she'd compiled on her laptop. During the weeks following her conversation with Rob, her attempts to contact Wade diminished slowly but surely. She still wanted answers, but when he didn't respond, she decided his claims about being telepathic had to be inflated.

Blake sounded a bit annoyed whenever she called to ask whether he'd heard from Wade or anything about him. He suggested, just like Rob and everyone else, she forget about the guy for her own good.

Thinking back to her accident, she remembered the excruciating pain in her chest and head. The pain almost paralyzed her and she remembered moaning his name. Before she'd lost consciousness, Jui distinctly heard him ask, "Can you hear me?"

Did he hear me?

Then she considered the mysterious syringe and its equally mysterious contents. Diaphanous memories of Wade holding her seemed so real, but the more time that passed, the more she wondered if they were just a brain injury-induced confabulation.

Jui walked to her bedroom windows. She crossed her arms over her chest and let out a deep sigh, mindful of how doing those two things hurt badly only a few weeks ago. Her thoughts returned to Wade as she gazed over the lake. *If he hadn't heard me, why would he contact Rob, of all people?* Jui wanted to believe it wasn't just coincidence.

After some prodding, the ski resort manager recalled that a man with a slight German accent asked for information about her. *He wouldn't give his name but told me he said he'd gotten a message from you. He was worried because he couldn't reach you. We only told him you weren't here.*

Detective Ambrose from the Memphis Police Department contacted Jui a few more times, too. He still wanted to know whether she'd heard from Kevin Marks, the man who supposedly told her about Carl Spafford dying in the limousine explosion. Of course she hadn't heard from the man since Kevin Marks didn't exist any more than Carl Spafford did, but Detective Ambrose didn't need to know that. At the end of their last conversation, Jui felt confident she'd convinced the snoopy detective that rumors of Carl Spafford's death were a sick prank. At this point, Jui had no reason to think Wade was involved in Christophe's death. How Christophe got in the limo remained in the "mystery" column.

What about the heartbeat – or lack of one? Did I ever hear one at other times? She thought about being in Wade's arms in the vineyard hut and on the hotel balcony. She'd rested her head on his shoulder, kissed his neck but couldn't specifically remember hearing a heartbeat. She chided herself asking, "Who the hell takes their lover's pulse?"

Then the odd questions resurfaced about why he didn't eat or sweat and couldn't ejaculate but could still have amazing sex.

She closed her eyes and remembered being in his arms. An unbidden sigh left her lips as she relived their night together. God, how making love with Wade had changed her. She remembered being so spent he nearly carried her out of the shower and back to bed. Exhausted, they slept wrapped in each other's arms until sunrise. She loved the way his caramel-colored hair took on spun-gold highlights in the morning sunshine. She studied him while he watched the day dawn and the way he looked at her afterward was something she'd never forget. His hazel eyes smoldered with a longing that stole her breath. *You didn't want to leave me, Wade, I know it. I felt it. I didn't imagine it.* She wiped away the inevitable tears that always came when she got to the stone wall with his name etched in it.

Somehow you kept me from dying. Was it the strength of your love or something more? Relief settled in her bones. She denied what she felt all these months because the guy was completely out of her life. *I don't know where you are or how you could have helped me, but you did.* The bedroom lamp backlit her sad reflection on the windowpane. *I still love you wherever you are. Maybe sometime I'll be able to tell you in person.*

Back on her bed, Jui resumed searching the Internet for Wade. A newsfeed about Christophe Strasse popped up. Jui scanned a short legal notification regarding Christophe's estate and Wade was named as the executor. Jui copied the legal firm's name into her browser and did a search. With shaking hands, she dialed the number only realizing after the firm's voicemail answered that it was in the middle of the night in Munich. She disconnected the call, suddenly giddy over the possibility of finding Wade.

Her thoughts ran away like a child chasing a puppy, lighthearted and playful. She checked into flights from Seattle to Munich. If Wade was in the vicinity, nothing would stop her from going to him. She made a reservation for the next afternoon and then logged off. *I've got packing to do.*

After a restless night, she got out of bed at four-thirty a.m. and made coffee. Her body filled with anxiety over calling Urs Lamburg and asking about Wade. *What if it's just another dead end?* She sipped the mug of hot brew and hoped her German and their English would be good enough to get through a conversation.

She dialed the phone number and rapped her fingers impatiently on the kitchen counter while waiting for somebody to answer.

"May I speak to Urs Lamburg, please," Jui asked in German.

"I'm sorry, Herr Lamburg is unavailable. May I take a message?" the woman replied.

"When will he return? I have an urgent question."

"Perhaps another member of our firm can help you."

"It has to do with an estate Herr Lamburg worked on. Did anyone assist him with the Christophe Strasse estate?"

"Karl Steiner handled many of the details."

Hope filled Jui. "May I speak to him?"

"Just a moment, I'll transfer you."

Jui explained she was a friend of Wade Kairos and had been searching for him for months.

"How may I help you? We are not a lost and found," Mr. Steiner said in a snobby tone.

"I appreciate that fact, Mr. Steiner. I wondered if you knew how to contact Mr. Kairos. I have his cell phone number—"

The uppity lawyer cut her off. "I'm afraid I cannot help you. The cell phone number is the only contact information we have for Mr. Kairos."

"You're sure? Would you please take a minute to be sure?" Jui heard him let out his breath in an irritated huff. After clicking and several sharp taps on what Jui assumed was his keyboard, she heard him muttering words in German and figured he was reading documents on the screen.

"I'm sorry, there is nothing. I have a bank account for him but that is all."

"Can you please tell me the name of the bank?"

"I cannot. Frankly, I have spent too much time discussing a matter of no legal concern or interest to me. Good day."

The haughty lawyer hung up before Jui could get in one more "but." With a frustrated screech, she flung her cell phone toward the living room and watched it bounce, the hapless victim of her rage.

She calmed down and dialed Urs Lamburg's office an hour later. This time he was available. While sympathetic to her plight, Mr. Lamburg couldn't provide any help either.

"His private affairs are precisely that, Fraulein Fabrice. I have no right to divulge any information," Lamburg said.

"Can you tell me if the bank is in Germany?"

"It's not."

"Moscow?"

"No, and I won't play the game you Americans are so fond of—twenty questions."

Jui was getting desperate. Lamburg had information she needed. She tried a different strategy. "If you won't give me the information, could I impose on you to give Mr. Kairos a message?"

"I have no reason to think he will contact me. Our business is finished. His will is in order as well."

Jui gasped. "Is he ill? I knew he was. He has so many peculiar issues."

"Stop, please stop. I shouldn't have said that but to ease your mind, to the best of my knowledge he is in excellent health. He merely wanted to put his affairs in order. A man of such wealth should do so," Lamburg said.

"I don't care about his money." Jui squeezed her eyes shut, frustration overwhelming her. "If you hear from him, would you please tell him I said thank you for helping me. I was very sick and nearly died. If it weren't for him, we would not be speaking today."

"I'm glad you are recovered but as I said...."

"I get it. Please do what you can. That's all I ask." She hung up believing the conversation was her last hurrah.

And in Bucharest, Wade wished she'd give up before it was too late.

Chapter Fourteen

A few weeks passed with no word from Urs Lamburg, or, more importantly, Wade. Jui slouched in her office chair on Friday afternoon, feeling depressed. *It's time to let him go.* She wondered why their relationship failed. *Why did we even have to meet?* She tossed her pen across her desk in frustration and it rolled off the edge. The pen reminded her of her truck sliding through the snow bank and down the mountainside. *Did he save my life or was it just a crazy, coma-induced dream?* She packed up her things and left the office without a word to anyone.

At home, she booked a flight to Beaufort, North Carolina. The last time she packed for Harkers, she and Rob were going to have a romantic weekend together. She thrust out her lips in a pout, undecided about whether she regretted the way things turned out last fall. Her night in Wade's arms was the most amazing of her life but every day since was laced with personal challenges and melancholy. And she'd hurt Rob. She tossed the last handful of clothes into her suitcase and sat on the edge of the bed in a huff. *Maybe I should just pack black clothing. I feel like I'm going to a funeral. Mine.* As she zipped the bag shut, Jui decided going back to Harkers *was* a funeral of sorts. She would bury her memories of Wade there and by Monday, she would start life, brand new.

She boarded a United flight out of Seattle and settled in her window seat in first class. Turning off her phone, Jui drifted asleep until the airline attendant's soft voice awakened her. She told the attendant her dinner choice and then reached in the front seat pocket for a magazine. The cover photos featured the teen heartthrobs from the newest vampire movies and she glanced at the date. *October.* The center article described the cinematic evolution of Dracula, beginning with the ugly Count Orlock in Nosferatu, to Dracula, to the romantic actors in today's television and movie hits. She learned Count Orlock's castle was in the Carpathian Mountains. Thinking about the horrible tragedy at Carpathian Studios and its similar name gave her the willies. The mystery of Christophe Strasse's death popped into her brain and she wondered for the hundredth time how he managed to get into the limo undetected by anyone or anything.

A picture of Bela Lugosi as Dracula holding a tall, beautiful blonde in his arms captured her attention. "Dracula's" long fingers rested on the woman's shoulder while his exposed fangs poised over her neck "ready to suck her blood." The woman looked unconscious or in some kind of dramatic swoon, Jui wasn't sure. She remembered Wade and Rob in her own spooky dream. Her eyes narrowed as she squinted at the magazine picture, unable to ignore the contrast between the romantic image from the Silver Screen and the shocking image of Wade with fangs bared. Jui gulped and shut the magazine. After stuffing it back in the seat pocket, she crossed her arms over her chest, scolding herself for acting foolish. *Vampires are a legend.* She reached forward and flipped the magazine cover around so it couldn't "stare" at her.

* * * * *

By the time she pulled into the driveway in Harkers Island, Jui was beat. She brought in her suitcase and the groceries she'd picked up on the way. The fridge kicked in with a soft hum as Jui put away her food. A bottle of Australian merlot sat on the counter, begging to be uncorked.

"I'll be right back," she said to the bottle. "Stay put."

She hauled her suitcase upstairs, dropped it on the bed, and then considered sleeping in the guest room to avoid the memories of her passionate night with Wade. Jui decided against it. "Time to put him behind you, girlfriend," she said to the empty bed.

No moon illuminated the balmy, early spring sky. Jui opened the French doors and let the sea breeze in and four months of stale air out. The ocean called to her, its peaceful cadence relaxing her spirit and mind.

Downstairs, Jui uncorked the wine and then took the

bottle and a glass to the beach. Afterward, she carried down two armloads of firewood and skillfully built a fire. A few large pieces of driftwood lay on the beach, washed ashore from winter storms and Jui put them next to her fire to dry. The wood crackled and popped; cinder flittered into the sky like crazy lightning bugs. Jui poked the fire with one of the long pieces of driftwood and sipped her wine.

I came to say goodbye, Wade. I don't know if you can hear me. Maybe. I can't keep searching for you, waiting for you. I don't know why you left me or whether you were really at the hospital with me.

She prodded the burning chunks of wood with a long, thick branch and then plopped another split piece on the flames. A glittery cinder column rose and dissipated in the sky. The seagulls' gleeful cries pierced the silence and Jui thought it odd to hear the scavengers so clearly at night. She drank her wine and slouched in her beach chair, watching the flames shimmer in blue, red, orange, and yellow.

This is where it started, Wade, and where it ends. I should have taken your advice and moved on with Rob or somebody else, but I haven't. I couldn't. I still love you.

"Jui."

Her head snapped in the direction of that familiar voice. Wade Kairos stood ten feet behind her and Jui nearly tumbled backward trying to get out of her chair. "What are you doing here? How did you...?"

He stepped toward her. His hazel eyes glimmered in the firelight, full of serious purpose. "I, too, came to say goodbye."

Tears stung her eyes. "Where have you been? Why didn't you call me?"

"Shh, you know why."

"I don't, you selfish bastard. You're nothing but mysteries and riddles."

"I needed to protect you."

Jui's questions tumbled from her lips in disarray. "From who, from what? You saved my life. How did you know where I was and how did you get here so fast?"

"I'm risking everything to be here. My life is in danger, but I had to see you one last time. I couldn't die without telling you."

Tears rolled down her cheeks. "Urs Lamburg said you're fine and now you're admitting you've been sick all this time. You should have told me last fall." She turned away from him and hugged her arms against her body. "You're really cruel, you know that?" she whispered through her sniffles.

"I'm not sick, believe me, but they want me dead."

She whirled to face him. "Who? Let's go to the police if you're in trouble."

"It's not that kind of trouble."

"Then what is it?" she nearly screamed. "Complete a sentence—complete a thought for god's sake! Help me understand just one thing about you."

"I saved you and that's why they want me dead."

"You saved my life. What is so wrong about that?"

"I saved you from a life with me. It pissed them off. You're a threat to our safety."

"Holy shit, Wade, if you don't stop talking in circles I'll kill you myself!"

Wade inhaled deeply. The end was near; he felt it in his cold bones. "I'm a creature you cannot imagine."

"Cut the gothic crap. Say something I can understand."

Emotional pain tore through him as he prepared to destroy her love with the truth. Seagulls gathered; their shrill cries filled the air as they circled above. A few landed nearby as though taking front row seats in the drama. "I couldn't stay with you last fall no matter how much I wanted to. I can't give you a life because, Jui, I am not alive."

Her brows furrowed and she started to laugh. "Are you insane?"

"Touch my heart," he said, reaching for her hand. She jerked it from his grasp. "It doesn't beat. You weren't imagining it, my minx."

"Don't call me that."

"That's it," he said, "let rage and fear loose."

"You're an asshole. If you didn't want me, you didn't need to come back and taunt me." She turned on her heel to leave.

"Stop! Hear me out."

She froze in her tracks.

"I won't hurt you, I promise, but you need to know what

I am to understand why we can't be together." Wade lowered his head and clenched his fists, marshalling his energy into the transformation that would answer her questions.

He raised his chin and opened his eyes, showing her the golden flames leaping in them. He drew back his lips, revealing long fangs and hissed at her while his head danced on his neck, cobra-style.

Jui stepped backward, shock overwhelming her.

"It's not a legend. We live among you," he said in a wooden voice she didn't recognize.

She smelled mold and shivered from a sudden chill. Jui backed up farther and grabbed a long piece of burning wood. "Stay away from me, whatever you are," she stuttered.

"That's it, minx, do it yourself. The fire will set me free."

Waving the burning branch in front of her, she ordered, "Get back. I don't know what you are, but get away from me."

"Set me on fire, Jui, set me free from this hellish existence. I have no soul, no purpose, except to feed on humans and treat them as playthings."

Her face contorted with pain at his hurtful admission. "Was I a plaything? Did you feed on me?"

With head held high, he admitted the truth. "You weren't a plaything but I fed on you before I knew who you were."

"Who I am? What has that got to do with anything?" The realization dawned on her. "Grandma Claire—you were going to marry her."

Wade nodded.

"I visited your grave," she shouted. "How disgusting. Did you compare the two of us in bed?" She gave him an ugly sneer. "How'd I do?"

"Don't demean what we shared. You are nothing like Claire. Our relationship, yours and mine, cannot be compared to what Claire and I had."

Her tone verged on hysteria. "That's for sure, because you weren't some kind of—creature—with her."

He took a step toward her. "Don't, Jui."

She couldn't take her eyes off him and what he'd become. Her voice and body shook with fear. "I saw you with Rob that night. I didn't imagine it. What are you? Some kind of a vampire?" When he nodded and advanced another step, she waved the flaming log at him. "No you don't. Stay away from me! Go back where you came from—hell! Don't touch me!"

The flock of seagulls came nearer and the dank odor of mold filled Jui's nostrils. She pressed the back of her hand against her nose as bile rose in her throat.

"That's it, hate me. I could turn you into a creature like me. We could spend eternity together feeding on the living, living with the dead." He came closer, taunting her softly. "Do it for me, please. I'd rather you did than the Prophets. They're waiting to kill me," he said, indicating the assembling flock.

Tears streamed down her face and she repeatedly warned, "Get back."

The gulls followed Wade, seeming to march in unison toward her. She fell backwards, dropping the thick, charred stick. Using her elbows and heels to shove herself backward in the wet sand, she kept moving while Wade and the gulls advanced. Jui screamed bloody murder as the harmless gulls turned into large, black vultures and attacked Wade. White maggots instantly crawled out of the sand by the thousands and squirmed their way onto his feet. The air filled with her blood-curdling screams when he fell to the sand and the birds pecked at his body, which vibrated as if a powerful seizure possessed him. His skin turned glaucous and slid back from his cheekbones and hands, waxy and dead-looking.

The ugly, bareheaded, red-faced vultures cawed victoriously and flapped their large wings while dancing around his prone body. Their talons shredded his oilskin coat and shirt and Wade covered his eyes with his forearm to protect them from the carnivorous birds.

The macabre sight paralyzed Jui. She watched in stunned silence as the birds pecked mercilessly and the maggots covered his legs and kept climbing. They were already boring into his putrid, exposed flesh.

He croaked, "Jui, do it! Set me on fire, please, now. It's the only way to stop the Prophets."

His plea cracked her frozen brain. She rolled over and then crawled on her hands and knees to the smoldering branch lying on the sand. The birds paid no mind to her as Jui reignited the branch in the fire and crept toward the carrion that used to be the man she loved.

She waved the flaming wood in the air and screamed, "Get off him." The burning log singed their wings and scattered the evil birds. Their swift return made her frantic. She screamed again, "Get off him!" The lit branch left contrails of smoke as she waved it in crazy patterns, disseminating the vultures along the beach. "Get back!" The wave of menacing birds retreated only a moment and then pursued her as well. They flew close enough to throw her off balance as she dodged their attacks. Burning stick in hand, Jui, covered Wade's wounded body with hers. "Turn me into whatever it is you are. I can't...I love you...I can't let them do this to you."

Maggots marched onto her body in waves. She slapped them away, squishing the disgusting white worms by the handfuls. The scent of mold turned to something much more putrid and Jui gagged as her stomach rebelled and she vomited. Flies arrived and swarmed around their heads in a buzzing, black, angry cloud.

"Wade, please, there's no time."

The vultures came back. The first bite pricked her shoulder, followed by another on her ribs. She screamed in fear and pain. "Wade, please, I love you, take me with you. Make them stop!"

His arms wound around her body. "It's too late. I'm powerless. This is the price I have to pay for loving you." His body convulsed beneath hers and his face contorted in agony. Throughout the vile attacks, he made no sound, no cries for mercy or pity.

"It can't, it can't be too late." She rolled to her side waving the burning wood in the air, keeping the birds at bay with every ounce of strength she possessed. "I love you. I can't lose you this way." She gazed into his face. "Wade, oh my God, Wade, you're bleeding!"

His body pressed against the wet sand like a vacuum was sucking him underground. Jui again became so distracted by the unholy sight that the vampire-killing things—'Prophets', Wade had called them—found another chance to attack. She burned several of the horrid black birds and they screeched as they flew out of her reach.

"Wade, you're bleeding," she shouted once more.

The powerful vibrations ceased and Wade's body ached from the forceful attack. He felt every bite from the ravenous birds. His mind raced with a new consciousness. *It isn't possible.* Slowly he raised his hand to his cheek and touched a wound. He opened his eyes to examine what his fingers found.

"You're bleeding," Jui kept repeating.

He gazed at her, incredulous.

The maggots dropped off their bodies and lay in the sand like rice kernels after a wedding. The huge black flies joined the vultures circling high above.

"It's blood, Jui," he said, examining the red liquid on his fingertips. His eyes opened wide. "I can't bleed. Vampires can't bleed."

"But you are," she exclaimed as happiness replaced fear on her face. "You're bleeding everywhere and you're alive."

Wade pushed himself up on an elbow. Pain like he'd never felt before wracked his body. His black shirt hung in tatters from his shoulders and blood streamed from bites on his torso and face.

"We have to get you to a doctor."

Wade's brain refused to form a coherent thought. His mouth contorted to speak but nothing came out at first. Finally, he regained his composure. "It's not possible. All these years and I never heard any vampire say it could happen. Christophe would have told me." He wiped the blood dripping from his forehead with the back of his hand. "Shit. Maybe he did. He must have known."

"Known what?" she asked.

"Just before he died, Christophe told me telepathically I was a lucky bastard, and love changed everything. I didn't know what he meant."

He met her teary gaze. "He was telling me if we loved each other it could reverse vampirism. I wonder if he kept it a secret so I wouldn't live with false hope. He spent his entire vampire existence hating Gerhardt Meuhler—the vamp who turned him. It took Christophe hundreds of years to kill

202

the bastard. Christophe didn't want me to spend eternity hopelessly chasing after love." Wade pressed his fingers on his carotid. "My heart beats. Feel it," he said, taking her hand and placing her fingers where his had been. "My skin is warm."

Jui felt his pulse beneath her fingers, steady and strong. She drew his battered body into her arms and wept against his shoulder. "We need to get you to a hospital," she said, sniffing back her tears. "Come on, let me help you up. You look like hell."

Wade got to his feet. "You raised me from the dead with your love. This is where I get to kiss the girl, isn't it?" he asked with a hopeful smile on his bloody face.

Jui's heart raced and she couldn't find her tongue.

He stood on unsteady legs and said, "It's over and you're safe. I'm simply a man now, Jui, and I love you."

"They won't come back and try to take you back, turn you again?" she asked in a shaky voice.

"No."

"Are you sure?"

"No, but the Prophets—the beasts sent to kill me—aren't vampires. They're exterminators used by us, I mean vampires and other creatures, to exterminate rebels and eliminate problems."

"There's more of you—other creatures?"

Wade nodded. "Most vampires don't turn humans. Eternal life is desolate and we—they—never forget what it felt like to be human. What we lost."

Tremors ran through her body as she stepped into Wade's embrace and lifted her tear-soaked face to his gaze. The first touch of his lips was unfamiliar and after a few seconds, Jui realized the difference was his body temperature. He felt real. "Can you still read my mind?" she asked timidly.

"Think of something."

Jui studied his face while concentrating on a message.

"Nothing."

"You aren't lying are you?"

"What did you try to tell me?"

"Distance means nothing to the soul."

He cupped her jaw as their gazes met.

She trembled beneath his touch but didn't push him away.

"Thank you for giving my life back to me." Their kiss deepened from tentative to tender. "I love you."

"And I love you." She put her arm around his waist, and winced when she felt the sting from the wound on her shoulder. "I have no idea what we're going to tell the ER docs."

"I know," Wade said, giving her a wink. "We'll tell them they're love bites."

~The End~

About the Author

Margie Church has a degree in writing and editing and has been a professional writer and editor for more than 25 years. She works as a copywriter and editor for a small direct marketing firm specializing in the credit union market and writes freelance articles for business-to-business magazines. Her first novels, *Awakening Allaire* and *Avenging Allaire*, were released in August and November 2009. She has contracted a nursery rhyme with Guardian Angels Publishing, too.

Margie lives in Minneapolis, Minnesota, is married, and has two children. Vegetable and flower gardening, biking, walking her dog, listening to music, and making people laugh are some of her passions.

Learn more about Margie at:
www.site.romancewithsass.com

Made in the USA
Charleston, SC
31 May 2013